# PRAISE FOR THE

"Therese Beharrie's books are some of the most thoughtful romances available, full of warmth, wit, and careful consideration of her characters' lives and desires. She's a fresh voice romance readers will adore and one that our genre very much needs."
—Olivia Dade, author of *Spoiler Alert*

"Building [this] kind of depth in the swift, sleek category form is just—woof, I have no idea how Beharrie does it, but let's let her keep doing it as often as she wants."
—The Seattle Review of Books on *One Day to Fall*

"Therese Beharrie is a stunningly talented writer."
—Smart Bitches, Trashy Books on *One Day to Fall*

"The magic of the story comes from Gaia learning to choose that real, scary, vivid life over the safety of her imagination. In Beharrie's wonderful romance, real love is even better than magic."
—Bookpage on *And They Lived Happily Ever After*

"This richly emotional rom-com is electric enough to kick-start even the most cynical heart. Achingly real, unexpectedly whimsical, and wholly original."
—Talia Hibbert, *New York Times* bestselling author, on
*And They Lived Happily Ever After*

"Clever and charming, *And They Lived Happily Ever After* is a tribute to what so many of us see in romance: the escape and the insight, the layered experience of learning how to love in all areas of our lives."
—Kate Clayborn, author of *Love at First*, on
*And They Lived Happily Ever After*

"Therese Beharrie writes the tenderest romances, and I love the sprinkle of magic she's infused into her people-pleasing heroine, Gemma, and hero Levi, a man of few words, as they embark on an unconventional journey to help and understand not only each other but themselves and their own honest needs. A sexy, emotional tale with a fun dash of the paranormal."

—Sarah Hogle, author of *Just Like Magic*, on
*A Ghost in Shining Armor*

"Their slow-burning will-they, won't-they combined with Beharrie's laugh-out-loud narration makes this a surefire crowd-pleaser."

—*Publishers Weekly* on *A Ghost in Shining Armor*

"*A Ghost in Shining Armor* is as richly imagined as it is deeply moving—and quite a lot of fun as well."

—*Bookpage* on *A Ghost in Shining Armor*

# Single Dads Club

# OTHER TITLES BY THERESE BEHARRIE

## *Harlequin Romance*

*The Tycoon's Reluctant Cinderella*
*A Marriage Worth Saving*
*The Millionaire's Redemption*
*United by Their Royal Baby*
*Falling for His Convenient Queen*
*Tempted by the Billionaire Next Door*
*Surprise Baby, Second Chance*
*Her Festive Flirtation*
*Second Chance with Her Billionaire*
*From Heiress to Mom*
*Island Fling with the Tycoon*
*Her Twin Baby Secret*
*Marrying His Runaway Heiress*
*His Princess by Christmas*
*Awakened by the CEO's Kiss*
*Finding Forever on Their Island Paradise*

## *One Day to Forever Series*

*A Wedding One Christmas*
*One Day to Fall*
*One Last Chance*

## *Paranormal Rom-Com Series*

*And They Lived Happily Ever After*
*A Ghost in Shining Armor*

# Single Dads Club

## THERESE BEHARRIE

Montlake

Published by Montlake, Seattle

www.apub.com

Amazon, the Amazon logo, and Montlake are trademarks of Amazon.com, Inc., or its affiliates.

ISBN-13: 9781662511783 (paperback)
ISBN-13: 9781662511776 (digital)

Cover design by Kris Beecroft
Cover illustration by Louisa Cannell

Printed in the United States of America

*To my husband, whose dedication to being the best*
*father inspired this book—and makes me*
*love him even more.*
*And to my children.*
*You are loved more than you can possibly imagine.*
*Everything we do is for you.*

# AUTHOR'S NOTE

Please be aware that this book deals with potentially triggering topics, such as parental abandonment and neglect, white-collar crime (off page), and accidental pregnancy and discussions thereof.

I've tried to handle these with care, but please, put your mental well-being first.

# PROLOGUE

No one had prepared him for this.

They'd warned him he'd be tired.

He was.

They'd warned him he wouldn't understand the love flooding his body because he had a son.

He didn't.

But no one—and Rowan Quinn thought this was particularly important—had told him that in the first few days of his son's life, there'd be a thick, sticky black substance coming out of his son's body, and Rowan would have to clean it up. And pretend to not be completely, utterly grossed out.

"It's normal!" the bright-eyed nurse had told him and Mckenna the first time it happened. "And good. Your son's bowels are working. That's a good sign."

Yeah, it was a good sign. Also, a really gross sign.

"It should last no longer than five days."

And she'd winked at them.

Now, he'd only been a parent for three days. He'd had little sleep during that time, jumping at every sound and peep—which babies made a lot of—but looking back at that conversation, he didn't think winking was appropriate.

Parenting wasn't the kind of thing he'd associate with winking. It deserved gravitas, and if he'd been in the right state of mind, he might have told the nurse that.

But he hadn't been in the right state of mind. Not since Mckenna had told him, after their fluke of a one-night stand, that she was pregnant and he was the father.

He was a father.

He was a *father*.

His biggest nightmare.

Rowan took a breath and lifted Declan's legs. One wipe . . . two wipes . . . five wipes later, he'd cleaned most of the mess. And as he put the new diaper under his son's bum, he got sprayed in the face. With urine. For the third time in as many days.

"Really?" he asked Declan, who didn't even have the decency to look him in the eyes. "You're really going to take that shot today, huh? Didn't think yesterday and the day before were good enough?"

Ignoring the pee on his face—not a sentence he'd have predicted he'd think—he finished changing Declan's diaper and got a wet wipe for his face.

"Your aim's getting better," he said, cleaning his forehead and nose. "Or worse, I guess."

Declan didn't say anything. He had his pacifier in, was making cute sucking sounds, and Rowan's heart filled in a strange and unfamiliar way. It scared him, how big his heart grew. How full it felt when he simply looked at his son.

Surely that wasn't healthy? Surely it meant something was wrong with him, that he needed to see a doctor or a psychologist or whatever kind of professional to make sure he was okay?

But he didn't need a professional to know he wasn't okay. He was a father. He'd never thought he'd be one. After growing up the way he had . . . no. He didn't want to be a father. And if he were going to be one, this wasn't the way he'd want it to happen. He wanted to give his son what he'd never had: Stability. A normal family.

Except now Declan would never have that, and it was Rowan's fault.

Rowan's phone rang. He grabbed it off the bed, afraid it would unsettle Declan even though it was on vibrate. He'd turned the ringer off on the day Declan was born and hadn't turned it back on since.

He put Declan in his bassinet and waited a minute to see if the kid would cry, and when he didn't, Rowan slipped into the other room, taking the monitor with him. His eyes didn't move from it as he answered.

"What?"

"Is that any way to speak to your grandmother, Rowan?" He opened his mouth, but his grandmother continued. "I suppose that sort of curtness answers my question about how you're doing."

It wasn't a question, not really, and yet somehow, he felt compelled to reply.

"We're hanging in there." He paused. Did it matter how honest he was? Would his grandmother hear what he wasn't saying like she usually did? He relented. "It's hard. Harder than I thought."

He was embarrassed to admit it. *Of course* it was harder than he'd thought. Of course it was.

"How's Mckenna?" Linda asked, her voice neutral. She'd never met Mckenna. Now Mckenna was a part of the family.

"She's fine."

"Really?"

"No." He snorted. "She just had a baby, Gran. Pushed it out. Right through her . . ." He threw out a hand, as if somehow, his grandmother could see. "It was an experience."

Linda chuckled. "I do so enjoy hearing people talk about that experience. My friend witnessed her grandchild's birth the other day and told me she finally understood why her husband fainted. Seeing a baby leave the birth canal *is* an experience."

He smiled. It felt . . . foreign.

"You still don't want me to come?" Linda asked softly, as if somehow she'd heard that thought and wanted to come for the sole purpose of making him smile.

"No," he answered, emotion thick in his throat. "Mckenna would feel . . ."

He wasn't sure, actually. He hadn't brought up his grandmother's offer because he didn't want Mckenna to think he didn't believe she was capable of mothering. He was helping as much as he could. Taking care of the food, doing all the changes. But they'd been out of the hospital a day, and already he felt out of his depths.

He should have said yes to his grandmother. He should have brought it up. But not wanting to step on Mckenna's toes was a direct result of the fact that he didn't really know her. Hadn't really known her when they'd had sex, either, but it was too late to dwell on that.

"You two shouldn't be doing this alone."

"We're not."

They were.

Mckenna's family lived on the other side of the world, and he only had his grandmother to rely on. Linda lived two hours away.

What would happen when Mckenna went back to her high-powered job and Rowan had to take care of Declan full time? If he was struggling to manage it now, when both he and Mckenna were temporarily staying together, being by himself when he went back to work, even if it was from home . . .

He should have taken his grandmother up on the offer.

"We have a problem." Mckenna interrupted his ruminations from the doorway of the bedroom. Her phone was in her hand, and there were two large milk stains over her boobs. "A work problem. They need me."

As she said the words, Declan let out a wail.

"I'll call you back," he said into the phone.

# CHAPTER ONE

"Your boyfriend's here."

Delilah Huntington looked up at the singsong words of her friend and colleague Kirsten, even though she knew who Kirsten was referring to: Sugarbush Bay's newest resident. Her stomach swooped, but she caught it, gently pressing it back to its rightful place inside her body.

*No swooping,* she told it firmly. *Only admiring. From a distance.* And from where she stood behind the counter, she distantly admired the sharp angles of his face . . . the brown of his skin . . . that full beard . . . his curly hair. Not to mention the grim expression on his face. What was it about his frown that appealed to her? It should have repelled her.

It did not repel her.

Neither did the baby strapped to his chest.

"He's not my boyfriend," she muttered.

Delayed, true, but good enough to act as a warning. A man with a frown and a baby was not a reasonable crush. And while she believed in the Law of Crushes, namely that the best crushes had no reason, this one felt . . . messy.

Kirsten winked at her, then called out the two coffee orders she'd finished while Delilah took the order of the next person in line. They worked at the Blue Café, one of two cafés in the small town of Sugarbush Bay, where Delilah had been living for the last eighteen months.

The café was unusually busy for a Tuesday morning because of a bus passing through. Travelers from Cape Town, she'd managed to glean from their chattering, and her heart gave a pang.

She missed Cape Town. Missed her home with its beautiful mountain, sun-drenched vineyards, glowing beaches. She missed the place more than she did the life she'd had there.

A familiar lick of shame flicked out at her.

No, she didn't miss the life she'd had there. Not when it had done such damage to so many people.

She shook her head and focused on her work. She had two more people to help before she got to the man. Plenty of time to build her defenses so the sight of him with his baby didn't melt her heart and make her slip, hit her head, and forget that he ordered two coffees every time he came to the café.

Still, she kept stealing glances at him. His obvious tiredness did nothing to detract from his handsomeness. *She* looked like a creature from a horror movie when she was tired, but he looked like his tiredness was a result of being too good looking. What a burden.

She could appreciate his good looks. She *had* been appreciating his good looks since he'd first come to the café two weeks ago. She'd made the mistake of mentioning how cute he was to Kirsten, even joking that he must have thought the same thing about her when he returned a few days later.

But after his third visit, his fourth, she started thinking that maybe he wasn't one of the holidaymakers in town. And then she remembered Linda, one of the women she'd befriended since moving here, had talked about how her grandson and great-grandson were coming to live in Sugarbush Bay, and she'd stopped making jokes altogether.

Kirsten, however, had generously taken the baton from her and run with it.

Which was fine. Jokes about her crushing on an effortlessly good-looking man with a cute baby were harmless. Perfect, in fact. He was unavailable and unattainable, two things she deeply related to. So maybe the crush itself was harmless, too.

But there were flutters in her stomach when it was his turn to order. She was almost relieved at the distraction of his baby's fierce little cry.

"Sorry," he said, trying to put the pacifier back into his child's mouth, bouncing a little. He succeeded, but it only stayed there long enough for him to look up and open his mouth. The pacifier now hung from a chain of plastic rings clipped to the carrier. The baby started crying in earnest.

"I'm sorry," he repeated, this time a little more panicked.

"It's fine," she said, already punching in his order. "Two large cappuccinos, one decaf with oat milk, right?"

She knew the second coffee could be for anyone, but the possibility of it being for a partner—though Linda hadn't mentioned anything about *that*—was another reason this crush wouldn't go anywhere.

Good thing she didn't want it to.

He blinked up at her. "Yeah. Yeah, that's it."

He fumbled with the carrier, trying to get the baby out, and she bit her lip.

"Go," she told him, amused by his fumbling. "Sort that out. I'll bring the coffee to your table. Takeaway," she added when he opened his mouth, "and the bill, which you can pay over there while you take care of your baby."

He gave her a nod, said "thank you" distractedly, and walked away, the carrier half-loose, the bag on his back half-off, his baby firmly in his arms. She couldn't help the fond look she knew was on her face. Didn't even get upset that Kirsten was openly grinning at her.

"You didn't offer him today's special," Kirsten said softly. "If you order two cappuccinos—one decaf with oat milk, coincidentally—you get a server free, frothing at the mouth, ready to cater to your every need."

"Ha ha."

Kirsten's smile widened, but the next customers came forward, and they switched positions so Delilah could start with the man's order.

"He *is* cute with that baby," Kirsten said after she'd helped the two women. The café had gone quiet again, the only people at the tables their regulars who usually worked there and had already had their breakfasts. The other customers were waiting for their coffees, which Kirsten would start with when Delilah finished.

"Undoubtedly," Delilah said, steaming the milk. "Which is why I like him, isn't it? That whole unavailable thing."

"He isn't wearing a ring."

"It doesn't matter." She lifted a shoulder. "I came here to start an uncomplicated life. That . . ." She paused. "That is not uncomplicated."

"Tell me about it," Kirsten muttered.

"Oh, no, I didn't mean—"

"Too late," Kirsten interrupted. "You said dating with a kid is complicated. I have a kid. I hate complicated. Ergo, you need to stop telling me to date."

"Ergo?" Delilah repeated. "You think using a word like that is going to distract me from what you said? Because it did, but only a little." Kirsten snorted. "I'm still going to tell Anne that whenever dating comes up, even for me, you somehow end up making an argument for how you shouldn't date."

"I should have never given you my therapist's number," Kirsten growled.

"Too late. We're therapy sisters now. Connected for life."

Kirsten's stormy expression cleared, and she let out a laugh. "This job was so boring without you."

"And my life was boring without you." Delilah waited a beat, trying to figure out if what she wanted to say next would be weird. "I'm glad we're friends," she settled on, instead of the word vomit that wanted to come out. "Thanks for being so kind when I got here."

Kirsten's cheeks reddened. Beneath her sass, Kirsten was a sweet woman with a soft heart. When Delilah had started working at the café, Kirsten had taken Delilah under her wing. She'd covered for Delilah when Delilah had messed up, and hadn't once during that time said a cruel word.

If the positions were reversed, Delilah didn't know if she would have done the same.

She wouldn't have—before. But the before Delilah was behind her. The now Delilah would have helped. Because that was what people like Kirsten had taught her to do.

"Get back to your man," Kirsten said sharply, but there was a soft look in her eyes. "I've got it from here."

Delilah nodded, offering her a small smile, and tried not to let her nerves show as she carried the coffees and card machine—as well as the chocolate chip cookie she always added to his order—over.

It wasn't *exactly* nerves. It was just those darn butterflies. No matter how logical she was about the situation, about this man, they remained.

She supposed it was only natural when she hadn't been attracted to anyone since her last relationship. Her boyfriend had cheated on her. And though she hadn't been particularly invested in their three-month relationship, the insecurity she'd felt after being betrayed that way—for a second time; the first had again been with a man she hadn't cared much about—had done a number on her.

She'd stopped dating. Wanted to figure out why she kept being attracted to assholes. Her life had fallen apart shortly after that, and she'd had no desire to date since.

It reminded her that there were no stakes involved here. She was merely serving a customer. A customer she had a silly, innocent crush on, yes, but the emphasis was on *innocent.*

For one, it was one sided. For another, she didn't want anything romantic. In fact, she'd rather be friends with the man. Hell, she'd befriend his partner, too, if he had one. She was sure he was Linda's grandson, but she'd wait on confirmation before she offered to show them around town. Do what people had done for her when she'd first moved to Sugarbush Bay.

Nerves calmed, she fixed a harmless smile to her face.

He was sitting in the corner, far away from the closest customer. His baby was drinking from a bottle, their little mouth moving in the cutest way. The man was looking down, staring at that scrunched-up face as if he were witnessing a miracle. There was no grim expression now, no frown, only wonder.

And Delilah could swear she heard her heart sigh at the sight.

Her crush might be innocent, but it had quickly become serious. A natural occurrence with him looking at his baby like that.

*No,* she commanded.

*LOL, nice try,* her heart said and went back to staring dreamily at the man in front of her. It thudded when he lifted his head, caught her eye, and gave her a half smile.

A half smile.

This one said, *I don't have the energy to give you a full smile, but I still have a little something-something for you.*

*See,* her heart said, sticking out its hands triumphantly. *This does not deserve a no. This deserves a yes. A yes, please.*

Hurriedly, she put down the coffees.

"Thanks," he said.

"You're welcome."

She turned to leave.

"Hey. Hey, wait."

She spun back around. "Hmm?"

"Don't I have to pay?" He gestured to the card machine still in her hands.

She swallowed. "Oh, yes, but I can see you're still busy, so I thought I'd come back when you were done."

His gaze flickered down to his kid. He gave her a curt nod. "Thank you."

"Yeah, no, of course." She staggered back but realized he had his hands full and he might need some help. "You probably want to drink that, huh? Which is yours?"

His frown was back. "The coffee?"

"Yes."

"The normal one."

She took it out of the cup holder for him. Because it was an easy thing to do. A small thing to do. And because she was good at her job.

It had nothing to do with his stupid smile.

"Sugar?"

He shook his head.

"Okay." She stepped back but leaned forward again, hands clutched together. "I got you a cookie as well. I thought it might make you feel better. Can I take it out for you?"

He lowered his head, eyes resting on the bag she'd put the cookie in. "You brought me this."

"Yeah. No cost. Do you want me . . ." She cleared her throat. "Do you want me to take it out for you?"

He gave a slow, thoughtful nod. She took the cookie out the packet, laid it in front of him next to the coffee. And stood. For much longer than she should have, waiting for . . . she wasn't exactly sure.

"Oh!" she exclaimed. "You can't even drink this. You have your hands full. Do you want me to—"

She mimicked drinking and, as she did, felt her eyes grow wide. Was she . . . was she actually offering to feed him his coffee? As in, bring it to his lips, let him drink? *What?* What was she *doing?*

"As much as I appreciate the offer," he said, his tone mild, "I've got it."

"Of course you do," she replied quickly. "I'll just . . . go now."

She turned on her heel, immediately making eye contact with Kirsten. *Wow,* her friend mouthed, her expression the kind Delilah imagined people wore when they witnessed a disaster happening right in front of them.

Or more accurately, the kind worn by people *filming* the disaster instead of helping.

"Why didn't you come save me?" Delilah hissed when she joined Kirsten at the counter, resisting the urge to look at the wreckage she'd left behind.

"You looked like you had it covered?" came the chagrined reply.

She groaned. "Words kept coming out of my mouth. I offered to bring the coffee to his lips! What is wrong with me? I don't do stuff like that. Talking to people is *easy* for me."

"There, there," Kirsten said, patting Delilah's arm. "It'll be okay."

Delilah narrowed her eyes. "You're going to need a wingperson when you start dating someday, and—"

"I'm not dating," Kirsten interrupted.

"You will."

"Delilah," Kirsten said, her voice a warning.

Delilah heeded it, but only because now wasn't the time to push. She'd been working on Kirsten for months, urging her friend to put herself out there after her husband's death. Not because Kirsten needed a romantic relationship but because Kirsten needed something for herself. She poured her life into work, into her two-year-old son, and did nothing for herself.

"Look on the upside," Kirsten continued, her tone light, as if trying to make amends for her sharpness. "At least you didn't offer to bite off a piece of cookie and chew it for him before directly transporting it to his mouth."

"It was bad, wasn't it?"

"It was pretty bad."

Delilah groaned again.

"Another upside," Kirsten said, straightening as the bell of the café door rang, "is that you'll have a chance to redeem yourself." She elbowed Delilah out the way so she could help the customers who'd come in. "He's calling you."

Rowan was burping Declan when his phone went off. It was a text from Mckenna.

Where are you with my coffee? Dying over here.

The phone pinged again.

Also with my son. I was thinking of my son first, and then about the coffee.

He snorted lightly, then stilled because it felt so unfamiliar. Did Mckenna feel the same way? Did she worry that if she laughed or talked with friends or engaged with the world in a noncritical way, she'd be using up the energy meant for Declan?

There was so little energy these days. He saw the lack of it in the bags under his eyes when he looked in the mirror. In the expression Mckenna wore beneath the lightheartedness she projected. He could see it—the weight of having a newborn—on her, even though she tried to hide it. The weight of not only having a newborn but having one with a man she barely knew.

They'd tried, over these last months, to get to know one another. Even tried to date. But it all had felt forced. Awkward. Everything was awkward between them. *He* was awkward. They'd eventually agreed that a romantic relationship wasn't going to happen between them. They'd decided to be friends instead.

But that didn't make him feel any more comfortable in their relationship. In his life. He still wanted to run. Far away from his stupid choices. Back to a time when he knew what to expect from his days.

Guilt struck him in the chest, even as warmth spread across it. A physical warmth. Declan. His son was still there, making sweet little noises as he tried to get his wind out. Rowan sucked in a breath, rubbing a hand gently over Declan's back, murmuring softly.

The decisions that had led him here might have been stupid, and he might no longer recognize his life, but he had a child. A son. Declan Black-Quinn. Rowan wouldn't spend time dwelling on what he couldn't change. No, he'd focus on his son. On what he could give—not what had been taken away from him.

He took a long drag from his cappuccino, closing his eyes for a second. There were good things in this new life of his. Like coffee, which he'd never particularly liked before but which somehow now made all the sense in the world.

He drove across town regularly to get it from the Blue Café, an innocuous little place that was decorated in honor of its name and proximity to the beach. Light sprawled in from the glass that stretched midway from the wall to the ceiling, and the wall below was painted white with blue waves, plants crawling out from blue pots in every corner.

He wasn't sure why he'd come here the first time, when he put a crying Declan in the car and drove and drove.

But now he came here for the peace and comfort, the familiarity in a town that he still didn't know, despite having lived there for two weeks.

*And for the quirky little waitress who makes you smile every time you see her.*

No. *No,* he thought again. That wasn't true . . . was it? Sure, she was pretty. He'd noticed it in a very distant kind of way. His brain knew her features were pleasing to the eye, but beyond that, he hadn't really been interested.

But he had noticed the extra cookie he was getting every time, which was a huge perk of coming here, but he'd thought it was a special the café had running. Now he realized it was . . . kindness. Or something more, he thought, as his eyes rested on the woman.

She had her back to him, her hair exploding in a pouf of curls at the top of her head. She was gesturing animatedly to her colleague, a woman with a strange hair color, somewhere between brown and orange and blonde. The amused expression on the strange-haired woman's face as she watched his waitress—and the fact that her eyes darted to him more than once during the conversation—made it clear they were talking about him.

So maybe the cookie wasn't only kindness. It was . . . what? Some form of . . . flirting? If it was, she obviously knew the key to flirting with him: feeding him dangerously sweet things.

Then again, she had offered to bring his coffee to his lips, like he was a child, so flirting might not be her thing.

A smile tugged at his lips, but he shook his head. It didn't matter if she was flirting with him. His life was too complicated to think about romance.

Fortified, he gestured for her attention. The brown/blonde/orange-haired woman said something to the waitress and nudged the woman out the way so she could serve their next customers, and his waitress turned and looked at him.

Yeah, she'd been talking about him. The nerves and guilt skipping over her face were too strange a combination for her not to have been. A warm, odd feeling spread in his chest.

*No,* he told himself again. *It doesn't matter.*

She skipped over to him—not quite literally, but close enough— and smiled. "Ready to pay?"

He nodded, standing up to get his wallet from his back pocket.

Declan burped.

At first, Rowan smiled. That was exactly what he'd been waiting for. Then he felt it. Something that had him pulling Declan from his body slightly. Declan burped again, and again, thick white spit-up bubbled from his lips—and all over Rowan's T-shirt.

There was a beat of silence before Declan let out the loudest wail Rowan had ever heard. Everyone in the café turned to look at them, and he'd never felt so helpless in his life. He couldn't comfort Declan without covering him in spit-up, and he couldn't do anything about the spit-up with Declan in his arms.

Panic flooded him, his heart thudding, because he knew everyone was looking at him, and if he didn't come up with a solution fast, everyone would think he was a bad father and he didn't want that even though he probably—

"I can take the baby for you," said a quiet voice beside him.

He looked down. The woman. The waitress. She'd moved to his side, shielding him from the view of the other patrons. Her eyes were kind. There was no judgment, no condemnation. And she waited. Patiently, even though Declan was still screaming and Rowan's heart was still thudding.

She smiled. A small smile that was comforting and reassuring, and something inside him broke.

"Please," he rasped.

She nodded, took Declan, and began to bounce him gently, talking to him softly. A minute passed, maybe more, before she looked at Rowan.

"Can I have the pacifier?"

Rowan scrambled to get it, pulling it from the carrier he'd thankfully taken off completely before feeding Declan. He used too much force, and the pacifier snapped back. He pulled it again, this time unclipping it, and handed it to her. She offered Declan the pacifier. After a few seconds of cajoling, he took it, and there was quiet again.

Sweet, sweet quiet.

"I'm sorry," Rowan said, as everyone went back to their business. His heart rate slowed as they did, and he'd managed to find his voice again.

She smiled at him, so brightly he almost blinked. "Don't apologize. They're a baby. You have no control over their actions, and you were in an impossible situation. Do you have a spare shirt?" she asked, wrinkling her nose, as if she hadn't exploded his world with her reasoning.

"No," he said, bewildered.

"Hmm." She pulled her mouth to the side. "Would you like to clean that off?"

"No."

"Yeah, you'd probably leave with your entire shirt wet if you tried to clean it," she agreed, again so reasonably. As if that *no* hadn't been a curt, borderline-rude answer. "Hey! We have spare uniforms at the back. There should be a T-shirt in your size there."

The "uniform" was black pants and a black T-shirt that had **THE BLUE CAFÉ** in blue lettering at the breast.

"No," he heard himself say. "No, I don't want to put you out."

"Oh, please, you won't be putting me out."

She looked around for her colleague and tilted her head to him and then to a door that said **EMPLOYEES ONLY**, shifting Declan's weight to one arm so she could lift her T-shirt with the other. Her colleague's eyes swept the café before she nodded. The waitress turned to him.

"See? Easy peasy. Bring the bag; leave the coffee. I'll have Kirsten watch over it."

With those words, she turned.

Rowan pretended not to see the smirk on her colleague's face as he followed.

# CHAPTER TWO

Delilah worked on weekends. Lately, she'd been helping to prepare for the town festival, which was about two months away, but she tended to do anything people asked her to. She liked to help. She especially liked to help people who needed it. So when she'd seen the baby spit up all over their father, when she'd seen the poor man's face—and witnessed bewilderment turn into panic when he realized people were looking at him—it was natural for her to step in.

*Natural, huh?* a voice that sounded eerily like Kirsten's said in her head.

*Yes,* she replied with a mental sniff. *None of this has anything to do with the crush. I would have done it for anyone.*

*Lots of protesting for someone who would have done it for "anyone."*

Okay, she was arguing with an imaginary voice in her brain. She needed to relax. And focus.

She needed to relax about holding his cute-ass baby and focus on finding him a T-shirt.

She needed to not think about being in the small storeroom with him.

If she did all those things, it would become a story she and Kirsten laughed about. Or Kirsten would tease her about.

But it certainly wasn't the tale of a tryst.

She shifted the baby to her left, leaving her right hand free to rummage through one of the boxes on a shelf in front of her. It took three tries to find the right box—and every ounce of her strength not to fill the quietness in the room. The baby was quiet, the father was quiet, and she was quiet—a fact no one in her life would believe.

She was also willing to bet she was the only one freaked out by the quiet. By how it amplified the tension exuded by the man standing at the door. Or how it made her imagine being in the storeroom with him under entirely different circumstances . . .

"Here you go!" she cried triumphantly, interrupting her alarming thoughts and, more importantly, the undesirable silence.

She turned—and found him shirtless.

He'd taken his shirt off.

This sexy man had taken his shirt off.

In a storeroom.

With only her—and his baby—to witness it.

Her instincts told her to turn around, to give him privacy.

The horny monster inside her declared war against her instincts. The two of them were too busy fighting for her to listen to either, so she half turned, giving him privacy in an empty gesture because she could still see him.

His strong shoulders, the beautiful brown skin stretching over them, spreading over muscles that swelled and dipped down his arms to his forearms. She had never cared much for that part of a body, which now seemed like a rather significant oversight.

This man had *good forearms*. They looked as if they'd been designed to model watches or work shirts where the arms were rolled up. They looked like the kind of forearms that could lift a woman onto a pedestal and gently take her down when she'd gotten whatever she wanted from the top shelf.

His chest was almost as broad as his shoulders, almost as defined as his forearms, but there was a softness to it, just like the softness to his stomach. As if his abs had gone into hibernation for the winter.

Which was fine with her. She didn't mind the cold. Enjoyed it, frankly. When else could she wear her favorite boots? The coat her mother had bought her that was one of the only remnants she had from her previous life? Plus, she had a ton of scarves and a cute pair of earmuffs that she could only wear in the winter, and really, she was ready to go into hibernation, too, if it meant sleeping next to this man.

"Can I have it?" he asked, his voice soft and silken, a caress on her skin.

"What?"

"The T-shirt."

She looked down at her hand. Oh, right. She hadn't given him the T-shirt. Which likely meant he'd been watching her as she'd been watching him and he probably thought she was a creep. Exactly the kind of person he'd want holding his child.

"Of course," she said quickly, handing him the shirt and averting her gaze.

She turned around again, focusing entirely on the baby, whose eyes were blinking slowly, their mouth sucking the pacifier intently for a few minutes, then pausing and starting again as if stopping had been a mistake.

*Cute,* she thought for the umpteenth time. She wondered what their name was. Would it be weird if she asked? Probably. Hell, everything had been weird since this man and his baby had come into the café. All because she had a stupid crush making her act like a teenage girl, not the strong, capable woman she was.

The strong, capable woman she fought to be.

"Can I have your bag?" she asked now. "There's some spit-up on your baby's clothes. I'll try to get it off with a wet wipe."

A sound behind her told her he'd slid the bag over to her. She turned, still avoiding looking at him, took out wipes, and cleaned the baby as much as she could, describing everything she was doing in what she hoped was a soothing tone.

"I can take him now," the man said from much too close.

Her head whipped to the side, and there he was. So close to her she could smell the slight pine scent of him, mingled with bacon frying from the kitchen next door in a ridiculous yet tempting combination. It didn't help that he looked absurdly good in that **THE BLUE CAFÉ**

T-shirt, or that when she handed the baby over, there was a slight spark at their contact.

In her head, she told herself. It was all in her head.

And she needed to snap out of it.

"Thank you," he said, his tone stiff. "For the shirt. And for helping."

"Yeah, of course. It wasn't a problem. I loved holding—?" She broke off questioningly.

"Declan."

"Hi, Declan," she replied, unable to keep from moving closer. The baby was content in his father's arms, and Delilah couldn't have anticipated how *right* they looked together in that moment. "I'm Delilah. It was very nice to meet you."

There was a pause before Declan's dad said, "Delilah."

She straightened at that, ignoring the thrill going down her spine, and stepped back to a safe distance. "Yes."

"Rowan."

"It's nice to meet you, too, Rowan."

There was a moment then. A long, tense moment when they held one another's gazes. When she *felt* his gaze, her skin covered with goose bumps, her nipples pebbled.

"Thank you again," he said abruptly and, with a curt nod, left the storeroom.

Delilah sagged against one of the shelves.

That had been a bit much. But at least it cured her of her crush. Because there was no way she could call what she'd felt for Rowan in the last fifteen minutes a crush. And if it wasn't a crush, it couldn't be anything else. Her life didn't allow for it. Neither, she bet, did his.

She took a deep breath and went back into the café. Rowan was gone.

"He paid for the cookie, too," Kirsten said, whizzing past her with a tray in hand. "And you got a big fat tip."

"That's nice," she murmured.

"It is," Kirsten called over her shoulder. "Now, get back to work."

And so Delilah did.

"You're back! Finally! What—"

Mckenna stopped talking as soon as she saw the car seat in Rowan's hand. Declan had fallen asleep on the way home, and Rowan was fully planning on following suit for however long this moment would last. Gingerly, he lowered the seat in the living room of their cottage and went back to the car to fetch the coffees and baby bag.

Delilah's face flashed in his mind as he grabbed the drinks and the bag, and he shook his head, desperate for the image to bounce right out. He didn't want to think about her. About the way she'd looked at him when he'd taken his shirt off. He'd been too tired to remember politeness, had wanted the smell of curdled milk off him, and then he'd seen her face.

The flush on her golden-brown skin, creeping up from the graceful column of her neck and blooming on those sharp cheekbones. Her mouth, full and sensual, parted, allowing him to all but feel the warmth of her breath on his lips . . .

His skin prickled, the blood heavy in his veins, heading to a part of his body he'd disowned after everything had happened with Mckenna. The thought was as good as an ice-cold shower. The arousal dissipated, leaving only the memory of Delilah's kindness behind. Rowan worried that was more lethal.

"Gimme, gimme, gimme," Mckenna chanted in a whisper when he came in with the coffee and gently pushed the door closed behind him.

"It's cold," he whispered back, but she shook her head.

"I don't care."

And with those words, she downed the coffee, closing her eyes and making a gruff little sound in her throat.

He'd have found that sexy ten months ago. He had long before then, too. When he and Mckenna had reunited almost a year ago, he hadn't been able to take his eyes off her.

They'd gone to school together, though they'd never run in the same circles. She was popular, and he was . . . quiet. He kept to himself mostly, but like every other guy in their school, he'd had a huge crush on her.

So when he'd seen her for the first time in ten years at a work party he'd been obliged to attend, he thought it was fate.

She'd been drinking from a flute of champagne when their eyes met across the room. Recognition had flared on her face, then interest. Her mouth curled up at the side, and she'd licked the lip of the champagne glass. Slowly, torturously, her gaze never leaving his, even when she took her next sip.

He wasn't proud of the way his body had responded to that in public, but when it had continued to respond that way in private an hour later when they'd been in the bathroom making love, he'd been quite proud.

Two months later she'd tracked him down and told him she was pregnant. Eight months after that, they were living together in the small town he'd only visited twice since his grandmother had moved there. They'd come for his grandmother's help, which Rowan would need when Mckenna left the country to attend a conference in London in a few weeks.

When he'd be a full-on single dad for a fortnight.

Nerves whirled in his body, making him jittery.

"Sweet, sweet caffeine," Mckenna said softly when she was done drinking.

"It's decaf."

"It's the spirit of the coffee that counts." She smiled as her eyes swept over his face, his T-shirt. "What happened?"

"He spat up on me."

Her eyebrows lifted. "So you applied for a job at the café?"

He almost smiled. "No, the waitress offered me a spare shirt."

"Kind of her."

He didn't respond to that. Declan made a soft noise, and they both glanced over. But he only sighed, still sleeping. Mckenna's gaze shifted to Rowan, and she disappeared into her bedroom—Mckenna had insisted they each get separate ones, since they weren't, in fact, a couple—and brought out the baby monitor.

She placed one camera on the coffee table in front of Declan, gripped the other to her chest, and dipped her head to his bedroom, which was the farthest away and where they'd be less likely to wake Declan up if they talked.

He walked to the bedroom with a small sigh. With each moment, sleep seemed like less of a reality.

"Are you okay?" she asked when he closed the bedroom door. "You've been acting weird since . . ." She trailed off. "Actually, I'm not sure if you've been acting weird. I don't know you, really. I mean, I know we tried after we found out I was pregnant, but . . . I don't know. It changed me. The pregnancy. It probably changed you, too, so . . ." She exhaled. "I don't know what I'm saying. I'm sorry. Ignore me."

"No," he said, because she was right. Beneath her words was genuine concern. For him, maybe, but certainly for Declan. Perhaps even for herself. "You're right. It has changed me. My life is . . . different now. And I don't have the right to complain because so is yours. And you did more. You carried him and you feed him. I will never not be grateful for that."

"Gratitude isn't enough to build a family."

"Is that what we're doing?"

"Isn't it?"

He didn't reply. He couldn't. No answer felt right. They were building a family, but not a family he'd ever associated with the word.

"I know you and I are never going to be together," she said quietly, and for the first time, he noticed how small she was. He took in the fatigue in her eyes. Realized the hands she had propped against her lower back were probably there to help with her pain.

She was dressed in a black shirt that stopped above her knees, and she'd put black tights on beneath it. The buttons of the shirt were white, and the top two were untied.

For easy access, he thought, and guilt hit him in the gut. Mckenna had sacrificed as much as he had for their child. More. But here he was, being broody that things were no longer in his control while she managed to keep her good humor.

"I don't want to be together in that way," she continued, her voice stronger. "But I want us to be friends."

"I want that, too. I want that more than anything."

And he did. In fact, if he could manifest feelings for her based purely on will, he would. If they could have a healthy romantic relationship—not one where they were obsessed with one another, ignoring their son in the process—Declan would have the perfect family.

But Rowan and Mckenna *had* agreed they couldn't be together. That neither of them wanted to be.

For one, they had little in common. She was outgoing and ambitious, always looking for more in life, in her job. He was quiet and content with exactly the way his life was. Or had been, he supposed.

For another, their chemistry . . . no longer existed. They hadn't clicked on any of their dates. It seemed the physical attraction that had brought them together at first had burned to ash.

But he respected the hell out of her. That was an even better foundation for a family than love. Love was a distraction. A weapon, too, he thought, in the wrong hands . . .

Besides, he *was* grateful. No matter what she said, he'd never not be grateful to her for giving him a child.

"I . . . I didn't think it would be so hard," she said. "Taking care of him. Us." She gave him a small smile and plopped down on the bed. "I thought . . . I don't know. I guess I thought we'd be able to do this without help. And that going back to work would be easy. I convinced myself that it would be like before."

He waited for her to go on, knowing there was more.

"I hate that I have to leave in two weeks. I think about him all the time. How am I going to focus on work?"

He sat down beside her, gripped her hand. The mere fact that she was worried about that made her so much better than either of his parents. They'd worked all the time, had gleefully put their legal careers—and one another—ahead of Rowan.

He'd worried Mckenna would do the same with her high-powered job at an NGO, but she hadn't. The only reason she was leaving was because their annual conference had unexpectedly been moved up, and it was the most important fundraising event of the year for the organization.

It did a lot to raise awareness for the cause, too, and since she was a part of the board, they needed her.

"We'll call every day."

"I know," she said softly.

"I'll take care of him," he vowed after a bit, squeezing her hand.

"I know that, too." She smiled. "I'm glad you're his father. I don't think I could have chosen a better man for the job."

As if hearing them, Declan let out a squeal. Rowan made to get up, but Mckenna put a hand on his shoulder. "No, you take a break. Nap. I got this."

When she left, he curled up on the bed, trying not to think about his son's tears in the other room.

Worrying desperately that Mckenna was wrong and that he was the very worst man for the job.

# CHAPTER THREE

Delilah's brother was waiting for her when she got home.

He was standing by her front door, leaning against it as he stared off into the distance. Delilah sighed. Matt couldn't even do something normal like check his phone while he waited. Heaven knew how long he'd been waiting, too, and he'd almost certainly spent that entire time staring. What a freak.

She adored him.

They hadn't been in touch for years. Not when their cruel and exacting mother had kept them apart. Matt had disappointed her, failed to meet her too-high expectations when he'd gotten his high school girlfriend pregnant at sixteen. She'd treated him horrendously after that, and Matt had only been able to escape it when he'd turned eighteen.

He'd been old enough to get a steady job in a small town two hours away from Cape Town, where they'd lived. The cost of living in that small town was less, and the job he'd gotten was able to provide the basics for his daughter, Irene, and Vanessa, Irene's mother.

Their own mother had threatened to disown him—and had, when the threat hadn't worked. Delilah had been banned from seeing him. They'd tried to keep in contact over the years, but somehow it had fizzled out to only the occasional message about Irene.

She'd known very little about her brother because of her mother, and she'd never seen it for how bad it was until her mother was arrested.

Then the scales had fallen off Delilah's eyes. Cruel had become criminal; exacting, calculating. Geraldine Huntington had known exactly what she'd done by banning Delilah from seeing Matt. She'd isolated Delilah, made her believe there was no independence outside the family.

Matt was struggling, she'd always told Delilah, and maybe that was why Delilah had never asked Matt about how he was doing. She felt guilty about him suffering when she . . . hadn't been. Not with her mother's wealth and the life that wealth had built her.

Delilah shook her head, trying to shake off the guilt, but it lingered, a faint layer of emotion over everything she did.

Matt had reached out after the arrest, offered that she come stay with him until she figured things out. She'd only been in town for a few weeks when he'd told her about this cottage. Turned out her brother hadn't been struggling at all. He'd gotten into construction, fixed up houses and sold them for a profit, and built a decent life for himself.

He kept the cottage for Irene so she'd have some place to stay when she was older, and he was letting Delilah stay there until Irene needed it.

It was more generosity than she deserved. *He* was more than she deserved. A good, kind big brother she hadn't known for over ten years because she'd allowed her mother to dictate her choices.

A gust of wind hit her in the chest. The joy she felt at coming home to her cottage, to her brother, was swept away with it.

No, she thought fiercely. No, she wouldn't allow thoughts of her family, of her mother, to rob her of her joy. She worked very hard for her joy. For this tentative relationship she was forging with her brother. To earn back what her mother had taken from her. Not only with her brother but with everyone.

*That doesn't make sense,* a voice whispered in her head, but she ignored it. Instead, she got out of her car, walked the small rock path to the wooden door, and grinned.

"Hi," she said.

Matt grunted.

"You know this is your house, right? You have keys. You don't have to wait."

He shrugged.

She bit her lip to keep from smiling. "Want to come inside?"

He bent to pick up packets she hadn't noticed on the floor. "I brought food."

Matt's voice was low and gruff, which made everything he said sound vaguely like a threat. Except to her, it only sounded like her brother. The one she'd lost touch with, who'd given her the biggest, most unlike-him smile when they'd first seen one another again, and wrapped her in his arms.

Overcome, she went up on her tiptoes and kissed his cheek.

He frowned, even as his cheeks reddened. "Why?"

"Because."

He grunted again, telling her it was an unsatisfactory answer.

She shrugged. "That's all you get. Why didn't you use the spare set of keys?"

"Didn't want to scare you."

She rolled her eyes and pushed open the door. The first sight that greeted her was Teddy. Teddy was a gamble. He'd been a baby when she'd gotten him. Barely old enough to stand up straight. But now, he was taller. He was bolder. He had leaves and everything.

Look at her, being a plant mom. A successful plant mom. She was delighted.

She murmured a hello to her beloved plant. She didn't know what kind of plant he was, having only remembered the instructions on how to feed and water him when she'd gotten him.

Now, it felt exciting not knowing. Who would he become? Who would he grow up to be? The possibilities were endless.

Her brother snorted at her side, as if he could see the hopes and dreams she had for her plant in her eyes.

"You have Irene; I have Teddy," she said defensively. "Not everyone's kid has to be human, you know."

Matt muttered something that sounded suspiciously like "bullshit," but since he had gone straight to the kitchen while she'd greeted Teddy and was currently packing out the most delicious-looking meal she'd ever seen, she decided not to call him out on it.

"You made this?"

He nodded.

"What is it?"

"Beef short rib, slaw with sesame dressing, garlic bread."

"You made the bread?"

He gave her a look to say, *I already answered that.*

She shook her head. "I am constantly amazed by you, Matt, my darling brother. Your talent surpasses my wildest expectations. You are the chef I never knew I wanted—because we had a chef growing up and he was pretty good. Plus, Sonny taught us the basics about cooking, but everything you make is better than his food. Not that I'd ever say that to anyone besides y—"

"Are you going to eat this, or are you going to keep talking?" he interrupted.

"Eat."

"So eat," he barked.

Obediently, she took the plate he offered her, and began to eat. He held a hand up when she opened her mouth to tell him how amazing it was, his eyes telling her he already knew, and she laughed.

Light played on his face, the expression so rare and precious that she stared an extra moment before dropping her eyes to her plate again.

It had been eighteen months since she'd moved to Sugarbush Bay, since they'd reunited, and she still got a little nervous around him. The talking, the teasing? It was a coping mechanism. An *I hope I'm not messing this up* mechanism. And since he seemed to enjoy it—if the small smiles she sometimes saw playing at his lips were anything to go by—she'd keep doing it.

"How is Irene?" she asked, at the same time that Matt said, "I have a favor to ask."

She blinked. He never asked for favors. So she said, "Anything," at the same time he said, "Fine."

There was a beat of silence.

"You go first," she said.

He shook his head.

"No, really. I was asking you a question anyway."

There was another beat of silence as he considered this.

"Irene is fine. Challenging."

Delilah laughed. "You're parenting a sixteen-year-old. What did you expect?"

"She's still fifteen."

"Her birthday is in three weeks."

"Fifteen."

She didn't laugh this time, but oh, how she wanted to. "Fifteen it is. Now," she said, pivoting, "what's the favor?"

"You have new neighbors. Two houses down."

"I do?"

She hadn't noticed, which she supposed made sense. She worked a lot and sometimes missed out on things happening in the neighborhood. Not for long—Sugarbush Bay was a small enough town that most news made its way to her whether she wanted it to or not. But she hadn't heard anything about a new neighbor. Hadn't seen anyone new around either.

"Since when?" she asked.

"Two, almost three weeks now."

"Three weeks?" That *was* a long time not to have noticed someone new. "And the favor's for them?"

"For me." He paused. "Actually, for them."

"Anything."

Matt tilted his head, studying her. "You mean that."

"Of course I mean it."

"Wasn't a question," he said and briskly moved on. "They have a kid. Irene was supposed to babysit on Saturday. But she has an exam on Monday that she is not adequately prepared for."

"Why would she agree to babysit if—" She broke off at the stormy look on his face. Clearly, Irene was trying to avoid studying. Unfortunately her father was a drill sergeant who knew too much about her business to allow it. "Yeah, of course. It'll be a nice chance for me to welcome them to the neighborhood."

"Great." Matt nodded. He grabbed his keys from the table and began to walk to the door.

"Wait," she said. "That's it?"

"What more do you want?"

Delilah opened her mouth, then turned to look at all the containers behind her, finally realizing how much he'd brought. "That's too much for me."

"Three more meals," he said simply. "Three different sides, but the short rib stays the same. I put them each in a separate container with instructions on how to heat it. Dinner tonight, lunch tomorrow for the café, dinner tomorrow night. Put them in the fridge."

With that, he left.

Delilah stared after him, and smiled.

At precisely twelve noon, the doorbell rang.

"At least she's on time," Mckenna said, nerves jumping across her face despite the calm words. "Should I open, or should you? Who says 'Please take care of our kid as you would your own, and if you don't, we'll kill you' more?"

He laughed. "You. Definitely you."

She stared, lips curving. "It's nice to see you smile again."

Immediately, his smile faded. So did hers. She opened her mouth but shook her head and went to open the door.

Rowan could have kicked himself. Things had been less awkward after the conversation they'd had that day he'd come back from the café. They were easing into some semblance of normality, but he was constantly worried he'd do something to spoil it.

Not intentionally. Never intentionally. He just didn't know how to act. How to be normal when he felt . . . so disjointed.

And here it was. Something so small, so simple, but he had spoiled it. What was wrong with him?

"Hi, I'm Delilah." A vaguely familiar voice came from the direction of the door. "I think Irene told you I'll be standing in for her?"

"Oh," Mckenna said. "No."

"No?"

"No," Mckenna said again. "We hired Irene based on Rowan's grandmother's recommendation."

Mckenna pushed the door open wider and gestured to Rowan with her head. He took a step forward. Another, when that first step wasn't enough and he couldn't see who was at the door. And when he did see, he thought maybe he'd recognized her voice, and that first step had been some form of denial.

Delilah's eyes widened when she saw him. There was a short moment, so short he was sure it couldn't have been longer than a few seconds, when their eyes held. Just . . . held.

And the world faded around them, his thoughts stilled, that constant buzz of anxiety that clouded his mind, weighed down his heart, quiet.

Soon the moment was over. Delilah cleared her throat and offered them both a smile. "Wow. Okay, yeah, this makes a lot more sense."

"What does?" Mckenna asked.

"Oh. I . . . um . . . I live a few doors down, and I hadn't heard we had new neighbors, which was weird because I usually find out about these things long before . . ." She trailed off. "Sorry, I'm surprised. I knew Linda's grandson was in town, and I thought it might be you, Rowan, but up until this moment, I didn't know for sure. But it makes sense that you, the new person around town, are also my new . . . neighbor."

She ended off slowly. Awkwardly. Rowan felt a pang of empathy. He understood what it was like to stumble through surprise. Hell, he was sure he'd have sputtered in the same way about finding her at his door if he'd been the one talking.

Only Delilah didn't seem to care that she'd been awkward. She took a breath and laughed a little, before shaking her head.

"I'm sorry. That was a mess, wasn't it? I really didn't expect the guy I occasionally make coffee for to be my new neighbor."

"Oh," Mckenna said slowly. "Oh! You're the waitress who helped Rowan when Declan spat up on him."

Delilah brightened. "Yes! That's me! And you are . . . ?"

"Mckenna." She offered Delilah a hand. "I'm Rowan's . . ." She pursed her lips. "I'm Declan's mother."

Delilah took Mckenna's hand, her eyes going from Mckenna to Rowan. They stayed on him, softening a bit before she smiled.

"It's lovely to meet you. I'm sorry about the confusion. Linda recommended Irene to babysit, I know, but Irene has a test to study for, and I'm her aunt, so I'm stepping in. But Linda knows me, too. Please, feel free to call her. I have several other references as well, if you need them."

"How?" he heard himself ask. It was the first time he'd spoken since he'd seen her, and Mckenna shot him a strange look.

It didn't seem to bother Delilah, though. Her smile widened. He had the most dramatic desire to put on sunglasses.

"For the references? Oh, I'm a babysitter."

Mckenna frowned. "I thought you said you were a waitress."

"I am. A waitress and a babysitter. I also work as a carer, sometimes, and an assistant, which, honestly, means anything. Admin, practical jobs like painting, getting someone's groceries, whatever. Would you like to call my references, or—"

"Oh, well, we trust Rowan's grandmother, so I'll just give her a call," Mckenna said. "Sorry."

"For making sure you're leaving your child with someone safe?" Delilah shook her head. "Don't apologize. And let me know if you need anyone else's number."

Curiosity shone on Mckenna's face as she excused herself to make the call. Delilah still stood at the door. Rowan was at a loss on what to do next. He should invite her in, shouldn't he? Yes. Yes, that was the most logical next step.

But it felt wrong, somehow, to have her inside his house. She was the woman in the café. The one who'd been so patient with him and his gruffness the other day. Who always gave him an extra cookie. She'd been kind, patient, and he . . . he'd been a jerk.

So maybe the next logical step was to apologize.

"I'm sorry," he said bluntly.

She frowned. "Like I told your son's mother"—he heard the hesitation before she settled on the term Mckenna had used—"you don't have to apologize for—"

"Not that," he interrupted. "For the other day."

Her frown deepened, her head tilting. *Cute,* a voice said in his head. It belonged to a small creature, grinning at him from some part of his brain he hadn't had access to since he'd found out Mckenna was pregnant.

Rowan showed it the middle finger, then flicked at it with that same finger. It disappeared back into the part of his brain he didn't want access to. The same part of his brain that controlled certain other parts of his body.

"I don't understand."

"I was rude," he elaborated, not letting himself feel the embarrassment of the facts. "You were trying to help, and I was short with you. You didn't deserve that. I'm sorry."

"Oh." She blinked a couple of times. When she spoke, it was through slightly curved lips. Perplexity or amusement, he couldn't tell. "Thanks, I guess. Although I didn't take offense to it, really. I thought it was part of who you are. All gruff on the outside but goo on the inside."

It was his turn for surprise. "Goo?"

"Yeah. Warm and supple. Sticky." She wrinkled her nose. "Okay, I'm not sure where I'm going with this. My point is, you were so soft with your son, and that's really all that matters, isn't it? At least to me. I'm a stranger, but he's your blood. I get it."

It was a frustratingly compassionate answer—and it confused him. Was that really how she saw him? As being soft with his son? Because right now, he felt like he was doing everything wrong. He was treating Mckenna strangely, felt . . . distant from himself, and how could that person be good with his son?

Then again, she hadn't said *good*; she'd said *soft*. Those weren't the same things. Or were they?

"Oh no," she said softly. "Are you malfunctioning?"

His eyes met hers. The teasing he saw there made him want to smile. Made him smile, in fact. "A little."

"Ah, I was worried it was a lot. A little is much better. I'm sure some kind of brain engineer could fix you right away."

"Brain engineer," he repeated.

"You *are* malfunctioning, aren't you?"

It was a strange way to put it but also a simple way. Because he *was* malfunctioning, on a much deeper level than he was telling her. And there *were* brain engineers—psychologists. Was that the answer to coming back to himself?

He shook his head.

"No," she said quickly. It took him a second to realize she thought he was answering her question. "No, of course not. I'm sorry. That was over the line."

It wasn't. It was so far from the line that he didn't understand why she thought it wasn't. But he didn't get a chance to say that to her when Mckenna stopped at his side.

"You've been approved."

Delilah smiled. "Wonderful."

"Come inside," Mckenna said after a beat. She shot him a look that asked why he hadn't invited Delilah in earlier.

He shrugged.

How could he explain that it didn't feel right to invite sunshine into this dark and gloomy place he was in? And he wasn't talking about the house. That was all light and bright with its textured white walls and green couches. The sleek modernity of the kitchen; the homey comfort of the bedrooms.

No, he was talking about himself. About how inviting her into his home felt like he was inviting her into his life.

He needed to shake this off. He'd be sharing space with this woman for the next four hours. If he didn't stop thinking about how she was the stars to his night sky, he wouldn't be able to focus on work. And he was already going to need every inch of his willpower to do that.

"Okay, both Rowan and I have to work," Mckenna was explaining when he joined them in the kitchen. He leaned against the wall, content to let Mckenna do the talking. "I'm going to work at his grandmother's house. She won't be home, and I need quiet for the three-hour meeting I'm about to attend." She rolled her eyes. "And Rowan has some emergency at work as well, and he can't be jumping to attend to every need Declan has until he sees to that emergency."

Delilah nodded. "Yeah, of course. So he'll be going with you."

"No," Mckenna said. "He feels more comfortable"—she shot him a quick look—"*we* both feel more comfortable if he stays here. He'll be around if you have any questions, but you'll primarily be looking after Declan. I'm sure neither of them will bother you too much." Mckenna gave him a wry smile. "Quiet, these guys of mine."

A subtle hint of possessiveness, but Rowan noticed it all the same. As did Delilah. Her expression was pleasantly blank, but acknowledgment had darted across her face.

He didn't understand what Mckenna hoped to achieve by claiming him. They'd already established that things between them were platonic.

Could it be that she was sensing the tension between him and Delilah? It was faint, delicate, but it was still there. From his side, certainly, even if it confused him. And from Delilah's side, too. He could sense it, though he had no idea why he was so sure about it.

If Mckenna *had* sensed it, perhaps she was merely warning him. Reminding him that he wasn't available. His life was a mess. Everything seemed overwhelming, unsure, confusing, and that was the shit he was aware of. Beneath that . . . well, he didn't want to think about it.

No, he wasn't available.

But what the hell was it about this woman that made him want to be?

# CHAPTER FOUR

Delilah was cleaning the living room when Rowan asked her what she was doing.

She looked at him. Down at herself on her hands and knees, scrubbing something that looked like spit-up out of the thick beige carpet.

"Isn't it obvious?" she asked.

He reconsidered. "Wrong question then. Why?"

"Yes, that does make more sense. Well, I changed and fed Declan, we played for a while, and now he's sleeping. You're not paying me—well, not me, my niece, since I plan on giving the money to her for being so studious"—she grinned, thinking about what Matt would say about that—"to sit around and scroll on my phone."

"No," he said carefully. "We're paying you to take care of Declan. Which you have." He blinked at the monitor showing the sleeping baby. "How long did it take for him to go down?"

"Ten minutes? He was tired."

"Ten minutes," he mused. "You had to rock him?"

"A little. Mostly I walked up and down, singing him some lullabies, and he fell asleep."

"Ten minutes," he said again.

"What? Is that long or is that short?"

"We usually spend at least twenty minutes on the task."

"Ah, I'm sure I was lucky." She shrugged. "Babies are weird. Although I probably shouldn't say that to you, his parent, who believes he's the moon and stars." At the conflicted look on his face, she straightened. "What? What is it?"

"Nothing."

She opened her mouth, about to tell him that there was clearly something wrong, but she knew it was none of her business. Instead, she went back to her cleaning, trying hard to ignore the fact that he was standing there, staring at her.

After a few moments, he left. Relief pooled inside her. She'd been off, tense, since discovering Rowan was her new neighbor. Although now that she knew it, she wondered why she hadn't realized it before. She'd only known about one new person in town, and she'd made the connection to Linda based on that alone.

How hadn't she made that same connection when Matt had told her she had new neighbors? And why hadn't Matt told her her new neighbors were Linda's grandson and his family? He must have known, with Irene babysitting for them. If he did, he clearly didn't think it was important enough to mention. Why would it be?

*Because you have a crush on Rowan.*

No, no. That was no longer a thing. She'd pretty much talked herself out of it at the café the last time he'd been there. And though he clearly wasn't with the mother of his child—Mckenna deliberately hadn't introduced herself in relation to Rowan, which she wouldn't have done if they were in a relationship—the situation was complicated.

How could it not be? They had an infant together. They were living together. After witnessing Matt go through the same thing with Irene's mother when Irene was first born, Delilah knew the complexity of having a child together. She didn't even blame Mckenna for being possessive of Rowan. He was hers in ways Delilah would never understand.

None of that changed that she still felt charged around him. As if the mere acknowledgment of his attractiveness had energized every cell in her body. It was how she knew he'd returned to the living room before she heard him set something down on the table in front of her.

A cup of tea and a cookie.

She looked at him. "What's this?"

"Tea." He paused, a blush on his cheeks. "And a cookie."

It was so endearing she almost died.

"Why?"

"You deserve a break."

"I . . . no. No, Rowan, I work for you. I'm working for you. You don't have to—"

"Delilah."

The sheer surprise of hearing her name in that smooth, deep voice of his stopped her talking. Why did it sound so good?

"What?" she asked.

"It's okay to take a break." He pushed the cup and plate toward her. "I'll leave you alone to take one."

But he didn't move.

Delilah didn't know how to feel about it. Any of it. Her crush—ex-crush—and, technically, her employer had brought her a snack and told her she deserved to take a break.

That type of kindness wasn't unusual in Sugarbush Bay. It was the general culture of the people here. But this . . . this felt specific. Special. Rowan hadn't brought her tea because that was what people here did. He'd done it for her.

It distracted her enough that she didn't realize he was still standing there. After even more silence, she couldn't ignore it.

"Thank you. For this. I didn't expect . . ." She cleared her throat. "I should have said thank you sooner."

"That's not why I'm here."

He stuffed his hands in his pockets. He was wearing a pair of black sweatpants—Delilah kept her eyes away from the groin area; she was *not* prepared to see anything like that—and a black T-shirt.

Stay-at-home-dad chic, she thought with a smirk. But really, the smirk was hiding the fact that he looked hot and did sweet stuff like bring her tea. She was usually the one doing sweet stuff for people. Rarely did they return the favor—she wouldn't allow them to. She didn't deserve kindness in that way, and yet, when Rowan offered it, it felt . . . good.

She couldn't think about that. He had a child and a complicated relationship with the child's mother, and now, he was her boss. Sort of. She really shouldn't be thinking about the crotch area of his sweatpants or how hot he was.

"Why *are* you here?"

"You spend a lot of time with kids, right?" he asked softly.

"Yeah."

"Babies?"

She nodded, unsure of where this was going.

"And you know . . . their parents, right?"

Again, she nodded.

"Okay." He stood for a couple of moments. Shook his head. "Okay, thanks."

He turned.

"That's it?" she asked before he could flee. "That's all you're going to ask?"

He paused but didn't turn around. There was a stretch of silence, and she searched through his questions to try to anticipate what he was going to say.

"Do you want to ask me something about other parents?"

He still didn't turn around, but he nodded.

She waited to see if he'd give her more. He didn't. So she reached for her tea and took a sip before saying, "It's hard. For all of them."

He turned around, and the conflict in his eyes . . .

She set the cup down. Her hands weren't quite steady as she did, and it was because of him. It felt as if his turmoil were living in her own body. She didn't understand it, and so she said, "Is that it? Are you having a hard time?"

"I . . ."

His voice faltered. She put aside the brush she still held in one hand, stood—and promptly fell over. She'd been sitting on her legs for too long, and they'd lost feeling. And so of course, during this very important time, she fell.

And of course, he caught her.

Her breath swept out her lungs. She was overwhelmed by everything about him. The way his eyes searched her face, as if looking for any sign that she wasn't okay.

The way his arms, stronger than they looked, softer than they looked, held her against him.

The way his body felt against hers, hard, comfortable, perfectly aligned, as if they were made for one another . . .

She sucked in a breath.

Big mistake.

Because now she knew how he smelled by himself. Pine. Pure pine, as if he'd been leaning against trees in a forest.

She loved trees. She loved the forest.

And she was once again fantasizing about a man she had no business fantasizing about.

"Thank you," she said, testing her legs. They still felt unsteady, but she wasn't sure that was because they'd fallen asleep. "I . . . fell."

His lips twitched. "Yes."

"Yes." She rolled her eyes. "Yes, of course. You know that. You . . . um . . . you caught me." She shook her head. "Sorry. You were saying?"

"I wasn't saying anything."

The twitch disappeared.

"Oh." She went back and forth about saying what she wanted to say and ended up ignoring the voice warning her not to say anything at all. "It's hard, being a parent. I see it all the time. With the parents I babysit for; with my friends, my brother . . . I think it's probably the hardest job out there. Especially at this age."

She tilted her head toward the monitor.

"When my niece was Declan's age, my brother used to stare at the monitor the entire duration of her nap to make sure she was okay. And if she made the slightest noise, he'd jump and try to cater to her every need. Granted, he was seventeen then and a little bit of an idiot, but he loved her so much and . . ." She let out a breath. "It's hard now because they need you so much. But if you feed them, change them, love them . . . that's enough. And that's what you're doing. You're doing enough."

He blinked, slow, steady. "And what about later? When feeding and changing and love isn't enough?"

"You figure it out," she said softly.

"Just like that?"

"No. It'll be a long, tedious process."

"Yeah," he said after a bit. "Yeah, that's what I'm afraid of."

"You won't be alone," she added quickly. "You have Mckenna."

"Yes."

"I like her," Delilah offered. "She seems really nice."

"She is. We . . ." He frowned. "We weren't a couple when we found out about Declan."

She waited, but he didn't elaborate. She wanted to ask why. Why they weren't a couple, if they had been before, why he'd told her about it.

Instead, she focused on telling herself that it was fine. She didn't have to ask any of the questions his statement provoked in her head.

And she believed that. For a second. After that second, she was asking, "Are you a couple now?"

He stared at her.

Through her.

In her.

Her skin grew tight. Hot. Her stomach flipped. Dipped. Melted into a pool of lust, pure and simple lust, that gripped parts of her body that had been dormant for a long time. For too long a time, if a single look could make her feel this . . . this wanton.

This *wanted*.

43

The side of his mouth tugged up. A sultry, knowing half smile that echoed the one he'd given her in the café and yet was so far away from the cutesy meaning she'd assigned to it then.

"No, Mckenna and I are not a couple."

"Right. Okay."

Her face was flushed. She resisted the urge to fan herself.

"Thank you," he said quietly, angling his head. "For your reassurance."

He turned and walked back to his office, but his presence lingered. Delilah wondered at it. At him. How he'd gone from uncertainty to . . . to whatever he'd been when he'd looked at her that way. It was the look of a man who was aware of attraction. Aware of it and wanted it. She couldn't quite wrap her head around the change, but she . . . liked it.

At the same time, it terrified her.

She gave in to the urge to fan herself now, blowing out a breath. When she felt normal again, she thought about what Rowan had said before he'd stared at her. About what she thought might help. She pulled out her phone and sent a text to her brother.

The guy I'm babysitting for is freaking out about parenting. I think you should talk to him.

A minute passed, and her brother answered,

No.

To which she replied,

You owe me.

A faster reply this time:

Fine. But no buddy buddy stuff.

She laughed.

I don't know what that means. But thank you.

Matt didn't reply to that, but he didn't have to. He was probably rolling his eyes at the request, at her thanks, because of course he'd do something she'd asked him. He was like that. It was what she remembered about him when he'd still lived at home.

He'd tried to make their parents' indifference tolerable by making himself present. Her memories of when she was younger, before he'd left, were filled with him.

And after, the memories were empty.

She hated that when Matt had left, she'd become a typical rich girl with a family who didn't care about her. Her mother and father worked almost constantly. Her mother because Geraldine was a workaholic who enjoyed the challenges of her job  and the challenges of defrauding hundreds of clients. Her father because he didn't want to spend any more time with his family than he had to.

Delilah had always known her parents didn't like one another, that they barely tolerated their kids, and that their professional and societal connections prevented them from getting a divorce. If they'd had any clout as individuals, she had no doubt that they would have separated.

But they'd amassed their wealth and power together. The public was riveted by the Ice Queen and her Prince Charming. That was what the media referred to her parents as: royalty. Merely because they had money. Merely because they seemed important.

It disgusted her as much now as it had then. Of course, she'd only realized it after Matt had left. He hadn't played by the rules her parents had established for their family, after all. They'd kicked him out. And with that action, they'd cracked the Huntington family veneer.

Delilah felt the echoes of it in her heart to this very day. Along with the damage her mother's arrest had done.

But what was the point of thinking about that now?

She was saved from having to answer when Declan woke up. She'd drunk her tea, eaten her cookie, and finished the carpet by then. The rest of her day was spent taking care of him.

At 4:59 p.m., she heard a car pull into the driveway. At five, her phone went off. Matt. He'd offered to come fetch her, and he didn't want to ring the doorbell in case the baby was sleeping.

"Good thinking," Delilah said softly when she opened the door to him. "He's snoozing now. I think he misses his parents. He's been restless all afternoon."

Matt took in that information with a nod.

"I'll tell Rowan I'm on my way out, and as I leave, I'll be like, *Oh, look, it's my brother, a single father since he was a teenager, with the best daughter I know, who did it all while co-parenting, but a lot of it was really him. You guys should talk.*"

She bit her lip to keep from laughing at her brother's dark expression. "Honestly, I'm surprised you haven't reached out to him already. You knew he lived here, and Irene was babysitting for him. In fact, I'm sure Linda arranged that so the two of you could meet." She didn't wait for him to answer. "Anyway, I'll make it seem like you're this fountain of parenting wisdom who can't help but take him under your wing and—"

"Delilah," Matt growled. "I don't care how you do it as long as you tell him I'm not here to be his friend."

"What do you have against friends?"

"I already have two. One I work with and a spare. That's enough."

"Are you saying Lucas is your spare friend?"

"Yes." Matt said it so casually she didn't bother threatening to tell Lucas. Lucas probably already knew. "Let's get this done. I have a pork belly slow cooking in the oven. I need to be home in thirty minutes so it doesn't dry out."

She almost second-guessed asking him now, but maybe Rowan would appreciate Matt's honesty.

She hoped, anyway.

"Hey." A soft voice came from the vicinity of his office door. "I'm heading out."

Rowan blinked as the words filtered into his head. His brain processed them, even though a part of it was still working on fixing code for his client.

Some genius at the man's company had messed with the product page, wanting to make a "quick change" that resulted in shoppers being unable to add anything to their carts. Rowan had spent the last five hours dealing with that, and though it was mostly done, he'd wanted time to check that no other issues had cropped up.

He'd also wanted a word with the developer he'd delegated the client to. Apparently, customer service had "decreased in quality" since Rowan had gone on paternity leave, which was unacceptable.

He'd built his business on the quality of both his work and the relationships he had with his clients. In those early days, it had just been him, and advertising had largely meant word of mouth. He'd been determined to build a stellar reputation. He *had* built a stellar reputation. That wouldn't change because he'd taken a step back.

He turned, his body responding to seeing Delilah in the doorway before his heart did. The pulse of awareness, of desire, that went through him was less alarming than his heart going thump.

In and of itself, that thump wasn't alarming. Hearts beat, didn't they? Except that thump was in his ears, as if he could literally hear it. It vibrated through his body. And it was a reaction to something. To *someone*. Delilah.

It probably didn't mean anything.

It was probably fine. Normal, even.

He was fine. Normal.

Everything was fine and normal.

"You're leaving?" he repeated hoarsely. It barely sounded like him.

"Yeah. It's five." She smiled. Tilted her head to the side. "You're going to be okay, right? Mckenna should be home soon?"

He blinked. Right. She was asking him if he was going to be okay because of Declan. Because she had been there to take care of Declan. Now she was leaving, and he had to take over because Declan was his son. He'd gotten so caught up with work he'd forgotten.

A thick lump sat in his throat. Unease trickled down his back.

This was how it began. He'd lose time, get caught up in work. Before he knew it, he'd be hiring Delilah full time, and another nanny when Delilah inevitably quit, and another, and another, until his son's life became a revolving door of people, all because Rowan thought work was more important.

"Rowan?" Delilah's brow was knit. "Are you okay?"

He nodded, not trusting himself to speak. He was spiraling. His thoughts had done so often enough in the last ten months that it had basically become a hobby. Only he didn't enjoy this hobby, could see that it was destructive and robbed him of his sense of self. The sense of self he desperately needed to be a good father.

And a functioning human being.

"I'll walk you out," he said, his voice gruff but working. He'd take it.

"He's sleeping," Delilah said as they walked to the door. "He's been a bit restless, so I don't think this nap will last for much longer. A bottle of breast milk is defrosting in hot water in case Mckenna doesn't get home in time for the feed. And if she does, tell her to take a shower and pump instead. I'm sure she'll need and appreciate the break."

She paused. "Although I don't want to be presumptuous. I put the bottle in the water a few minutes ago. Maybe I should—"

She turned around, walking right into Rowan. He'd been following too closely behind. Though it was too late to consider that, since her nose was already smooshed in his chest.

"Sorry," came the muffled sound of her voice.

"Don't worry about it."

"Hmm."

The vibration of that sound reached into his body, clutching his veins, freezing his blood. His thoughts flickered back to that moment earlier, when Delilah had asked him if he and Mckenna were a couple. She'd wanted to know because he'd been right, and she did feel whatever was happening between them, too.

It had given him a sense of satisfaction that he had no right to have.

But it hadn't stopped him from imagining what it would be like to touch her.

He was touching her now. It was innocent, of course, but it was contact. Only he didn't feel what he'd thought he would. There was no heat, no overwhelming sense of desire. His blood remained frozen.

But it pulsed. Resuscitated after being dead for so long.

Idly, he thought about how warm Delilah felt. Warm and soft.

She smelled like cinnamon and vanilla.

"Sorry," she said again, this time more clearly. She was standing in front of him. At some point, she'd moved and he hadn't even noticed. "I got stuck."

"Stuck?"

"Yeah."

"In my chest?"

"It's like a maze in there."

His lips twitched, despite the absurdity of the statement. Or maybe because of it. But Rowan didn't get a chance to indulge it because he heard a grunt coming from the vicinity of his front door.

When he looked over, a man was there. Tall, brown skin, full beard, heavy brows, all glowering at him.

Rowan had never been on the receiving end of a look with so much . . . resentment? Or contempt. Perhaps fury? None of those fit exactly right, but he got the gist of it anyway.

*Warning! Warning! Warning!*

He pushed Delilah aside, shifting so his body shielded her, and barked, "Who the hell are you?"

"Oh! No, no. No, Rowan, this is me. Mine. I mean, he's mine."

Delilah pushed him out the way and went to stand at the man's side. Rowan took it in. How the man leaned toward her as she looked up at him adoringly.

He gritted his teeth, actively trying not to curl his hands into fists. If he did, he was afraid he'd beat his chest, scream in rage, because this woman—*his* woman—was with someone else.

But she wasn't his woman. She was nothing to him at all. He had no right to feel any of what he did, and he knew it. Could only blame the primal part of him, the part *she'd* woken up, for the irrationality of his thoughts.

He struggled to keep his voice neutral. "I didn't realize."

"Why would you?" Delilah shook her head. "It's not like he said anything. Only stood there staring at us like we're a movie he's watching."

"And didn't particularly like," Rowan said under his breath, still staring at the man, who stared right back.

He appreciated that. Respected it, even. Delilah had had her face pressed against his chest, and clearly her boyfriend didn't like it. But the man obviously wasn't upset at Delilah. He was upset at *Rowan*. That Rowan had dared touch the woman he saw as his own.

Rowan couldn't blame him.

"Anyway, I wanted to introduce you two," Delilah said brightly, seemingly oblivious to the tension in the room. "Rowan, this is my brother, Matt. He's Irene's father. She was meant to babysit for you today. He had Irene when he was pretty young. Sixteen."

"Seventeen," Matt said.

"That depends on who you ask," Delilah replied.

"Me."

"You can't ask you. You're not exactly the most reliable."

"The first time I held her in my arms, I was seventeen."

"Yeah, but you conceived her when you were sixteen, so—"

"Delilah."

Matt managed to infuse a world of meaning into that single word. She blinked and nodded.

"My dear brother became a father at seventeen." She smiled at Rowan mild-manneredly. "He is well versed in the bumps of parenthood. You two should chat."

Rowan had gotten lost somewhere along the way, but with those words, he was finally caught up. Matt was Delilah's brother, not her boyfriend.

Something akin to relief washed through him, but it wasn't quite as reassuring as that. Not when Matt clearly saw Delilah as his own. Rowan could now see what had been obvious before: the possessiveness wasn't romantic. It was familial. It was . . . protection. Matt was warning Rowan against pursuing Delilah.

Some wicked and unfamiliar urge made him want to do it all the more.

He shook his head. This wasn't who he was. It wasn't who he was at all. Or it hadn't been—before Delilah.

But then her words finally settled in his head.

"You asked your brother to come talk to me about fatherhood?" Rowan asked, his spine stiffening.

"No." Delilah shook her head vigorously but stopped. "Well, yes, I asked him to talk to you, but not because I thought you couldn't—"

She broke off. Took a step forward. Something about it seemed like a plea.

"Look, I know things are rough right now, and this might seem like it's me . . . overstepping, or whatever. And maybe I am—"

"You are," her brother informed her.

"I think it'll be worthwhile," she finished, ignoring him. "In my experience, going through difficult times can be isolating. Reaching out, asking for help? It's easier." Her eyes looked so sad Rowan forgot about being offended. He wanted to grasp her hands and ask her what had hurt her. "Let it be easy, Rowan."

His indignation fading, he saw the appeal. It was tempting, so damn tempting, to ask for a hand that could pull him out of this . . . this . . . hell, he didn't even know.

And it *would* be easier. To know that he wasn't the only person feeling this way. That he wasn't the only father flailing, afraid of failing. It was why he'd asked Delilah about the parents she'd babysat for in the first place.

He'd almost forgotten about that, and now that he remembered . . . this was probably his fault. He'd allowed Delilah to see his insecurities. And for some unknown reason, she'd taken it upon herself to help him through them.

He couldn't be offended, yet he still was.

"Tomorrow. The Blue Café. One p.m."

Matt nodded at him, turned on his heel, and left. Delilah gave Rowan a helpless smile. "You better be there. He'll be pissed if you're not, and you won't like him pissed."

With a little wave, she was off.

Rowan had the distinct impression he'd been ambushed.

# CHAPTER FIVE

Matt was quiet on the way home. That wasn't unusual. What *was* unusual was that his quietness was very loud—and very judgmental.

"Just say it."

Matt didn't even have the decency to pretend. "He's wrong for you."

"I'm sorry?"

"You heard me."

"Yeah, I heard you. But I'm trying to figure out why you'd say something so . . ."

She couldn't find a word. Probably because she couldn't identify the feeling that had tightened her stomach at Matt's warning.

The rest of the drive was somehow quieter. Tenser, too. Delilah's fingers curled in her lap, her heart thudding so hard that she had to take a breath to calm herself when Matt eventually stopped at his house.

"You still want to do this?" she asked, her voice coming out thin, losing weight so that it could move past the huge lump in her throat.

"What?"

"Dinner."

"I cooked, didn't I?"

"Yes, but—" She broke off and decided to try another tactic. Directness. "Do you still want me here after what you said to me about Rowan?"

Matt's frown deepened. "What did I say about Rowan?"

"That he isn't right for me." She swallowed. "Not that we . . . I mean, we're not . . ." She didn't know how to make him see. "There's nothing there, Matt. Don't be upset with me because—"

"I'm not upset." His gaze swept over her. "But you are."

"No."

"Yes."

"No."

He grunted. Took a breath. "I only meant that he doesn't deserve you."

He reached out and squeezed her hand, though it might as well have been her lungs based on how they reacted.

"Now, come inside and eat the pork belly I made."

He got out of the car and walked to the house without looking to see if she was following. And that was the thing about Matt. He didn't linger in the madness.

When he'd reached out after their mother's arrest, Delilah had been surprised. She'd fully expected to never hear from him again. Or if she did hear from him, she thought he'd be mad. Gloating, even. Because she'd stayed behind after he'd left. She hadn't called him more than a couple of times a year. Hadn't checked in with Irene as often as she should have.

Matt, by every right, should have enjoyed the life he'd carved out for himself. It was a damn good life. She got out of the car, looking up at the house he'd built. Literally. When Matt had started working in construction, he'd been one of the builders, before moving up to foreman. Some years after that, he'd taken over the company from his mentor.

It had been controversial, she'd heard from the town, because there'd been others who'd worked for the owner, Hans Smit, for longer. Back then, Matt was an outsider. And he was young.

But now, five years later, no one doubted him. He knew every part of his business because he'd worked in every part of his business. Smit was still his mentor, still owned part of the business, albeit a minority share. Matt was smart with his money. He'd made investments, bought properties, flipped them.

And this one? The one where he now lived with Irene, a few kilometers from the beach and from town? He'd built it to look nothing like the house they'd grown up in.

It was a double story, white, with a balcony on the second floor that stretched from the front of the house to the side. There were glass windows on the top floor, sliding doors leading to the balcony, and a black roof that somehow made the house feel modern and homey at the same time.

At each corner of the balcony at the front of the house stood a large potted plant, green and lush, and around them, Delilah knew, though she couldn't see them from here, were flowers of different colors.

Irene planted them and cared for them. It was something she and Matt had done together initially, but as she'd gotten older, she'd asked for the responsibility for herself. Something about her dad not having the right touch or the necessary patience.

Delilah laughed to herself, even as her heart ached. She'd lost out on so much of Irene's childhood. She'd lost so much time with Matt. But now, through the grace of her brother, she was a part of their lives again. They were a part of hers.

So though she knew he hadn't meant it that way, Delilah thought Matt was right. Rowan didn't deserve her. Neither did Matt and Irene. They didn't deserve to have someone as selfish as her in their lives.

She'd done all she could to make sure she wasn't selfish anymore, but . . . was she succeeding? Would she ever?

"Dad," Irene said as Delilah walked into the house, "I think something died in the garage. I was in there earlier, and the smell was bad."

"I'll check it out later."

"Is this later as in *after dinner* or later as in *when I remember*, which is likely to be three days from now, when the smell has permeated the walls and soaked through every piece of furniture?"

There was a long silence.

"I'll do it now," Matt said.

"Great!"

Delilah smiled. She might not know if she was succeeding, but she would do everything in her power to keep trying. Anything to continue having her brother and niece in her life.

Anything.

Rowan got to the café before one o'clock. Exactly fifteen minutes before one o'clock. He would have come even earlier if he could. But Mckenna had offered to take care of Declan while Rowan met with his "new friend"—her words, not his—and she'd had some work to do first.

Declan had been antsy before Rowan left, too, but Rowan knew that was because of him. He was nervous. He couldn't stop pacing. He hadn't been able to get a word out to Mckenna. She'd laughed gently, patted his shoulder, and told him it would be okay.

It would be okay.

That was something people often told him. But social interactions were never really okay for him. He always said the wrong thing or did something stupid or . . . or got a woman pregnant.

He blew out a breath. Fifteen minutes early didn't change that he'd be awkward, but it did mean he wouldn't be late. And if he could sit at the café, if he could find a table, settle, before Matt came, things might be easier.

*It wouldn't hurt to talk to Delilah, too.*

He took a breath. She infiltrated his thoughts. The idea of her, the memory of her. Knowing that they could bump into one another if he left his house put him on edge. That had always been possible in a town as small as Sugarbush Bay, but knowing that she lived walking distance away . . .

It taunted him in the middle of the night. When he was feeding his son, he thought about her. About how easy it would be to walk to her house, talk to her. That was the worst of all: He *wanted* to talk to her. He didn't want to talk to anyone he didn't know, but he wanted to talk to Delilah. About anything. About everything. With her, talking seemed easy.

It wasn't. Not for him.

It confused him as much as wanting her confused him. He could still smell her, feel her body against his. Remember what it had been like to learn that she was interested in him, too.

But whatever desire that knowledge awoke in him, he squashed it quickly. Brutally. He'd taken the physical side of him offline after Mckenna, and he didn't miss it. He refused to miss it now, even if Delilah did make him feel things he hadn't for a long time.

But he had self-control.

And he'd have the opportunity to practice it, since they wouldn't be able to avoid one another.

No one could avoid their neighbors, no matter how much they wanted to. And if Matt and he were going to be friends, Rowan would definitely bump into Delilah. Then again, there was no guarantee that he and Matt would be friends. With his skill—or lack thereof—this meeting would amount to nothing more than a man doing his sister a favor.

It was a reality Rowan had to face. This was the first time he'd been out with anyone since . . . since he and Mckenna had decided dating wasn't for them. Before that, the last time he'd been out with people had been the party he and Mckenna had conceived Declan at.

His social clumsiness was a vicious cycle. He didn't go out much because he was worried about messing up, and because he didn't go out, he never got the chance to improve.

Not that he thought he needed to improve. At least he hadn't—before. Now he was a father. He didn't want Declan to grow up as iso-lated as he had. When he'd been a kid, he'd never gone to parties, never had playdates. His parents would have had to be involved for that. They would have had to take him to parties and arrange playdates. But they hadn't been that kind of parents.

Rowan would make sure he was.

Which meant that at some point, he'd have to start interacting with people. Delilah had helped him get a head start, so he would try not to dwell on why she'd introduced him to Matt, only that she had. He'd try to make conversation with the guy, and he'd go home. Easy peasy.

But when he walked into the café, Matt was already there. Rowan immediately stopped, his heart tripping at this unexpected development.

Should he walk over? Sit down? Matt had a half-eaten sandwich in front of him. Would Rowan be interrupting if he did walk over then? How weird would it be if he sat at a different table and waited for Matt?

He could have kicked himself. If he'd come exactly on time, he wouldn't have been in this predicament, and he—

"Rowan? Hey."

Rowan turned. Delilah. It was Delilah. She gave him a questioning look, and he realized he hadn't said hello back.

"Hello."

"Hello," she repeated with a small smile. "You know you've been standing at the door for at least five minutes?"

He looked at his watch. Twelve fifty-one. Yeah, that checked out.

"He won't bite," Delilah said, her eyes resting on Matt. "He'll bark, though. Really gruffly. And you'll be afraid in the beginning, but really, it's not that scary. He's not that scary. Think of it as a poodle's bark. It seems really intimidating, but that's only because you haven't looked at the dog yet. And when you do, you see its curly hair and its cute face, and you're like, 'This? *This* is what I was afraid of?' You get over it pretty quickly after that."

She smiled, and his lips curled. *No*, he told them. *Don't you dare.* But they didn't care for that instruction, widening instead, and before he knew it, he was smiling properly and basking in the broader smile he got in return.

It was warm and comforting and he felt like he'd been itching in a spot he couldn't reach for ages and finally someone was scratching it.

He blew out a breath and told himself to get a grip.

It helped when her smile got smaller. A slight curve of her lips. Hesitant, instead of the confidence of a few seconds ago.

It helped that she was holding herself a little taller, her shoulders pushed back, as if he'd put her back up.

Yes, it helped. Because it was familiar. He was used to people being uncomfortable around him. He was used to *making* people uncomfortable. Delilah's ease with him had been there from the very first cup of coffee she'd served him. It was why he felt so . . . unlike himself around her.

Someone he didn't know couldn't be easy around him. Not with his flaws. And before her, his experiences had proved that. People in the grocery store avoided his gaze. No one ever greeted him when he walked down the road. That could only be because of him. Because of who he was.

Delilah was still staring at him. Waiting for an answer.

He cleared his throat. "I won't be bothering him by being early?"

"Of course not. He came early, too."

"Yeah, but he's eating."

"He's always eating," she said casually.

As if there weren't a lingering thread of tension between them.

As if with each word she weren't pulling that thread off the spool, leaving a mess Rowan was sure he'd get tangled in.

"I meant what I said earlier. My brother is a good guy. The best guy," she qualified. "I wouldn't have introduced him if I didn't think so."

"You have to think so," he commented. "He's family."

"How nice that you think that," she replied, her voice thin. "It must mean you get along with all your family."

She didn't wait for him to reply before she moved. He followed but didn't get the chance to tell her that no, he didn't get along with his family, and that he was an idiot for saying something he didn't believe in.

He didn't even get the chance to process the admiration and love she had in her voice for her brother. Didn't bother acknowledging the pang of longing that gave him.

*But this is why you're here,* a voice in his head said. *To make sure your son never feels that longing for family. Because he'll already have it. He'll have you.*

*If you can manage to do it right,* an opposing but familiar voice said back.

His heart thudded in response.

"Matt, Rowan's here," Delilah announced when they stopped at Matt's table.

Matt stuffed the last bite of his sandwich into his mouth. The bite had been big. For an amount of time Rowan couldn't quantify but was surely *at least* an hour, Matt chewed. He watched Rowan as he chewed. His eyes never left Rowan's gaze.

Rowan had never, ever in his life experienced anything like it. No one, and he meant no one, had ever looked at him this way while chewing.

It was chaotic. It was compulsive.

He couldn't look away.

"Matt," Delilah said patiently. "Be nice."

He looked at her, confusion streaking across his eyes.

"You're doing that thing," she continued in the same tone. "Where you do something normal but you're glaring."

Matt wiped his mouth with a serviette. "That's just how I look at people." To Rowan, he said, "Sit."

Rowan narrowed his eyes, but he sat.

"Matt," Delilah said, her voice sharper now.

"He's fine," Matt said. "We're fine. Aren't we, Rowan?"

They were staring at one another now. In his head, he heard the music that usually played during a standoff in a western. Still, he said, "Yeah, we're fine."

Delilah sighed. "Did I make a mistake introducing you two? Because I swear—"

"You have a job to do, Deelee," Matt said.

The pet name had Rowan looking at Delilah to see how she'd take it. Her face had softened, but she was frowning. At him. She was worried about him.

"Go," he said softly.

"You're sure?"

He nodded. She gave him one last look and sent her brother a warning glare before walking to a table behind them. There was a long silence. Rowan didn't say anything. He didn't know what to say. The tension that hung in the air made it that much worse.

And then Matt spoke.

"It's scary, isn't it?" he said, his voice rough. Vulnerable. And just like that, the tension disappeared. "When they put your kid in your arms for the first time and you realize, *This is it. This is the rest of my life.*"

Rowan's lips parted. He immediately pressed them together again. But it was too late. His breath had escaped in one sharp exhale. Matt nodded, taking it as a reply. Correctly interpreting it as a reply.

*It's the scariest thing I've ever done.*

"My daughter, Irene. She's almost sixteen." He frowned, as if he couldn't quite believe this. "When they put her into my arms, I was seventeen. I was . . . a kid. I look at her now and think to myself that I was pretty much her age when I had her. It's a miracle she ended up being the kid she is now."

"So I pray for a miracle?" Rowan asked dryly.

"Yeah." There wasn't a hint of sarcasm in Matt's tone. "Every single day you pray that you won't screw things up. One day becomes the next, and before you know it, sixteen years go by and you've turned that baby into a real human being."

"That's it? Prayer and hope?" Rowan shook his head. "Are you telling me that every single day prayers and hopes work?"

Matt studied him before leaning back in his chair, looking out the window. "When she was eight months, she ate a shitload of bum cream. It was on the floor after I'd changed her. I didn't close the container properly, and I looked away for . . . a minute, maybe."

He paused, his gaze unfocused.

"I still remember how panicked I was when I saw her. My heart . . . it stopped. And she gave me the biggest smile and kept giggling to herself, like she'd done the most amazing thing of her life."

His lips twitched.

"I rushed her to the doctor. They told me the cream wasn't poisonous, that it was unlikely to do anything but make her throw up or have diarrhea. They told me to hydrate her as much as possible and that if she kept doing it and wasn't keeping anything down, to come back. She was fine, after a day, but I didn't sleep for weeks. I watched her like a hawk. I made sure she was breathing and . . ." He trailed off, met Rowan's eyes. "I made sure she wouldn't ever suffer for my actions again. You know what I got for it?"

Rowan could barely catch his breath. "What?"

"A crayon stuffed up her nose when she was three."

Rowan blinked, then burst out laughing. Matt's own mouth curved into a smile, and he waited until Rowan was done.

"Was she okay?"

"Yeah. She really stuffed it up there, but the doctor got it out in minutes."

Rowan shook his head. "How did you handle that?"

"I waited until she was with her mother and downed a couple of shots."

"Did it help?"

"No."

Rowan snorted and felt his body relax. It was subtle, the easing of his muscles, the deceleration of his heart rate. But it was there, and it was because of Matt. This man, this cool, confident, intimidating man, was as knocked out by parenthood as he was. Things had happened to him that Rowan would kick himself for. That Matt *had* kicked himself for.

And yet Matt was sitting across from him, telling him this story, and it soothed Rowan somehow. Like maybe, sixteen years from now, he'd be telling similar stories to a new dad, and he'd be on the other side, too.

"I can't believe I'm leaving this meeting with hopes and prayers," he muttered, giving Matt a twisted smile.

"What did you want?" Matt asked. "A how-to manual?"

"Would have been nice."

Matt cracked a smile. It gave Rowan a ridiculous sense of satisfaction.

"Nah, there's no how-to manual. Anyone who tells you there is, is a liar." He went quiet again. "Rowan," Matt said after a while, "there's no way to know you're doing the right thing when it comes to your kid. But if you do your best, at least . . . at least you know there's nothing more you could have done."

Just like that, his ease disappeared. Disappointment hit him in the gut. His best? His *best*? His best wasn't enough. That was why he was there. That was why he was trying to improve: so that his best wouldn't be as inadequate as it was now.

Declan needed more than his best. Declan needed *the best*.

He looked at Matt and, for the first time, noticed how the man watched him.

"It's enough," Matt growled.

He blinked. "How could you possibly know what I was thinking?"

"Because I was you." He shifted forward. "*Do. Your. Best.* It's enough."

Was it? Because he was pretty sure his parents had done their best. They hadn't eaten dinner with him because they were always working, but there'd been dinner in the fridge. They hadn't spent much time with him, using their limited free time on each other, but someone took care of him. His nannies. His grandmother.

It was their best. It hadn't been enough.

Matt sighed. "I have friends. Two."

"Congratulations?"

Matt glowered but said, "They're dads, too. We're meeting at the bar down the road on Saturday to talk about the festival. You heard of it?"

"The bar down the road?"

"The festival."

He angled his head, thinking. His grandmother had mentioned something about the town festival when he'd first arrived. He might have said something about going to a crowded social event with a new baby over his dead body, and she'd patted him on the shoulder and said it was a few months away and he'd be ready by then. He'd forgotten about it seconds after.

"My grandmother told me there'd be a festival. That's about it."

Matt nodded. "The town hosts a Founder's Day festival. Three days: Friday night, Saturday, ends Sunday. Everyone gets involved. My friends and I are talking about what we want to do for it on Saturday. Join us. It'll help."

And with those words, Matt took out his wallet, threw some cash on the table, and walked out. He didn't even say goodbye to Delilah.

# CHAPTER SIX

When Delilah walked into Oasis on Saturday, the place was packed. That wasn't unusual. The bar was a favorite among the younger population in town, and Saturdays tended to be Oasis's most popular day of the week.

But since preparations for the Founder's Day festival had begun a few weeks ago, some of the bar's usual clientele were using it as an unofficial meeting place to discuss their contributions. Official meetings took place at the Blue Café during the week. But even during the planning sessions when they only brainstormed, things tended to be structured.

There was none of that in an unpressured setting on the weekend. Almost everyone in town was invested in the festival, and it was easier to talk things through with friends at a bar before presenting it to a planning committee.

The first time Delilah had become aware of this had been during her first year in Sugarbush Bay. Kirsten had insisted they meet at Oasis once a week.

Initially, Delilah hadn't understood it. Why would this woman she barely knew want to meet up regularly? Why would she want to meet with *Delilah* regularly? Had she heard about what had happened with Delilah's family? Did she want to sell information to the media? Post about Delilah online?

But Kirsten hadn't seemed to have any hidden motives beyond wanting to make Delilah feel welcome. Wanting to be her friend.

Delilah hadn't been able to trust it, to trust Kirsten, at first. She'd wanted to, though. Every Saturday she'd met with Kirsten because she wanted to believe it could be a real friendship.

Weeks passed, months, before she finally let herself relax. Kirsten was genuine. Except she did have a hidden motive: she wanted Delilah to become part of the town.

Meeting in a place that was so popular did that. Faces became familiar. Some Delilah had first seen at the café, others around town, and a lot simply at the bar. People greeted her. They talked to her.

No one asked her about her life before she'd moved to Sugarbush Bay.

It was strange, but she thought that maybe Matt had something to do with that. She'd mentioned Kirsten's invitation after her friend had made it. He hadn't had much to say about Kirsten, only that she seemed like a good woman, but he'd come to the bar every Saturday then, too.

When she'd asked him about it, he'd said he and his friends always hung out at the bar on Saturdays. Corey, one of those friends, had later told her that was a lie. But he'd winked at her after, thanking her for making her brother more amenable to doing friend-like things.

She'd realized then that Matt was protecting her even when she wasn't aware of it. The fact that people didn't talk to her about her past might have been him, too.

But it was Kirsten who'd gotten her involved with the festival. The other woman had pointed out the unofficial groups at the bar, talked about the festival a bit. And then, a few months after, she'd asked Delilah to step in and keep the café open for one of the planning meetings.

A year later, Delilah was on the planning committee herself.

She and Kirsten met at the bar less frequently these days. Kirsten didn't use a babysitter often now that Robbie was older, wanting to spend her limited free time with him. Even when Delilah offered her services, Kirsten declined.

"You need time for yourself, too," she'd told Delilah when they'd last talked about it. "Just this week you packed up Mr. Sharma's house for his move, did Mrs. Gerring's cooking and cleaning *and* grocery shopping after she broke her leg, and you had a festival meeting. When are *you* going to relax?"

Delilah had politely brushed off the concern because she didn't need it. She'd *had* time for herself. Most of her life had been filled with her. Her interests, her hobbies, her desires.

Before her mother's arrest, she'd shopped, been pampered, gone to events and parties. The only hard thing she'd done was get her degree, and she'd done it because she'd promised Matt she would.

So yes, she'd had time to herself once. And the only unselfish thing she'd done during that time had actually been selfish, because a degree would only benefit her. Not that she was using it now . . .

But that wasn't the point. The point was that she was done being selfish, and so her time would be used to help others. And since Kirsten had gotten a babysitter for the day, she'd start with her friend.

"How's studying going?" Delilah asked after she and Kirsten talked about the festival for a few minutes. Both of them were already involved in some capacity, and they didn't need the unofficial time to chat about details.

"Oh, you know," Kirsten replied, waving a hand.

Delilah raised a brow. "I don't, actually. That's why I'm asking."

Kirsten didn't respond, her face pulling tight, and Delilah straightened. The chatter around them faded. "What happened?" she asked quietly.

Kirsten shook her head. "Nothing."

Delilah waited.

"I mean that literally," Kirsten continued eventually. "There's no point, you know? I don't have time to study. My days are spent at work. When I get home, it's Robbie. And I wouldn't change that for the world," she added quickly, "but by the time I go to bed, I'm exhausted, D. Like, completely out of it. Sometimes, I wake up on the couch, the television still on or my book still in my hand, and I have no idea when that happened. How am I supposed to add studying to that?"

Delilah's heart ached. Kirsten had never gone to university. She and her husband had been high school sweethearts who married as soon as they graduated school. They'd moved to wherever he could find work, Kirsten barely settling in at her own jobs before her husband found a better opportunity.

After years of this, they'd finally ended up in Sugarbush Bay—where Kirsten had fallen pregnant almost immediately after the move. And then she'd been widowed at four months into her pregnancy, and her life changed again.

But Kirsten was good at doing hair. Excellent, really. She especially had a way with natural hair, which was a gift and a rarity. Despite being predominately a community of color, Sugarbush Bay's hairdressers tended to only have expertise in chemically or naturally straight hair. There was a gap in the market, and Kirsten knew it.

She'd broached the topic one day, tentatively, with Delilah. So they'd gotten out the wine and come up with a plan. Her friend was too shy to post videos of her talents on social media. Studying hairdressing full time was out of the question. The closest school was in Cape Town, and Kirsten refused to move Robbie away from his home.

Eventually, Kirsten had suggested an online course in business. It was short, one year, and it could be done remotely. She had enough money to take the risk. By the end of that evening, Delilah was convinced her friend was ready.

But every time she brought it up, Kirsten ignored her or changed the topic. Today was the first time Kirsten had actually talked about it, and now Delilah knew why.

"How long have you been practicing that?"

"What?" Kirsten snorted. "I did not practice . . . a month."

"A month? You made this decision a month ago? We talked about it a week before that!"

"It didn't take long for me to see the problems," Kirsten answered defensively. "Look, what I'm doing now is working. I have enough money for my kid, and I get to spend time with him."

"You've always had enough money for your kid," Delilah pointed out. "Darryl's life insurance and saving policies made that more than possible."

"Yeah, but that money needs to go into Robbie's college fund."

"Not if he takes after his mother."

"Hey!"

"Sorry," Delilah said, immediately regretful. She exhaled. "I'm sorry, Kirsten. It just feels like . . ."

"Like . . . ?"

She exhaled again. "Like you're making up excuses. I'm not saying your concerns aren't valid—they are. But . . . you could do this without studying. You said no to social media—"

"I don't have time to make videos, edit them, or post them."

"Fine. But you also don't want to start the business. Just start it."

"Would you want your hair done by someone with no experience? With no qualifications?"

"Yeah! If the way they did my hair looks like the way you do hair, hell yeah."

"You're only saying that because you're my friend."

"No, I'm saying *this* because I'm a friend: You're afraid. And I get it. There's been so much in your life that has gone wrong, and you're afraid this might go wrong, too. Because if you don't try, there won't be any chance of it going wrong. But there won't be any chance of it going right either, Kirsten. And . . . and I'm so worried that you're keeping yourself from everything that *will* go right."

Kirsten stared at her for a moment, and then, without warning, her eyes filled. Delilah got up and slid into the booth beside her.

"No," Kirsten said. "I'm fine. It's fine."

"No, it's not. I made you cry."

"You didn't make me cry," Kirsten retorted. "*I* made me cry. Because my brain is—"

"Dealing with a bunch of trauma?"

Kirsten snorted. "Are you seeing Anne to deal with your own shit, or do you spend your sessions talking about me?"

"I spend my sessions pretending to deal with my shit, but really, I'm there to help you through yours."

It was uncomfortably close to the truth. But when Delilah tried to steer the subject away from therapy, Kirsten gave a quiet chuckle. Her friend grabbed a serviette from the table and dried her tears.

"What?" Delilah asked with narrowed eyes. "What happened?"

"Nothing important." Kirsten's tone was nonchalant; there wasn't a sign of the emotion she'd had seconds ago. "I'm just glad I don't have to deal with this anymore."

"What do you mean?"

Kirsten tilted her head to the side, and Delilah finally got it.

Rowan was here.

Her lungs suddenly felt as if they'd bumped into one another, had forgotten their purpose, and were taking their own sweet time figuring it out.

In all fairness, he looked pretty good. He wore well-fitted jeans that looked like they'd seen better days, though those days couldn't be that much better if they didn't make his thighs look . . . like that. Thick and muscular, like he walked for a living. Or ran. Or did anything that required the leg muscles to be in use and expand. That was how muscles worked, right? They expanded?

It didn't matter. Because he paired those jeans with a simple T-shirt. It was gray. *Gray.* By all rights, no one should look that good in a gray shirt. The color should have washed him out. Instead, it brought out the rich tones of his brown skin.

*Impossible,* a voice in her head said, but then her eyes told it, *Okay, but look, it does*, and the voice conceded with a shrug.

Two things could be true at the same time. He could look good in gray, and it could be impossible that he did.

In truth, everything about Rowan was impossible. He had a young son at home; his job meant he worked all day at a computer; she'd never actually seen him outside since he'd arrived. So how could he look good, firm, tanned? How could he make her heart beat faster and her lungs struggle for air?

He was off limits. Even if he and Mckenna weren't together, his life was messy. So was hers. Matt had warned her against him, for heaven's sake! Though not after his and Rowan's coffee date, which was the first time Matt had actually talked to Rowan, and maybe Matt had changed his mind? If he was here, with Matt and his friends, then Matt must have liked Rowan.

Or did that make things even more complicated? Matt had once let it slip that Lucas had wanted to ask her out, but Matt had said no because he didn't think Lucas was good enough for her.

She hadn't cared much then. She hadn't been interested in dating, even with the sweet and sexy Lucas. But now that she saw Matt's over-protective tendencies were a pattern—now that it was Rowan—she found that she didn't care for her brother's interference . . .

It didn't matter.

Rowan. Was. Off. Limits.

Now she only had to convince her body of the same.

Delilah dragged her eyes away, stood, and went to sit back at her side of the table.

"You're not going to get away from talking about it that easily," she told Kirsten primly.

Kirsten's eyebrows lifted. "Really? You don't want to know how things are going at that table?"

"No." Delilah ran a finger around the rim of her glass. "I'm not interested in him." There was a silence of probably a minute, which Delilah was extremely proud of, before she casually said, "But if you were going to tell me, I wouldn't be upset."

"Hmm." Kirsten took a sip of her drink. "Yeah, I don't think I'm going to say anything. You're obviously over your crush. You didn't mention him all week."

Delilah narrowed her eyes. "Is this payback?"

Kirsten grinned. "Yes."

Delilah couldn't even blame her. She laughed. "Fine." Another beat. "Okay, but seriously, does he look okay?"

"Hard to tell. He's frowning, but so is your brother."

She sighed. "They frowned at each other at the café, too. It's like they want to see who wears it better."

"Well, there's a clear winner in my opinion."

She wanted to resist. She really did. But she couldn't—and her friend knew it. She ignored Kirsten's cackle as she turned to look at her brother's table.

Rowan and Matt were frowning, but it didn't seem to be at one another. They didn't seem to be paying any attention to one another, in fact. Matt was lifting his hand to get their server's attention; Corey was shaking Rowan's hand; and Lucas was nodding at him.

She didn't know how, but she knew this meant they were comfortable with one another. Which she, funnily enough, didn't feel comfortable with at all.

She turned back to Kirsten. "You tricked me."

"You fell for it."

"I . . ." She shook her head. "This situation is weird."

Kirsten frowned. "Why?"

"Matt told me not to date Rowan. That he, and I quote, 'doesn't deserve' me."

Kirsten regarded her. "I think your brother is going to be an obstacle in your dating life. At least, with one of his friends."

"I have no interest in his friends. There's nothing going on between me and Rowan."

"Oh, there's definitely something going on." She continued before Delilah could protest. "But with Matt 'just letting it slip' that he didn't want you and Lucas dating either?" She shook her head. "I guess the interfering thing is a family trait."

"Excuse me?"

"You know you interfere in everyone's lives."

"To help! You make it sound like an insult."

"It's not." Kirsten reached over and squeezed Delilah's hand. "Everyone you help knows that, and we appreciate it." With another squeeze she blew out a breath. "But enough of this. How about we order something to eat and pretend to talk about the festival so people don't think we're slacking?"

Appeased, Delilah nodded. "I'd love to."

"Great." Kirsten lifted her hand, trying to get the server's attention. Her eyes darted to behind Delilah, and when Kirsten spoke again, Delilah was unsurprised by what her friend had to say. "He's looking at you."

She was unsurprised because she'd felt it.

Even when he was looking at the back of her head.

It was Saturday. The bar was crowded. It didn't feel too bad with the doors open to the outdoor patio, but Rowan still resisted the urge to pull at his collar.

He didn't know what he'd expected when he'd first arrived at Oasis, but the bustling vibe in the relatively small space wasn't it. The dark bar and wooden beams made the place feel dingy; the pictures of life in Sugarbush Bay up on the walls, nostalgic. The large television mounted on the wall felt like an odd piece of modernity against the dated decor while simultaneously being perfect for the younger crowd who gathered there.

He hadn't been there long, but he already wanted to leave.

But he supposed this was what he signed up for. Torture. The good kind. The kind that was necessary for a good result. That was what this was. He was being forced to talk to people he'd never met by another person he'd only met twice, and they wanted to know more about him.

And he was answering because he was here, and he wanted to know if Matt's friends had the same advice Matt did.

Because quite frankly, Matt's advice left a lot to be desired.

"You're from Cape Town?" Corey asked.

He was the tall one. Built like an athlete. A field athlete. Who did high jump or long jump or something else that required the use of long legs that regularly bumped into Rowan's even though he was sitting on the opposite end of the table.

"Yes," Rowan answered automatically, before he remembered what his grandmother had told him when she'd come over to take care of Declan while Mckenna packed.

*A one-word answer isn't going to make you friends, Ro.*

So he added, "Born and raised," and felt his grandmother's spirit pat him on the back for those additional words.

Corey didn't seem bothered by it. "Yeah, me, too. Lived in Bellville for a while, then moved to Claremont."

Rowan's eyebrows lifted. "Big difference."

Corey winced. "Yeah, there is a huge difference between northern and southern suburbs. But I got a job in Claremont, and I was old enough to move out by myself, so I got myself this tiny flat that cost an arm and a leg and lived there until I got a job in this town and met these assholes."

He grinned, tilting his beer in a toast toward Matt and their other friend, Lucas. Lucas didn't talk much, but Rowan didn't think it was a personality trait. Not based on the amusement glinting in Lucas's eyes. He was letting Corey take the lead . . . Rowan thought. Although honestly, he couldn't quite figure out the dynamics of the group.

Matt was quiet. That he'd know even if Matt hadn't spent the last thirty minutes not saying a single word. Lucas *seemed* quiet, but that spark of wickedness Rowan saw in his amusement only added to his . . . aura.

Rowan hadn't believed in auras until today. But it felt exceedingly real when it came to Lucas. The man was present, his expressions animated, his responses quick, yet rarely did he say a word.

Corey was clearly the extrovert here, talking almost constantly since Rowan had arrived. The three of them had distinctly different personalities, yet they all seemed so *easy* around one another. Like their personalities, introverted or extroverted, didn't matter.

Unless he was reading the situation wrong, which was entirely possible.

A faint hum of panic entered his blood. Restless, his eyes swept the room. There seemed to be even more people now than when he'd first arrived. He caught words of conversations here and there, and most people did seem to be talking about the festival.

Excitement jumped out at him as clearly as the words. It added to the bustling atmosphere—or perhaps created it. People were really looking forward to the event. Even his grandmother had started bringing it up more.

He wished she wouldn't. Not because he didn't want to attend it, though he still didn't. But because Mckenna was already having a hard time leaving, and talking about the festival seemed to make her sadder.

She was only leaving for two weeks, and by the time she got back, the festival would still be a month away. But it was a reminder of time moving on. Time she wouldn't be spending with their son.

And while she was packing, while his grandmother was at their house, helping take care of Declan, he was trying to make friends.

He wasn't even sure he was succeeding.

The panic intensified—and then, magically, it eased. It took him too long to realize it was because his gaze had rested on Delilah.

"Your sister's here," Lucas said, his words directed at Matt but his eyes on Rowan. It was the first thing he'd said since Rowan had arrived, and his voice was deep and soothing, something Rowan hadn't expected.

Luckily, he couldn't ponder that discovery, because Matt grunted and looked at Rowan. Rowan could feel the man's gaze boring into his skin. He met it with his own, and the staring standoff happened again.

In some primal part of his brain he understood their reactions were both because they were trying to protect Delilah. Matt clearly didn't want Rowan to get involved with his sister, but Rowan thought that should be Delilah's choice, not Matt's.

Even if the choice was superfluous, since there was nothing going on between him and Delilah, anyway.

The staring contest was interrupted when Corey said, "We should invite her over."

"No," Matt said. "We're here for Rowan."

"Maybe she is, too," Corey challenged.

"Mind your business, Corey," Lucas said with a twist of his mouth.

"What fun is that?" Corey grinned but changed the subject. "How old's your son?"

Rowan took a second to adjust. "Two months."

"A *baby* baby," Corey said with a whistle. "How much sleep are you getting?"

"Stupid question," Matt growled.

"Yeah," Lucas agreed.

"Yeah," Corey said after a second. "Sorry."

"When . . ." Rowan cleared his throat. "When does it get better?"

"Not until after the four-month regression," Corey said. "We sleep trained mine. She cried for literal hours. So did I, since I told her mom I'd do it. It was harder on her, and I was sure I could be a man of steel and stick it out." He chuckled, bringing his beer to his lips. "Idiot."

It seemed so easy for him to talk about it. About his kid crying, about himself crying. Why did that make Rowan feel so strange? Not quite uncomfortable but certainly not comfortable.

Though perhaps he did feel comforted.

"How old is she now?" he asked.

"Four." The grin on his face was big and dopey.

"And she sleeps fine?"

"Oh yeah. She slept fine after the second night of crying. It was hell, and I wouldn't recommend it to anyone. But it worked."

"For you," Lucas said. "We tried it, and we couldn't stick it out."

"Does that mean it didn't work or that you couldn't stick it out?"

Lucas gave him a casual slap on the head before looking at Rowan. "Even if you don't sleep train, things get easier after four months. They sleep for longer stretches. They're more likely to nap, and for longer. But until that day comes . . ." He shook his head. "It's absolute shit."

Absolute shit. Yeah, that about summed it up.

Maybe if people had been this blunt with their so-called advice, Rowan wouldn't have felt so unprepared. But the colleagues he'd told had only laughed and told him to enjoy his sleep while it lasted, as if it were a joke. And while his grandmother had said it would be hard, she'd told him not to worry because he could handle it.

No one had spoken to him so honestly. So unapologetically. Lucas had said it all like it was a fact, not a condemnation of his parenting style. Matt had the previous week, too.

Was Rowan struggling then a sign of how difficult parenting was and not of how bad he was at parenting? Could it be that simple? Or was he giving himself an excuse not to do what he needed to do?

If he was, he'd have gotten the trait from his parents. They'd given him reason after reason for why they couldn't spend time with him. Why they couldn't parent him. He didn't think they knew it, but each excuse had told him that he wasn't good enough for them to make an effort for.

He'd die before he did something to make Declan feel that way.

"The key," Corey announced suddenly and loudly, "is to know that things are supposed to be shit."

"What?" Rowan asked.

"He means that you need to talk to people," Lucas translated.

"He means you need to get involved," Matt added.

"I have no idea what you're talking about," Rowan said.

"You won't know everything about parenting," Corey answered. "You can't. It's too unpredictable, and every kid is individual. Plus, we all come into it with our own crap. My father left when I was a kid."

"My mother kicked me out when I was eighteen," Matt said.

"My parents were great," Lucas said.

They all looked at him.

"What?" he asked. "Is it a competition?"

Corey rolled his eyes. "His wife left him when their son was two."

"Cheated," Matt clarified.

Lucas glowered but sat back and didn't say anything.

"The only way we get through it is by having people around us. Support."

"Advice," Matt added.

"That honestly sounds . . . scary," Rowan said after a moment.

"So is parenting," Corey pointed out. "And has the stuff we've said to you made you feel better or worse?"

"You haven't really said much of anything," Lucas told Corey. "Assholes," he added, for good measure.

"We've said enough," Matt said, ignoring the snide remark.

And the truth was, they had. Despite his doubts, Rowan knew they were helping. He remembered everything Matt had told him a week ago. How there wasn't anything he could do besides his best. That believing things would work out if he did his best was the only way he could stay sane.

Even this short conversation he'd had with Corey and Lucas had helped. He didn't know what a sleep regression and sleep training were—he'd have to look them up—but he felt like there was a light at the end of the tunnel. That had to mean something.

Except what they were asking went against everything he was. He was quiet, someone who avoided social situations whenever he could help it. If it hadn't been for Delilah with Matt, he would have never agreed to that meetup. If both Mckenna and his grandmother hadn't insisted he come to the bar today, he wouldn't have been here either.

But if it meant he'd be a better father to Declan, he'd go against who he was . . . *right* after he worked through the anxiety the mere thought had thrumming through his body.

"I'll think about it," he answered after a while, since they were all still staring at him.

"The festival might be a good place to start," Lucas offered.

"I'll think about it," Rowan repeated, voice strangled.

Corey opened his mouth, but Matt put a hand on his arm.

"That's good," Matt said. After a second, Corey nodded. Lucas tilted his head in agreement.

"Hey!" Corey said suddenly, his gaze shifting. "When did they start making pizzas here?"

There was a faint smile on Matt's face. "They do it for Delilah."

"What?" Corey asked. "Since when?"

Matt shrugged.

"We should ask," Lucas said seriously.

Matt shrugged again.

Corey looked at him. "You have no desire for a slice of pizza?"

"Of course I do." Matt sat back in the booth. "I just know they aren't going to make it for anyone but Delilah."

"We'll see about that," Corey said determinedly. He lifted his hand to get the attention of their server. When she came over, Rowan saw it was the same woman who'd been serving Delilah and her friend.

She was short, with long black hair and a rounded nose that reminded him of a guinea pig. She offered them a smile.

"What can I get you?"

"Pizza."

Her smile didn't waver. "We don't serve pizza here."

"I saw you serve pizza to Delilah, Jill," Corey said.

"What?" Jill replied, her voice almost bored. "Are you sure? Because I was just over there, and I promise you there wasn't any pizza."

They all looked over Jill's shoulder to Delilah's table. Delilah and her friend—the other waitress from the café whose hair was no longer the strange color Rowan had first seen her with—both had slices of pizza in their hands.

They turned, as if sensing they were being watched. Delilah's eyes met his. There was a zing. He couldn't explain it any other way. A zing, a spark, something tangible and exciting. Something he absolutely couldn't pay any attention to.

His lips curved as she took a large bite of her slice of pizza and waved at them with her free hand.

"What do you call that?" Corey asked in a strangled voice.

"What?" Jill said. She hadn't bothered to look behind her.

"We're watching her eat the pizza!"

"We don't have that on the menu," Jill repeated. "We do have an array of bar food. Burgers, chicken wings, other fried foods. Our dipped wings are really popular, and they're currently a part of the special." She pointed to the blackboard mounted on the wall.

"Jill," Lucas said with an easy smile. "Stop treating us like we're new and you haven't known us for over five years."

For the first time, Jill looked something other than bored. "Ugh. I've been here for at least five years. That's . . ." She shook her head. "You're right. I know you. I know that you'll push your luck even when I say no. One more beer when we're closing up, one more game of rugby on the TV when everyone wants to watch soccer."

"That doesn't sound like us," Lucas said, easing back, as if he sensed this was no longer going in the direction he was hoping.

"Sure," Jill replied flatly. "Look, we don't do pizza, unless you helped the owners of the bar clean out their spare bedroom in eight hours because their daughter was getting divorced and needed a place to stay urgently." She waited a beat. "Have you helped Chuck and Portia clean out their spare bedroom in eight hours because their daughter was getting divorced and needed a place to stay urgently?"

Matt laughed quietly as Corey and Lucas shook their heads.

Jill nodded. "So we're doing the wings then?"

"Cheeseburger," Corey said, defeated.

"Two," Lucas added.

Matt nodded.

"Three cheeseburgers and a complimentary plate of wings—got it." Jill turned to Rowan. She smiled, and the sincerity made him realize that even when she'd come initially and offered them a pleasant smile, it hadn't been genuine. "Hi! I'm Jill. You're Rowan, right? Linda's grandson?"

Rowan opened his mouth, but he didn't quite know how she knew, and trying to figure it out was messing with his vocal cords. In the end, he nodded.

Jill's smile widened. "What can I get for you?"

"Same." The word came out soft and cracked. He cleared his throat. "The same. I'll have the same."

"Sure, no problem." She winked at him, glowered at the rest of them as she turned, and walked away.

It was quiet for a while after she left.

"We should have seen that coming," Corey muttered.

"I did," Matt offered.

Lucas showed him the middle finger.

# CHAPTER SEVEN

The events that led to Delilah knocking at Rowan's door about a week after she'd seen him at Oasis were simple. He hadn't been to the café in a while. She hadn't seen him around the neighborhood. Her brother hadn't heard from him. His grandmother was worried about him.

For some unknown reason, all of this made *Delilah* worry about him.

She'd talked herself out of it at first. So what if she hadn't seen the man around? Sure, she'd started spending more time outside in her neighborhood the last weeks, but that didn't mean she would see him.

It also had nothing to do with him. No, her garden was in a terrible condition, and since she was seeing to hers, she might as well offer her services to her neighbors.

Not to him, though. That would be weird.

Around this time, though, it occurred to her that the reason she hadn't realized he lived so close by wasn't because of her schedule. It was because he didn't seem to leave his house unless he was getting coffee, and he hadn't for a while.

Except that also didn't mean anything was wrong. He didn't *have* to get coffee. No one did. So the fact that he hadn't wasn't personal.

She, of course, hadn't believed it was.

She'd been desperate enough to ask Matt about him. She hadn't made it a thing, just asked if her brother had seen him around. Matt hadn't bought it. He'd studied her, given her a clipped negative, and ended the conversation by pushing a plate of food toward her.

She'd taken a huge bite so she couldn't ask any follow-up questions.

But what had really pushed her to his front door was Linda. Linda was taking Declan for a walk and had come across Delilah as she'd been pulling weeds out of one of her neighbors' gardens.

Delilah had warmly greeted Linda, but her attention had immediately shifted to Declan. The baby was catching air with his hands and looked so at peace doing it that she melted.

"He is gorgeous."

"He is," Linda agreed. "He got lucky with his dad's genes."

Delilah didn't respond.

Not to defend Mckenna, who was, objectively, stunning and had absolutely given some of that to Declan.

And not to acknowledge Linda's words about Rowan's attractiveness.

She wasn't an idiot. She knew how Linda's mind worked. The moment she even implied that she found Rowan attractive, Linda would start matchmaking. Subtly, at first, but soon, Delilah would go over to his house after some innocuous request from Linda and walk right into Rowan after a shower.

Which, of course, would be A Very Bad Thing because of course, she didn't want to see Rowan right after a shower.

She winced slightly, hoping that she wouldn't be struck by lightning for her lies.

Linda heaved a sigh. "I thought the worry would ease once he moved closer to me, but it hasn't."

Delilah's stomach dropped, but she still didn't take the bait.

"It's worse now," Linda continued. "He doesn't leave the house. Doesn't talk to anyone except Mckenna. He's busied himself with taking care of Declan, and he's forgotten about himself." The older woman shook her head. "I don't know what to do."

Delilah didn't either. "I'm sorry, Linda. That sounds awful."

"Thank you, dear. I'm sure something will change soon, though. It can't stay this way forever."

Declan began to cry then, and the other woman hurried back to Rowan's house to feed the baby after a quick goodbye.

And that was how Delilah found herself knocking at Rowan's door the next morning, on her day off.

She'd seen Linda on her walk with Declan minutes before, and she'd timed it so she could talk to Rowan and Mckenna without interruption. She was going to offer to babysit some more so they could take more breaks. She could bring them food, help with chores, do anything they needed her to. But when Rowan opened the door, she forgot about talking altogether.

He looked *rough*.

His clothes had very possibly been pulled straight out the laundry. Based on the stains, that was the dirty laundry. His eyes were tired behind the glasses on his face—she'd never seen him with glasses before, and damn it, it was *hot*—and his hair clearly hadn't been brushed. It was anyone's guess if it had been washed in recent times, what with that . . . sheen.

"Delilah?"

"Hi," she croaked. Cleared her throat. "Hi. I brought coffee. Your usual."

Rowan blinked, his head lowering to where she held the coffee in front of her chest.

"Why?" he finally asked.

"Because that's what neighbors do?"

"You brought two."

"Yeah. I've already had my cup."

His brow knit. "You didn't bring yourself coffee?"

"No," she said slowly and started to worry that perhaps his mental state was more fragile than his clothing let on. Which was incredibly worrying.

"No, Rowan, there are only two cups of coffee. One for you, and one for Mckenna. I think. She's the decaf with oat milk, right?"

He blinked a few more times. "Oh. Oh, you don't know."

"Know what?"

He shook his head. "I'm being rude. Please, come inside."

She opened her mouth to refuse but thought better of it. Linda was right to be worried about him. He was clearly disoriented from lack of sleep or from stress or something. She'd be doing a good thing by going inside and making sure he was okay.

But when she did, she had to stop herself from bumping into him when he abruptly turned around.

"Did you happen to bring one of your cookies? Not *your* cookie," he quickly added. "The cookie you give me. Gave me. Have given me. In the past, I mean."

Delilah watched in delight as he blushed. *Blushed.* If she were still crushing on him—which she wasn't—she would definitely be drooling right now.

Blushing suited him. Softened the harsh angles of his face, gave him a bashful look. With the glasses, he was giving real *nerd who took learning the secrets to pleasuring a human body very seriously* vibes, and it nearly took her knees out from under her.

Heaven only then knew why she said, "The cookies I was giving you . . . for free?"

He rubbed the back of his neck. "Yeah."

"You'd like one?"

"Please."

His voice was strangled.

So naturally she said, "How badly?"

His lips parted, drawing her eyes to them. Had she noticed how full they were? How they promised seduction, screamed desire fulfilled?

The insanity of those thoughts conjured up an image of him kissing her lips, her neck, her shoulder, making his way down to her breast. She'd buck under him, press her nipple to his mouth, and let him torture her. Let him take, take, take, with those luscious lips, with an undoubtedly skilled tongue, and oh goodness, she needed to calm down.

And yet, she was still teasing him.

Flirting with him.

"You know, I don't do this. Give my cookies out for free."

His jaw dropped.

"In fact, you're one of two men I've given my cookies free to in all my life. You and"—she lingered on the word—"my brother."

*Gross.*

She hadn't thought about the impact of saying those words out loud, and now that she had, she found that the mention of her brother had helped give her the perspective she needed. It just about took all the fun out of the conversation, too.

At least until Rowan said, "I never expected you to give me free cookies. I hope you know that. I never want you to think I'm taking your kindness for granted."

And maybe those words didn't bring back the fun, but they did soften her. He'd heard her teasing and responded with sincerity. Her heart skipped a beat.

"I brought you a cookie, Rowan," she said with a small laugh. "Mckenna, too. And don't worry about paying for them. Giving them to people I like is one of the benefits of making them. My boss doesn't care who I give them to as long as I keep doing that."

"*You* make them?"

"Yep."

"You make those biscuits," he said again.

"I do."

"Wow," he breathed. "They're amazing."

The reverence in his tone made her laugh again.

"Thank you."

He shook his head. "You shouldn't be so talented at everything. It's unfair to the rest of us."

She searched his face and, again, found only sincerity. And so she blushed, because it was the kind of thing people said when they were trying to get into someone's good books, but he was saying it simply because he meant it.

"I'm not," she said quickly. "Talented at everything."

"Sure, sure." It came just as quickly but much more sarcastically. She hid her smile. "I'm sorry," he said after a moment. "You must think I'm going out of my mind with how . . . strange this conversation has been."

"Not . . . very strange," she lied politely.

"Strange enough." He gave her a wry smile that disappeared as soon as it appeared. "Things have been chaotic since Mckenna left."

"She . . . left?"

He nodded. "Last week Monday. Before that we were trying to take care of Declan and make sure her leaving wouldn't affect him too badly and . . ." He trailed off with a long exhale. "It's been rough."

Well, wasn't *that* something Linda should have told her? That Mckenna had *left*? And here she was, bringing them both coffee and reminding him that he was going to be parenting alone from now on.

"I'm so sorry, Rowan. That's . . . I'm sorry."

"No, it's okay," he said with a small frown. "My grandmother has been helping a lot. She's basically been living at my place since Mckenna left."

"I'm glad you have her."

"Me, too."

There was an awkward silence. Delilah used it to formulate a plan.

"So here's your coffee." She took out his and handed it to him. "I'll have this one."

"Oh, you don't—"

"No, it's okay. I shouldn't have assumed you'd want coffee anyway."

"I *did* want coffee," he said gratefully. "Thank you for being . . . neighborly."

"You're welcome." She nodded. "But I have to go now, so I'll see you around, okay?"

They were basically still at the front door, so Delilah didn't have far to walk to leave after Rowan gave her a confused wave. Delilah used all her willpower not to apologize again, for being presumptuous—or for what he was going through.

It broke her heart knowing that Declan would grow up without a mother. That Rowan would have to raise his son alone. She knew from all that Matt had told her that co-parenting was tough. It was being a single parent but "luckier," though it never quite felt that way. And now Rowan *was* a single parent, completely alone with this daunting task, and . . .

Her heart broke for him.

She had to make this better. And luckily, she'd come up with a plan to do that in a small but important way.

She hoped.

The doorbell rang at around 6:00 p.m. Rowan looked at the clock in confusion, though the confusion had nothing to do with the time but the fact that there was anyone ringing the doorbell at all.

His grandmother was the only person who'd visit, and she had her own key. Plus, she'd already left for the night.

Which was as much of a relief as it was torture. She was doing so much for him. Too much. She'd spent most of the day—and every day since Mckenna had left—helping him with Declan. It was why he'd moved to Sugarbush Bay, and he needed the help. Welcomed it.

But the fact that he did was exactly why he felt guilty. The moment she left, the moment he was alone with Declan, it overwhelmed him. Taking care of his son *overwhelmed* him.

He was working on the bare minimum of sleep. Declan sometimes went three hours without waking, but Rowan woke almost hourly. Just to check that Declan was okay. Sometimes he got up to get diaper supplies, to make sure he had exactly what he needed, after which he couldn't fall asleep again, convinced Declan would wake as soon as he did.

He'd work then, until he had to prepare for Declan's next feed, and the constant cycle of it drained him.

He refused to let his grandmother help with laundry or cleaning the house. It pained her greatly, which she told him often. With that in mind, he made sure the house was clean so she didn't have to spend her days in dirt.

And he did laundry, only he focused on Declan's, leaving his own until the very last moment, which today meant he'd had to recycle a few items.

Of course today was also the day Delilah had decided to come visit. So she'd seen him looking unkempt—*and* he'd had his glasses on. He only wore them when he was tired and working. He'd forgotten they were on from the night before. Or technically, that morning.

*She'd* looked like a breath of fresh air. Her hair was tied back by a white-and-yellow scarf, she wore a white shirt and jeans, and there was a part of him that wanted her to twirl so he could get a look at the back of her. Only the minute he thought it, the very idea of it exhausted him.

He didn't even have the energy for *lust.*

If he'd had any ego or virility left after having a child, it surely would have sought refuge in some other guy's body after today.

He went to the door in a daze, his thoughts tiring him out even more than the baby gurgling on his chest.

"Delilah?"

"Hey," she said, offering him a shy smile that made the sky seem brighter. "I'm here to help."

He looked down when she shrugged, drawing attention to her hands. She carried four large bags, each filled to the brim with containers.

"Can I come inside?" she asked.

"Oh yeah. Yes, of course."

He tried not to inhale as she walked past him, but he still caught a whiff of her smell. Still that sweet mixture of vanilla and cinnamon, but now it felt whimsical, too. Exactly the kind of smell he'd expect from someone who made a dark night bright.

Was this what being her neighbor meant? Spontaneous visits? Reminders of how attracted he was to her, even when he didn't have the energy to be? Of how much her mere presence made him feel better about his life?

He tried to be annoyed. He really did. But he had no energy for that either.

*And you like it. You like seeing her.*

"I didn't mean to barge in like this," she said over her shoulder, putting the bags on his kitchen counter.

"You're not barging," he replied gruffly. "I let you in."

"Yeah, but I'm dropping over unannounced. Again." She winced. "Although this time, I'm not going to make things worse."

"How? How did you make things worse earlier?"

She bit her lip. "Bringing up Mckenna. I . . . I didn't know she'd left."

"Why would you?"

"Your grandmother . . ." She trailed off, eyes widening before she caught herself. "I just meant I'm here to help. But I wasn't sure you'd accept it if I offered."

He stayed quiet for a moment.

"My grandmother told you she was worried about me, didn't she?"

"No. Why would you say that?" she asked, completely unconvincingly. She grimaced. "Yes, she did. But I was already worried. I hadn't seen you around in a long time, and I wanted to check in anyway, so she kind of"—she made a pushing gesture with her hand—"nudged me along."

He was oddly touched. Oddly relieved, too. When the why of it hit him, he felt idiotic. And yet he still said, "So your brother and his friends didn't say—"

"No," she interrupted. "No, they haven't said anything. It's annoying, actually, how tight lipped they've been about your single dads club."

"Excuse me?"

"What?"

"Single dads club?"

"Oh." She wrinkled her nose. Cute, he thought almost idly. "That's what I've been calling you all behind your back. Because you're all single dads, and none of you want to talk about it, so it's all, 'What happens in single dads club stays in single dads club' . . ." She trailed off. "I think every single one of you would hate it, and honestly, that makes me like it more."

"I don't mind it."

He didn't. It made him sound like a part of a group. It made him sound like he had friends. And since he had, literally seconds ago, needed the assurance that his friends weren't talking shit behind his back, it clearly meant something to him.

Oh man. He was in more of a vulnerable place than he'd thought. Which explained the next words out of his mouth.

"You've been asking about it? About . . . me?"

For the first time since he'd met Delilah, she didn't have an answer. In fact, she seemed embarrassed. The light shade of pink staining her cheeks, growing darker the longer he looked at her, was confirmation. He should be polite, stop looking at her, but he found it fascinating.

This was because of something he'd said? Because of him?

This was *for* him?

"Okay, yes." She tossed her head back. "I have been asking about you. But only to my brother, *not* your grandmother. Because if I did that, we both know she'd be planning our wedding."

He tried not to react to the idea of her walking down the aisle.

"But I promise I wasn't asking Matt because of anything weird. I was . . . worried. Besides," she went on quickly, as if doing so would mean he wouldn't hear the admission of her concern, "I was the one who introduced you to my brother and so, indirectly, to his friends. If it wasn't working, it would be on me, so of course I wanted to know how it went."

"Why?"

"Why what?"

"Why would it be on you?"

"I just said—"

"I know what you said," Rowan interrupted. "But logically, it doesn't make sense. You have no control over my actions. Over your brother's or his friends'. If things didn't work out, that would be on us, not you."

She opened her mouth—and promptly shut it.

"You can only take responsibility for your own actions," he said quietly, almost apologetically, because it felt like something he needed to apologize for. Even though he firmly believed it. Was in the midst of taking responsibility for his own actions, in fact.

Did that mean he never wondered about what would have happened if he hadn't accepted an invitation to that party he'd had sex with Mckenna at? Did it mean he never thought about the client who'd invited him, who'd insisted, and what would have happened if Rowan hadn't been so desperate to get his business?

No.

But that man hadn't put a gun against Rowan's head. Hadn't forced him to make love to Mckenna. No, that had been *him* and *his* judgment.

When Declan started to cry at his chest, for a brief moment, he thought he'd said it out loud. That Declan was crying because he felt unwanted, like Rowan had, and that somehow he'd managed to mess his kid up before he even had a chance to try not to.

But Declan quietened when Delilah gently popped the pacifier into his mouth with a coo. When she straightened, she was smiling.

"You're right," Delilah said. "Of course you are. And my therapist will love to finally hear me admit it, though I'm not sure I should give her the satisfaction."

"Is that . . . is that how that's supposed to work?"

She snorted. "No. But I'm probably not doing therapy the way it's supposed to be done. I know I need it, and I guess I wanted to practice the habit for when I'm ready to do it the way it's supposed to be done."

She got a funny look on her face, as if she couldn't believe she'd said that. Neither did he. It was intensely personal and, at the same time, immensely helpful.

It had never occurred to him that therapy might need to be practiced. It had never occurred to him to go and get used to it before he actually dealt with all his baggage.

And if his unexpected journey to fatherhood had taught him anything, it was that he had a hell of a lot of baggage.

"That's pretty smart," he said softly.

"Is it?" She was smiling, but it was sad. "Anyway," she continued, shaking her shoulders, "confessing my deepest, darkest secrets isn't why I'm here. This is."

She spread out her hand, gesturing to the bags with flourish. He took a moment. Took a moment to figure out how she'd gone from the sadness to this . . . this ease. As if that sadness had simply been a moment. A bubble burst within seconds of being blown. And now she was moving on.

Would he ever be able to do that? Would he ever be able to move on from his own actions so quickly? From his emotions, even when they'd been as vulnerable as hers had been?

"Do I need to do something else for you to ask about what I've brought?" she asked. "A dance or something?"

*Yes,* his brain answered, instantly distracted from his other thoughts by the prospect of her dancing provocatively, moving her hips in front of his until he grabbed her and—

*Oh, so you* do *have the energy for lust after all.*

"What?" he asked in a strangled voice. "What did you bring?"

"*So* good of you to ask!" she exclaimed. "It's food. My famous breakfast wraps." She patted a bag to the left of her. "Several options since I wasn't sure about your dietary preferences, but trust me, they're all delicious. And then I brought lunch and dinner." She patted two other bags. "Along with some dessert options for when you're in the mood." She gestured to the last bag. "Oh! There are also cookies. So no more free ones, okay?"

Her eyes were twinkling, and Rowan simply stared.

This was all so amazingly kind. He'd done nothing to deserve it, so this kindness was all her. No one had ever done anything like this for him. His grandmother would, of course, if he asked, but he hadn't even thought of it because *he* wasn't this kind. They were virtual strangers, and she'd done this for him.

He kept staring then because that sparkle in her eyes made her look even more beautiful. Her eyes lit up in parts, turning into kaleidoscopes of different hues of brown. Her cheeks lifted, coaxing those eyes closed, making joy seem tangible. Like if he wanted to, he could reach out, grasp her face, and be happy.

"Thank you," he said hoarsely, because that thought was more disturbing than any other he'd had about her. More disturbing, even, than his physical attraction to her, which was, perplexingly, being resurrected the longer he stayed in her company.

"You're welcome," she replied cheerfully. Obliviously. "Have you had dinner yet?"

He shook his head. "I usually put him down first."

"Would you . . ." She bit her lip. A flash of heat pulsed through him, as if she'd done the action to him. He'd gone from being too tired to lust after her to being so tired he couldn't stop. "Would you mind if I held him? I was trying to be polite, but I've wanted to hold him since I got here. I mean, *look* at him."

The way she was staring at Declan, her face soft, glowing almost, was the real reason he looked down. Not because she'd said it but because he needed the reminder. Here was his son. His anchor.

Around her, he needed an anchor.

For the first time in his life, he had sympathy for his parents. For all their faults, they loved one another. Deeply, madly.

They'd met at work, and he thought that might have been the reason work was still such a huge part of their lives. It was inextricably linked to their relationship, and so they could offer as much of themselves to their jobs as to one another because it was simply another manifestation of their love for one another.

He, on the other hand, had tested their relationship. His grandmother told him how difficult his mother had found pregnancy, motherhood. Linda had hated how poorly her daughter had treated Rowan, which was why she'd stepped in and done what she could to help take care of him.

But during that time, his parents' relationship had suffered. A child tested bonds in a way that no other thing could, and his parents had chosen to remove that test by doing the bare minimum in raising him.

He'd judged them for it. Resented it, and them. Sworn never to be in a relationship that was so consuming nothing else mattered.

Other things *did* matter. Other people mattered. He refused to let this crush, or whatever was happening with Delilah, make him forget that.

"It's okay if the answer is no."

Her words brought him back to the present. "No."

Her face fell. "Of course."

"No, I meant no. As in, no, the answer isn't no."

She gave him a hesitant smile. "Yeah, that makes sense. Do you want to grab something to eat, and I can get him ready for bed? Would you like me to put him to sleep? Whatever you want, I'll be happy to do it."

An image of her on her knees in front of him, peering up at him with desire, flashed through his mind.

*Stop this,* he told it.

"Why are you being so nice to me?" he asked, more sharply than he intended.

"What? What do you mean?"

"Exactly what I said. You have no reason to be nice to me. I don't know you. You don't know me. We're not even friends."

She opened her mouth, as if to refute that fact, and when she didn't, Rowan told himself he couldn't be upset. He'd been the one to say it, to point it out. He couldn't be angry that she agreed.

"Because of me," she answered eventually. "Because I once went through a really difficult time, and no one helped." Her eyes shuttered. "No one brought me food; no one offered to take on some of my chores. I thought I had friends. And not a single one of them reached out when my life was falling apart.

"So," she said, her chin lifting, "forgive me for wanting to offer help to my *neighbor*, whether we know one another or not. Whether we're friends or not. You're a new father, you're struggling, and your baby's mother left you to raise your child alone. Let me help if I want to help."

Her life had fallen apart? When? Why? He wanted to know who the friends were who had left her stranded, who'd clearly hurt her. And he wanted to know—

*Wait a minute.*

"Did you say my baby's mother left me to raise him alone?"

She frowned. "Yes."

"Why?"

"Because . . . she did? That's what you told me when I brought you coffee today. You said she'd left and you've been alone."

Yes, he had said that. But he hadn't meant . . .

"She didn't leave *me*," he said in a rush. "Not like that. What I meant to say was that she left."

"Yes, that *is* what you said. That's why I'm here."

"No, she left the country."

Delilah gasped. "Altogether? Like, she fled?"

"What? No. No, she has a work conference. It was supposed to happen at the end of next month, but it got brought forward for . . . reasons." She didn't need to know why, which was handy, because he couldn't exactly remember why. "She's a pretty big deal in her business, so she couldn't not go, and so she went. But she'll be back in two weeks. A week now, I guess."

There, that was better. Wasn't it? Delilah was looking at him like he'd sprouted another head. Just when he thought he might risk embarrassment and ask her about it, she started to laugh.

"My gosh," she said with a shake of her head. "I got almost everything about this situation wrong. That's what I get for interfering." She narrowed her eyes at Rowan. "And if you ever tell Matt I said that, I will kill you. I'll regret leaving your son without a father, but when he's old enough, I'll explain the circumstances of your death, and he'll understand."

Rowan laughed, which was odd, since she was describing his murder, and she was dragging his son into it.

But it was coming from her, and she didn't mean a single word of it. Because he knew it, her threats ended up sounding cute, and man, he *was* losing it.

"I should probably go," Delilah said. "Before I embarrass myself any further."

"No, this isn't on you. I'm sorry. I should have been clearer."

"No, this isn't on *you*. Your grandmother told me you've been speaking with Mckenna. I don't know why that completely left my head after you said . . ." She rolled her eyes. "I'm an idiot. But hey—if you still want my help, the offer stands."

"Why?" he asked. "Because it would be rude to retract it?"

"Yeah, actually." She grinned. "I'm obviously going to leave the food. I spent all afternoon cooking, and I know for a fact that it's delicious and also that you're going to need it with Mckenna not being around to help. Which is another reason I'm not retracting my offer."

"I . . . thank you," he said, instead of asking her to stay for dinner because he had plenty of food and wanted to share. He wanted to hand Declan over, let her put him to bed, and while she was doing that, prepare their meal.

But he couldn't. There were too many reasons he couldn't.

It would come dangerously close to asking her out on a date.

He'd be shifting responsibility of his kid onto yet another person.

It felt like betraying Mckenna, when he'd never wanted to do any of those things with her, at least not in the way he wanted to with Delilah.

"You're welcome," Delilah said, her smile a little more unsure now. "Call me."

She gave one last longing look at Declan—and he felt like a dick for not letting her at least hold him, only it was too late for that now—and turned.

"Wait," he said hastily. "I don't have your number."

"Oh yeah." She pursed her lips, pretended to think. "How about next time you come to the café, I give it to you?"

"Why can't you give it to me now?"

"You might not come to the café then."

"So this is blackmail?"

"Yes."

She winked at him, and then she was gone, leaving behind the scent of sweetness and sunshine.

"I think we're in trouble," he whispered to Declan and got a hiccup in return.

# CHAPTER EIGHT

When his grandmother arrived the next morning, she was carrying a plate of doughnuts.

"I stopped by the bakery on the way over," Linda told Rowan, handing him the plate and reaching out for Declan. "They have the most delicious doughnuts. Which you'd know if you ever actually went out."

He accepted the plate and gave her the baby, then sheepishly followed her to the kitchen. It was becoming a pattern: women barging into his home, making proclamations, and bringing him food and him following behind. Not necessarily a bad pattern, since he benefited every time, but a pattern nevertheless.

"It's unlikely I would have gone to the bakery if I'd gone out, Gran," he said as he walked to the kettle and put it on.

His house didn't have a coffee machine, hence his trips to the Blue Café. He might invest in one soon, considering coffee had taken the place of his blood, but that would mean he wouldn't go to the Blue Café as much, and he'd just been blackmailed into doing the exact opposite.

"I know." Linda sighed and looked down at Declan. "I hope you're not as inhibited as your father."

"Don't tell him that."

"It's true," she said, looking at Rowan again. "You should be walking the streets of this town, stopping in the bakeries, the cafés, getting your hair cut at the barbers, walking on the beach. There's an entire town for you to discover, but you're confined to this house. Has he eaten yet?"

Rowan shook his head and went to get Declan's bottle ready. They were currently alternating between the frozen breast milk Mckenna had left behind and formula, so that when they ran out of breast milk, Declan would be okay.

They'd only started it after Mckenna had left, though, and the formula was still upsetting Declan's stomach somewhat. But the only way to stop that was to continue, and so Rowan made the formula bottle and watched as his grandmother walked to the couch with Declan.

She settled there, accepting the bottle from Rowan and offering it to Declan. She talked to Declan as she did, with the same love and patience she'd used with Rowan when he'd been a child.

It was unbelievable that his grandmother had birthed his mother. His mother had always treated him efficiently, almost clinically, as if he'd been an adult instead of a child.

Once—he must have been four or five—he'd fallen off his bike onto his hip. There'd been some bad scratches, and a large bruise had begun to form almost immediately after. His mother had cleaned the wound without saying a word to him, and then, when she was done, she sat him down at the kitchen table and told him about actions and consequences.

Rowan didn't know why that day stood out. There were plenty of other memories he could recall to indicate his mother's lack of compassion. But that day was . . . it was the first time he could remember wanting comfort. Wanting comfort from his mother.

He'd wanted her to hug him, to tell him she was sorry he was hurting. And yes, sure, she could tell him to be more careful, that recklessly riding his bike could hurt him, but she would tell him this because she cared about him. Not because he'd inconvenienced her with his actions.

He shook his head and made his grandmother tea, making an instant cup of coffee for himself. It was his third cup since he'd woken up for the day two hours ago, which was ironic since he was basically one-third coffee anyway.

"Have you eaten?" he asked his grandmother.

"No, honey. That's why I brought the doughnuts."

He turned. "You eat doughnuts for breakfast? Since when?"

"Since my grandson moved to town with his son and I spend most of my time at his place."

She'd said it matter-of-factly, not to make him feel guilty. Didn't stop him from feeling guilty, though. He hadn't thought about how much time she was putting in with him.

Well, he'd thought about it, but he hadn't considered how it might have affected her life.

"I can offer you something else before we get to doughnuts?"

He walked to the fridge and opened it to some of the food Delilah had brought. He'd had her chicken curry the night before, and he'd almost called her to thank her for blessing him before remembering he didn't have her number. Strangely, her talent for cooking only made him more interested in her, and he tried not to think about that.

"There's cream cheese and ham with bagels, or an egg-bacon-and-cheese wrap."

He took out the wrap, peering closely at the writing on it. Delilah had added a sticker to all the meals with a description of the exact ingredients. It had confused him at first, but he realized that if she'd been thinking about his dietary preferences, she'd also probably thought about his allergies. He didn't have any, but it was thoughtful and nice.

She made him feel *nice.*

"The wrap also has rocket."

He looked at his grandmother again. She'd finished feeding Declan and was burping him. She was also watching Rowan with a suspicious look on her face.

"Since when do you have options for me?" she asked.

"What do you mean? I give options."

"Yes," she agreed. "Options of takeout. This is different."

"I ordered a grocery delivery," he said defensively.

"And they had breakfast wraps? With rocket?"

"Well, no." He ran a hand over his head and tried to figure out how to handle this. "I ordered the bagel stuff from the store."

"And the wrap?"

Look at that. She wouldn't be dissuaded by vagueness.

"The wrap is from Delilah."

"Delilah! Delilah *Huntington?*"

"Don't pretend like you didn't send her to me."

"Yes, but I didn't think she'd act so soon." Linda leaned forward as if to get up, but Declan gurgled and she eased back. "I should have known, though. She's a darling girl, that one. Helped me when I hurt my back last year. Remember when I hurt my back?"

"Yeah."

He'd tried to drive down to Sugarbush Bay, but his grandmother had refused his offer, saying it wasn't too bad and that she had help. Now he finally knew who she'd been referring to, and oddly, the guilt he still felt about it eased.

"You're lucky she's your neighbor. In fact, we're all lucky to have such a good girl as part of the community."

"Why do you keep calling her a girl?"

"Oh yes, I forget that being older doesn't make you children." She rolled her eyes. "Imagine thinking of your generation in those terms when I'm holding proof that you aren't a child."

"Gran!"

"Did you think I thought Declan was conceived through immaculate means?"

"Why . . . what . . ."

She burst out laughing. "Oh, honey, it's the best thing to fluster you."

"Speak for yourself," he muttered.

Linda winked. "Now, tell me what you think about that *woman.*"

"She's . . . nice."

His grandmother narrowed her eyes. "Nice? A cup of tea is nice." She waited a beat. "Or is that exactly what you mean? She's *your* cup of tea?"

"No!" he said, possibly too quickly, but he wanted to get as far away from this topic as possible and would have even if Delilah hadn't warned him about his grandmother's potential motives. "No. We met a couple of times. She's nice."

Eyes still narrowed, Linda merely said, "Hmm."

"Really," he insisted. Why was he insisting? It would only make her more suspicious. "We met at the café, and remember Mckenna called you about her, when we were looking for that babysitter, and you suggested someone, but she couldn't come, so we called you about Delilah instead."

Something rippled across Linda's face. Was that . . . was that guilt?

"You planned it!" he accused.

"Of course not, darling."

"Your face says otherwise."

"Oh, my face is always saying things I don't mean."

"Gran."

"Rowan."

"*Gran.*"

"Okay, fine." She sniffed. "I happened to know Irene had an exam that Monday. Sweet girl. She brings me the latest romance novels from the library." Linda waved a hand. "Anyway, her father wouldn't allow her to babysit if she needed to study, but he wouldn't let me down—*you* down," she corrected hurriedly, "and I knew he'd ask his sister."

"Why?"

"She's a babysitter."

"No, I mean, Why did you do it?"

"She's lovely," Linda answered simply. "I wanted you to know someone lovely in town. Someone who isn't me, who would ease you into small-town living. Plus, she's your neighbor. It seemed like the best option, and look, it worked. You're friends."

"We're not—"

He broke off. What was the point? His grandmother would think what she wanted. Maybe he and Delilah *were* friends.

A traitorous voice in his head laughed.

"You do need more, though," his grandmother went on, shifting Declan to her lap. He was looking at her, making incoherent baby noises as she smiled at him.

"More what?" Rowan asked, leaning against the doorway, enjoying the show.

"Friends."

"I'm fine."

"You're not."

"I am. I've survived my entire adulthood with minimal friends. Childhood, too, for that matter. One friend is more than enough."

"It is not," she said sternly, looking at him, as if she didn't want the baby to think the admonishment was for him. "You're raising a child now. Children need friends, too. The way they get that usually is through their parents' relationships or day care."

"We'll put him in day care."

"He's not going to day care when he has us to take care of him."

"But you said—"

"It's not only for him," she interrupted. "It's for you and your mental health. You can't be isolated as a parent."

"I'm not. You took care of Rowan when I went out with the . . . guys."

There was that frown again. "I suppose you're right." She paused. "I probably shouldn't be so hard on you. You've seen some of the town and met some of the people."

"Yes," he said, exhaling in relief.

"I don't think it's enough."

He sighed. "What *will* be enough?"

"A normal, well-balanced life."

"That's asking a lot, Gran," he said quietly. "I didn't even have that when I wasn't a single father."

It was odd, the way his throat closed at that term. As if the words themselves had fingers, clutching him, making it hard to breathe.

He'd never imagined he'd be here. Not as a father, not as a single father. If he hadn't had Declan, he'd still be in his two-bedroom house in Cape Town. He'd be dealing with clients himself instead of delegating.

He'd be putting more and more of himself into his business, into the one thing that had been stable and successful since it started, instead of being on a tumultuous journey that was peppered with complicated emotions and unpleasant memories.

Normal and well balanced to him meant working all hours of the day, getting the satisfaction he needed from his accomplishments, and living his life on his own terms.

Hell, those *were* his own terms. What his grandmother was expecting was outside his capabilities.

Still, he was trying. He was trying so damn hard so that his son didn't one day find that "his own terms" meant being completely and utterly alone.

He'd thought he was okay with it. He'd always been okay with it. Realizing he wasn't, not anymore, had the fingers tightening around his throat.

"It doesn't have to be like that, Rowan," Linda replied kindly. "You already have people in your life who care about you. *Here*," she emphasized, "people you've met and become friends with. That life is closer than you think it is."

She stood, murmuring that she'd take Declan out for a walk, and slipped out the door with a soft click.

Rowan stared after her.

Was it true? Could he give Declan the life he wanted by himself? Was he capable of making friends when he'd never been capable of it before?

No one wanted to be friends with the shy, reserved kid in class. Even if they did, Rowan knew his parents' lack of involvement would eventually become a problem. A lot of kids had parents who cared about them, about who they were with. Those parents would want to speak with his parents or know they were there in case of an emergency. Nannies wouldn't suffice for that kind of parent. They had barely sufficed for him.

But maybe things would be different here. Delilah didn't know him, and she'd been kind and generous. Matt, Lucas, and Corey didn't know him, either, and they'd been kind and generous. And they'd insisted, at the end of that meeting at Oasis, that he do more things with them. That he "integrate" with the community. Get involved with the festival.

He hadn't committed to any of it. He hadn't even replied to the message Matt had sent him the night before. He'd wondered at the timing. That Delilah had come to see him, admitted that she'd asked her brother about him, and suddenly he was getting an invitation to Matt's daughter's birthday that weekend.

But that would imply that Matt was concerned about him, too. Or at the very least that Matt was okay with Delilah reaching out to him. Something told him it wasn't that last thing.

Despite the ambiguity of the situation—and despite his fears—Rowan finally replied to Matt's text.

I'll be there. Thank you for the invitation.

It was Irene's sixteenth birthday. Despite only being her aunt, Delilah felt an odd sense of nostalgia. She could still remember the day Matt had told their parents Vanessa was pregnant.

The day had started normally. Delilah had been woken up by the nanny, gotten ready for school, and eaten breakfast with her brother. He'd been quieter than usual, but at ten years old, Delilah couldn't figure out why that was, so she'd ignored it.

In fact, she'd been planning their weekly baking day. On those days, she and Matt baked something delicious together, with the guidance of

Sonny, the family chef, before sneaking up to their rooms and eating it before their parents got home.

It wouldn't have mattered if they'd been caught. Their parents didn't care about them spoiling their dinner. But it had felt good to pretend. Looking back, she thought Matt had pretended for her sake. Or maybe he'd needed it, too.

That day, when she'd come home from school, Matt hadn't been there. He usually told her if he'd be late, but he hadn't that day. She'd waited, and as the hour grew later, she began to suspect he wasn't coming home at all. A dramatic assumption, but a normal one for a girl whose parents frequently didn't bother coming home.

They had, that day. Around 5:00 p.m., her mother had shown up, greeted her, and with a frown, as if she'd noticed something was missing but couldn't put her finger on what, disappeared into her office.

An hour later, her father arrived. Patrick Huntington was handsome, smart, sharp, the exact kind of man who thrived on—and hungered for—money and power. He was also a terrible father who Delilah hadn't spoken with properly since . . . well, she couldn't remember.

It wasn't that different to her relationship with her mother, honestly. Only she did have conversations with Geraldine. How else would Delilah know what was expected of her?

Patrick had gone to his office, too, and shortly after, Matt finally arrived. He'd come over to her, apologized for being late and not telling her, and gone to his father's office. Seconds later, both Matt and Patrick went into Geraldine's office.

Delilah watched all this from her playroom, a wide-open space opposite all these doors. When her nanny tried to take her to her bedroom, she refused. Matt, hearing that, stopped in the door of Geraldine's office and told the nanny Delilah could come with him. She was part of the family, after all.

The warmth of that moment had quickly been eclipsed by her parents' coldness at the news. They'd informed Matt teenage pregnancy was not "Huntington" behavior. He needed to take care of it.

Matt firmly told them what to do with that suggestion—Delilah had never seen Geraldine that shocked, even at her arrest—and turned to leave when their mother sat down behind her desk and shooed him out.

Matt had taken Delilah's hand and led her out to his room, his palm damp. And though she'd rarely done it before because he didn't like it, she hugged him. His arms had enveloped her, his breath shuddering out his body, and in that moment, Delilah knew things would change forever. And they had.

Delilah didn't understand why she thought of those memories now and not the joyous ones. The celebration of Irene's life. That she was sixteen, healthy, happy—well, as happy as a teenager could be—and that she had a great relationship with her parents.

At sixteen, Delilah had been healthy, yes, but happiness had been a concept so foreign she hadn't even thought about it. She'd spent her teen years trying to keep up with people she didn't like, doing things she didn't want to do, and being a person she was ashamed of.

As for her relationship with her parents? It had been as nonexistent as when she was ten. Only then, she didn't even have a nanny or a brother to keep her company.

"No," she murmured to herself as she climbed the steps to Matt's house. "There will be none of that today. You're here to celebrate your niece's birthday, not wallow in the fact that you do not have her life. If you choose to do the latter, it's super sad, and you need help."

Satisfied, she rang the doorbell. Irene answered, as Delilah had known she would. She'd purposefully rung the bell so that Irene *could* answer, since normally she'd use the key Matt had given her.

But Irene needed to answer so she could pretend not to care that it was her birthday even as she secretly freaked out because her birthday was her favorite day of the year.

"Oh, hey," Delilah said, nonchalantly. "Is your dad here?"

"Yeah," Irene replied, as nonchalantly. "Why?"

"Nothing." Delilah put one hand on her hip and held three tickets up in the air with the other. "I just happen to have these tickets to a

Cape Town summer music festival. I thought I'd ask if he wanted to go. Maybe he could bring a friend and the three of us could—"

She got cut off by a fast, impactful hug that nearly took her off her feet.

"*The Serenity Festival?*" Irene shrieked in Delilah's ear. Delilah angled her head but couldn't get away from the high-pitched sound. "*You got me tickets to the Serenity Festival?*" Irene leaned back. "I don't understand. Dad said no."

"Dad said no so that we could pull this elaborate ruse and I could be the one to say yes. I'd be your favorite aunt, and you'd owe me your firstborn child."

"I'm not having children," she said, staring at the tickets that were somehow now in her hands. "But you can absolutely have my firstborn kittens."

She whirled, and Delilah had to rush after her to stop her from disappearing.

"Wait, hold on." She stopped in front of Irene. "There are rules."

Irene gave a long-suffering sigh but didn't speak, which was Delilah's cue to continue.

"One, you go with me."

"But—"

"That's the rule," a deep voice said from wherever its owner was lingering in the dark. It took Delilah a second, but she located him in the corner near the window. Her brother was a weirdo.

Irene rolled her eyes. "Fine."

"You get to take a friend."

"One friend."

"Yes," she said, giving Matt a look when he opened his mouth. "You get to take one friend. And we'll make a week of it. We'll go to Cape Town the Monday, do whatever you choose to do, no questions asked—within reason—and then we go to the festival that weekend."

Irene's brow knit, and Delilah's heart almost stopped. Oh no. She'd overestimated how much her niece liked her. Irene probably hated the idea and was now trying to find a polite way of letting Delilah down. Or just letting her down in general, since polite wasn't really in a teen's arsenal.

As much as she told herself it was okay, that it was normal for Irene not to want to spend time with her aunt, that it wasn't personal, Delilah couldn't quite believe it. It felt . . . important for Irene to like this gift. To like *her* for gifting it. She loved her family so much, and she wanted them to love her, too.

She knew it was desperate. Knew that she couldn't show Irene any of it if her niece decided she didn't want the gift. Delilah's fears, her feelings, were not Irene's responsibility. Delilah would handle the rejection with poise and—

"That's pretty cool, D."

Delilah barely stopped herself from squealing as relief dropped like an egg on her head, running over her body. She grinned instead. "Yeah? Well, great."

"For now," Matt said, pushing off the wall, "you give those tickets back to your aunt. She'll keep them safe."

"I am perfectly capable of keeping these tickets safe," Irene said with a sniff.

"Didn't say you weren't," Matt answered, offering no further explanation.

Irene rolled her eyes again but handed the tickets to Delilah and gave her father a kiss on the cheek before disappearing up the stairs.

They waited until they heard her door close before high-fiving one another.

# CHAPTER NINE

Rowan took a deep breath as he parked in front of Matt's house. The road was already filled with cars, and it took all his strength not to turn around.

Yes, there *would* be people at this birthday party. He'd known that the moment Matt had invited him. He'd even known that there would be a lot of people. Matt was popular, despite his gruff exterior. It was confusing but gave Rowan hope that he, too, could become . . . well, not popular, exactly. He didn't want that. He only wanted to be accepted.

He had no idea where that came from, let alone why it made him so prickly. So he ignored it. Instead, he looked at the house. The beautiful house of white and glass, with green potted plants on the balcony and a neat garden next to the driveway.

Rowan felt a pang of longing, and he wondered when Matt's life had become one he wanted. Maybe it was that Matt had survived raising his daughter for sixteen years while co-parenting. Maybe it was because he had people supporting him. Friends. A community. And yeah, maybe it was the enviable house.

*Or maybe it's having Delilah as a part of that life.*

He preferred not to dwell on that unwelcome thought. It was enough that he was seeing her today. But he'd been preparing for that since he'd told Matt he'd come.

It meant acknowledging how much space she took up in his head. When he saw her, he was taken aback by how attracted he was to her.

He'd try to understand it. How it was even possible to be attracted to her when he didn't care about feeling attraction to *anyone* anymore.

He'd try to convince himself it wasn't real.

When that didn't work, he'd try to stop himself from being attracted to her. He wouldn't indulge any fantasies about kissing her, touching her, caressing her . . .

It took energy. Energy he didn't—shouldn't—have. Not for this. Once he figured that out, he could come up with a plan. He *had* come up with a plan: he'd avoid her. She couldn't take up any mental space if he didn't see her.

The unforeseeable side effect of this was how badly he now wanted to see her. He resisted the urge to go to the café so he could talk to her, walk outside so he could see her—all while hoping she'd come over for a visit. Pop over to check why she hadn't seen him the last few days. It was the kind of situation he wasn't prepared for: such easy access to the source of his torture.

He wouldn't let it break him. His family depended on it, on him, and he wouldn't let them down by succumbing to temptation. Which was why he was here. At this party. He would go inside and talk to people. With his defenses in place, he'd even talk to Delilah.

He'd make connections, be social, and someday, he'd have a party for Declan, and the entire town would come.

With a deep breath he got out the car and went to the front door. He knocked, and beneath the pressure the door gave way.

It opened to a small reception area, which someone had decorated with a picture of a girl—Irene, since above the picture were the words **HAPPY BIRTHDAY IRENE**—and helium balloon bunches on either side of it. She didn't look much like Matt, though he could see the man in the shrewdness of Irene's eyes.

He turned to the left, to where he heard the sounds of a party, and stalled.

He could go in there. Should go in there. It was the first step to the life he'd pictured for himself and his son in the car.

He could also leave. Get into his car, go to his grandmother's house and hold his child, and spend the day with the two people in his life who actually loved him.

Before he had the chance to back out, Delilah came bounding down a staircase he hadn't seen. He didn't know it was her at first. He'd heard the footsteps behind him, and when he turned, she was there.

Because of course she was. She haunted him even when he tried to exorcise her.

Her eyes widened as she took him in, her gaze going from his head to his toes. "Hey! I didn't know you were coming."

"Matt invited me."

"Yeah, I figured you wouldn't swing by uninvited. That's more my thing, isn't it?"

She smiled. She *sparkled.* Rowan suddenly wished they'd met before he'd slept with Mckenna. When desire was simple. When acting on it wasn't irresponsible. When he had the time and energy for wanting.

"He invited my grandmother first," Rowan said slowly, forcing himself to talk about his family. Reminding himself of the stakes. "She didn't mention it until I asked her to look after Declan today. She insisted I go instead, so I guess I'm representing all of us."

"A worthy representative."

His mouth twisted. "Not sure that's true."

"Why wouldn't it be?" she asked, frowning. "You're a great guy, Rowan. Why wouldn't we want you around?"

*You're a great guy, Rowan.*

A little dazed, he said, "We?"

"The town," she replied vaguely, waving a hand. "We hold a monthly meeting about newcomers. Judge their general vibe, whether we believe they deserve to be a part of our community."

"You do . . . what?"

She immediately burst into laughter, and his resolve to resist her faltered.

She was magnificent.

Her entire face lit up when she laughed. She exposed her throat slightly, but enough for him to spot a splatter of freckles on the left side. Sunshine glowed from the creases next to her eyes, the rounding of her cheeks. Her mouth curved with happiness, with pure joy, highlighting the sensual fullness of her lips.

Desire punched through the walls he'd put up to defend himself, to *protect* himself from her. He tried to catch his breath, but the images flooding his mind didn't give him the chance.

He wanted to caress her face. Slide his fingers down, below her ear, over those freckles. He'd stop before he reached her chest. Or maybe he wouldn't. Maybe he'd lay a hand over her heart, feel it beating against his skin. See if he could make it beat faster, harder.

He wanted to kiss her. Move against her lips with his own, check if they were as soft as they looked. He wanted to know what she tasted of. Wanted it to be the benchmark of every other taste, which would no doubt disappoint in comparison, and he'd only be truly fulfilled when he tasted her again.

Where could he touch her that would make her moan? Her breasts? Her thighs? Between them? Would she be breathless and wanting or confident and demanding? Would she cry out in pleasure? Shout his name? Murmur?

This need *was* impossible. He *had* cut that part of himself off after Mckenna. He'd been foolish, impulsive, giving in to a momentary desire and ending up with a lifetime consequence. He wouldn't give his son up for the world, but that experience should have taught him what physical desire resulted in.

It *had* taught him that—he'd been celibate and frankly uninterested in changing that since he found out about Mckenna.

Until he met Delilah.

"I'm sorry," she said softly. He lifted his gaze, only then realizing he'd still been staring at her chest. That he'd been staring at her. "It was a joke."

"I . . . I know." He exhaled, trying to get a handle on his thoughts. "I'm sorry. I get the joke. It just—"

"Wasn't funny?" she interrupted, wrinkling her nose. "Yeah, I get that a lot. I think I'm a lot funnier than I am."

"I was going to say it took me by surprise."

"Okay." She shifted her weight, put her hands on her hips, and shook her head. "I should go? I mean, I'm kind of running things here." She rolled her eyes with a breathy laugh. "That's not true. Don't tell Vanessa I said so. Irene's mom," she answered after his questioning look. "I'm helping out, but I think she might need me." She paused. "I'll . . . um . . . see you around?"

He nodded, and she gave him a relieved smile before disappearing through a doorway around the corner. The party was clearly there, since that was where the noise was coming from, so he waited a beat, giving Delilah time to get away from him.

He'd made her uncomfortable with his staring, his intensity. It hadn't been like this before today. Today felt as if someone had taken their attraction and turned it into something tangible, and now its weight was pressing down on them.

On him.

He knew that weight was partly his reluctance; his knowledge that entering into a new relationship was the worst thing for his son, for his life.

It was that damn attraction. Forbidden and yet so damn tempting. He could feel it between them. Was so aware of it that he felt trapped in an invisible bubble whenever he was around her.

He took a deep breath. Then another. A third when the second didn't completely calm him. But it was the fourth that gave him the courage to walk through the doorway.

He found himself in a kitchen. It was a big open space, all white and modern, with a large kitchen island crowded with food wrapped in plastic. There were ice buckets with drinks on a counter beneath large windows. Next to it was a sink that was brimming with ice, too, though he couldn't see anything in it.

There were several people in the room, none of whom he recognized, walking between the fridges and the counters, dealing with food and drinks.

One of them, a woman who looked to be in her late thirties, looked over. "Hey! You're Rowan, right? Linda's grandchild?"

He wasn't surprised she knew who he was. Everyone seemed to, and he could blame it on the fact that it was a small town and word got around. But really? He knew it was his grandmother's doing. She was constantly taking pictures of him, of Declan, and though she never posted pictures of the baby to social media, the same didn't go for him.

He didn't mind it—or he hadn't, until he'd seen one of her posts:
*THIS IS MY GRANDSON. HE IS THE SWEETEST BOY. A FATHER NOW. I CAN'T BELIEVE IT—I USED TO BATHE HIM.*

For one, it was in all caps.

For another, she'd referred to bathing him.

And lastly, and this was really the one that got him, she'd posted a picture of him when he was a baby.

In the bath.

She'd put a sticker on his penis—he'd have to thank whoever had shown her how to do that—but it was mortifying all the same. When he'd asked her about it, she'd been suitably apologetic yet somehow managed to tell him how it had been one of the few pictures she had of him as a child. His parents hadn't bothered taking photos when he'd been younger, and so she'd tried to, but her camera had broken shortly after this very picture had been taken, and really, this was capturing history.

And then there'd been a spiel about how this was before camera phones and accessibility, and his eyes started to cross, and apparently that was exactly what she wanted, because when she stopped talking, she was smiling.

The woman was still staring at him expectantly.

"Sorry, yes. Yes, I am."

"Great to see you here," she answered with a warm smile. "Help yourself to something to drink. Nonalcoholic here"—she pointed to one side of the counter—"alcoholic here."

He hesitated but grabbed a bottle of water. He might need the liquid courage of alcohol, but once he went down that path, there was no going back. Because he needed *all* the courage.

Besides, he didn't want people to get to know him as a version of himself that wasn't really him. If he was going to be awkward, they should know that he was awkward.

And awkward was exactly what he was.

As soon as he got outside, it crept up on him. He lingered on the outside of groups, greeting people but never joining their conversation. He'd seen Matt with Lucas and Corey, but they were busy assembling a stage of some kind, and since he had no skills with that, he'd only be in the way.

Delilah flitted in and out of the house, nodding at him the first time she saw him in the garden but studiously ignoring him after. Not that he could blame her. He had made it weird, and even he would avoid the guy who made it weird.

Only he couldn't avoid himself.

He took a steadying breath. He could do this. He could. He'd built a company, hired people, worked with clients. He'd built a damn good company, too, and he wouldn't have been able to do that without dealing with people.

He would make at least one acquaintance today. He *would*.

He walked to the closest group. Small, three people, two of whom smiled at him as he joined them, not making him feel self-conscious at all. He recognized the third as the waitress who'd helped them at Oasis. Jill. She gave him a nod.

"Hey," he said as the conversation lulled. "I'm Rowan."

"Dean," one of the men said.

"Ronald," said the other. "You're Linda's grandkid, yeah?"

He nodded.

"She told me I should ask you to coffee," Ronald said with a small smile. "I moved here a year ago. I think she thought I could give you some acclimation tips."

"I moved here a couple of years ago," Dean said. "She hasn't asked me."

"Maybe she doesn't think you're good enough to help her grandson?" Jill offered.

Rowan opened his mouth to protest that but shut it as quickly. He didn't understand the dynamic here, and defending Dean when he didn't even know the man seemed like a dangerous game.

Dean swore. Jill smiled.

Yeah, he definitely didn't understand the dynamic.

"Anyway," Ronald said pointedly, "I know what it's like to start in this town. I'm happy to take you out, show you around."

"I'd . . . like that," Rowan lied, because he certainly would not. He could feel the faint beat of panic in his veins, the warning system he'd had in place since he was young. The system that told him he was out of his comfort zone and he had to retreat fast.

"Awesome. It's a date."

Rowan nodded and took a desperate sip from his water bottle. The beating was in his ears now, so loud he wished it had an off switch. Eager for something to distract him, he looked at Jill and Dean, who were both smirking, like they were sharing an inside joke.

He hated that. Genuinely hated it. Whenever he'd seen that look on people's faces, it meant they were sharing an inside joke, and usually, that joke was at his expense.

"Cut it out," Ronald said sharply. "You're making him uncomfortable."

Dean and Jill stopped smiling immediately.

"Sorry," Dean muttered, at the same time that Jill said, "We're asses."

Ronald offered Rowan an apologetic smile. "They've never actually witnessed me asking anyone out, so they think this is funny, like the immature assholes they are."

It wasn't that she was stalking him. She wasn't. In fact, Delilah had done her best to avoid Rowan since they'd shared . . . whatever it was inside the house when he'd first arrived. Only she kept finding herself near him, as if he were a magnetic surface and she were a magnet and she wanted to be on top of him.

Which, after the way he'd looked at her earlier, was not exactly untrue.

But she knew it was a bad idea. She'd already established her crush had veered into something more serious, and that went against everything the new Delilah stood for. It would be a fundamentally selfish thing to follow her heart, explore her feelings for Rowan.

She was no longer selfish.

She'd *fought* not to be, so that when she looked back on her life before, built with the money her mother had stolen from honest, hardworking people, Delilah knew she wasn't that person anymore.

Except she was only human. She would fail, despite her best intentions, and that failure meant she happened to be near Rowan when Ronald said he'd been asking Rowan out.

Of course, she understood what Ronald meant. Dean and Jill had been trying to convince their cousin to date since he'd arrived in Sugarbush Bay. The three of them had an odd dynamic, being cousins, all of whom had moved to this obscure small town for their own reasons.

It was all love and teasing, fighting and defending, and someone who had no experience with that wouldn't know what to make of it.

This was clearly the case with Rowan. He thought Ronald was asking him out romantically. The realization of what he thought he knew dawned on his face.

"I'm . . . I'm . . . not gay," Rowan spluttered.

The cousins stared at him—and burst out laughing.

It was an almost physical pain seeing Rowan's face. He was putting himself out there, and they were laughing at him.

She knew that was what was causing his discomfort. He didn't care that they thought he was gay but rather that they thought he was gay and were laughing. The indignation of being treated that way when he thought so carefully about how he interacted with people so he wouldn't offend them. The embarrassment of being laughed at when it already was so hard *to* interact with people.

Delilah was stepping in before she knew what she was doing.

"Hey," she said easily. She smiled at Rowan, bumping her shoulder to his, before looking at Dean, Jill, and Ronald. "What's so funny?"

"Ronald asked Rowan out," Dean said, still smiling as he took a swig of his beer.

"Oh, he did not," Delilah said, rolling her eyes. "I don't even know the context of this conversation, and I can tell you that."

"She's right," Ronald offered, his eyes sharp on Rowan, taking in the man's tension. Delilah lifted a brow when he looked at her. *Yeah, you did that,* she told him mentally. She didn't know Ronald that well, had only met him in a few social situations, but he seemed like a decent man. He didn't want to make anyone uncomfortable.

True to that observation, he continued, "I am gay, Rowan, but I wasn't asking you out romantically. My cousins were being idiots earlier because I haven't been out with anyone in town, and I don't intend to change that, because I like living here, and the small-town thing . . . well, I don't want people knowing my business."

He gave Dean and Jill a shrewd look.

"The point of that overly personal explanation is that they want me to date, and since offering to show you around town is the closest thing

I've come to a date in the last year, it amused them." His face softened. "I shouldn't have laughed when you said you weren't gay. I obviously didn't mean any offense by it. It was merely surprise, because of course you aren't."

His gaze flickered to Delilah. She resisted the urge to roll her eyes. The explanation could have done without that.

"I am sorry."

Delilah gave Ronald a quick nod before staring at Dean and Jill. Their expressions were comically similar in their blankness, but when Delilah narrowed her eyes, Jill snapped out of it.

"I'm sorry, too," she said quickly. "We were being jerks."

"In our defense, we thought we were being jerks to Ronald," Dean added. At Delilah's look, he said, "But we obviously weren't, and we're sorry."

Satisfied, Delilah smiled. "Well, that wasn't so hard, was it?"

"Speak for yourself," Dean muttered.

Jill poked him in the ribs. "No, it wasn't. Thank you for showing us the error of our ways."

"I hear the sarcasm," Delilah told her, "and it doesn't bother me one bit. You can always count on me to force you to be a better human being."

Ronald laughed while Jill gave her the finger with a smile.

"You love it," Delilah said before looping her arm through Rowan's. "Come on, let's go."

"I'm sorry!" Jill called after them, her tone chastised in a way it hadn't been earlier. Perhaps she'd realized how uncomfortable Rowan was. The fact that he hadn't said one thing since Delilah had appeared must have finally caught up with her.

He still wasn't speaking now, and his muscles were bunched beneath her hand. Privacy. He needed privacy to get over whatever was happening in his head. She took him to the house and up the stairs to Matt's office, closed the door, and waited.

It took some time—maybe five minutes, maybe longer—but eventually he said, "That was the most horrifying experience I've had in a long time."

He dropped to Matt's office chair and rested his head in his hands. "I had one thing to do today," he said, anguished. "One thing. I wanted to make things easier for my son. I wanted . . . I wanted to get to know the people in this town so they'd know him. And I . . . I messed it up."

She'd resisted many things when it came to Rowan. The attraction, the pull, the cute package of him and Declan together. But this? This strong, handsome man who looked so utterly defeated? So vulnerable?

She wanted to drop to her knees. She wanted to take him into her arms and comfort him. Tell him she was sorry it was so hard to navigate a world he felt so lost in.

It didn't take a genius to see Rowan struggled to talk with people. He'd barely spoken with her until she'd helped him in the café with Declan almost a month ago. Since then, she'd driven their interactions. She'd introduced him to Matt, who'd introduced him to Corey and Lucas. He hadn't initiated anything social, but he tried to attend what he was invited to.

She hadn't understood why until now. He wanted his son to be a part of the Sugarbush Bay community. He didn't seem to believe there'd be space for both him and Declan, and yet he was here, putting himself in what must have been a nightmare situation for him, so that the town would make a space for Declan.

And Jill, Dean, and Ronald had laughed at him.

It didn't matter that it hadn't been malicious or, strictly speaking, directed at Rowan. It didn't even matter that they'd apologized. Rowan saw this as a failure. He'd failed in doing what he'd come here to do. He'd failed his son.

"You're incredible," she whispered, getting down to her knees so she could face him. "You're an incredible parent. Declan is so lucky."

His brow furrowed. "Didn't you hear what I said? I messed up today. I couldn't even have one conversation with three people without—"

"I heard you," she interrupted. "I heard that you came here today even though it was hard. I heard that you joined a conversation with three strangers even though it was hard. I heard that you accepted the invitation from Ronald even though it was hard. Yeah, I might have been there a little earlier than I let on," she said with a quirk of a smile before continuing.

"You did all of these hard things because you wanted to make your son's life easier. How is that messing up? How is that you not being an incredible parent?"

"You're being nice," he said in a strangled voice.

"No, I'm not. If you were a bad parent, I would have said so." She paused. "Okay, no, I wouldn't have. I wouldn't have said anything at all. So I definitely wouldn't have told you you were incredible if I didn't believe it."

He shook his head. "You don't get it."

"I do. I do," she said again and took a deep breath. "I have terrible parents, Rowan. There wasn't a single thing they did that wasn't for themselves. They never thought about me or Matt."

Her mother hadn't thought of them when she'd been stealing money from innocent people. Sure, some of them had been Geraldine's wealthy friends. They'd gone on with their lives after her mother's arrest, the money she'd stolen from them only a fraction of what they had.

But the majority of the people her mother had defrauded had been middle class. People who couldn't afford to lose their savings, who couldn't afford to have a broker lie to them about financial policies and payouts.

People whose futures had disappeared before their eyes as they found out the professional they'd trusted with their money had been stealing it for herself.

Delilah hadn't known much about her mother's work before the arrest. But when she discovered who most of her mother's clients had been, Geraldine's crimes had seemed almost obvious.

Her mother would only work with the middle class if she was screwing them over. She believed she was better than them, believed she deserved more than them. And so she took it. Despite the fact that working with the upper class would have given her more than she could ever need.

Why would that be enough when it would never be more than what she wanted?

A woman that selfish didn't think of her children. When her mother had been arrested—when the police had pounded on the door, shouting that they had a warrant for Geraldine Huntington's arrest—Delilah's entire world had turned upside down.

Her mother had been cool even as they'd slipped the cuffs on her wrists, even as she'd instructed Delilah's father to call their lawyers. She hadn't looked at Delilah. Hadn't spared a single glance to the daughter who'd been watching with tears in her eyes, who'd known in that moment that her life would never be the same.

Her father hadn't thought of her either. He'd gone into his bedroom, returned with a suitcase, and left. He'd ignored Delilah's questions, her panic. Only that evening had he called her, told her the money currently in her bank account would remain hers and that she should use it to get out of town, and hung up.

There'd been no updates about her mother, nothing about whether he'd known what Geraldine had been doing, and not a word about their family.

Yes, she knew a thing or two about selfish parents. A man beating himself up over an uncomfortable social situation was not it.

"I'm sorry," he said quietly.

She stood. "Don't be. I'm here. I survived it." Barely, but she had. "Why are you being so hard on yourself?"

"I'm not—"

"Why can't you accept a compliment about your parenting?"

"I don't believe you," he said simply. "Even if I did, I'd still think I messed up back there. I messed up with you earlier."

"What? No you didn't."

"It was awkward."

"No." At his look, she snorted. "Okay, fine, it was a little awkward when you got here. But I didn't expect to see you."

"You and I both know you weren't the reason for the awkwardness."

"You don't know a damn thing."

"Sure. That's why you've been avoiding me."

"You weren't supposed to notice that."

He gave her a look. "I did."

"It's not you. It's not," she insisted.

"Then what is it?"

She couldn't think of a single lie that would answer his question. Not when he'd already made up his mind, seemed convinced it was him. So she didn't bother lying.

"There's this . . . thing between us. We're both ignoring it, and rightfully so. You have your stuff, I have mine, and we're ignoring it. But that makes things awkward."

He stared.

She shrugged. "Don't ask questions you don't want the answers to."

"I . . . didn't think you'd be that honest."

Neither of them said anything for a while.

"I'm not sure why I didn't think so," he said. "You were honest out there." He tilted his head to the door. "You didn't care if they liked you or not."

"That wasn't why I was honest. And trust me, I cared. I *care*. A lot."

"And you stood up for me even though you care?"

"They didn't mean any harm," she replied. "They're good people with misguided senses of humor. And they're idiots when it comes to family."

"Why were you honest?" he asked more directly now.

She folded her arms. "It doesn't matter."

"It matters to me."

It mattered to her, too. But she could hardly tell him she hadn't been thinking when she'd stepped in. She had only wanted to protect him.

Sure, she could—and probably would—lie to herself about her motives. Stepping in to protect a vulnerable person was what anyone would do. And while that might have been true, it wasn't why she'd done it. She'd helped him because she liked him.

She'd already admitted there was something between them. She couldn't tell him that something was her feelings.

It didn't help that he was so intently focused on her. His gaze, intense and disarming, had sparks running up and down her spine. It made her skin feel like it didn't belong to her. It was too tight, too flushed, too aware, to be hers.

"I know what it's like to feel out of place." Her voice sounded foreign, but she couldn't pinpoint why. "It helps to have a friend. Someone who can help you navigate the most uncomfortable parts of it, I guess."

He nodded. "That makes sense."

She exhaled. Good. He believed her.

"You can do that for me."

"What?"

"Help me. You're good in social situations. You don't care even when you care. You can help me."

"I'd be happy to help you, Rowan. But . . . um . . . what exactly do you want my help with?"

He fixed his gaze on hers. "I want you to teach me how to make friends."

# CHAPTER TEN

Delilah's expression made Rowan feel like a fool. Only he was a fool. He was asking a woman to teach him how to make friends. He was asking *this* woman. The one who made him hunger when he'd been intent on starving.

"I know what it sounds like—" he began, but she cut him off.

"It sounds like you've come up with a solution to your socializing struggles," she said, twisting her mouth. "But I don't know if it's a good one. I'm not . . . the right person for this."

"Every situation I've witnessed you in, you've navigated with authenticity and ease."

"Just because you haven't seen it doesn't mean it doesn't happen."

"Not the same way it happens with me."

"No, but . . ." She trailed off. Looked at him. "You think this is a good idea? Us spending more time together?"

He hadn't thought about it. He'd been too focused on the result. On building a home for Declan in this community. On making sure his son never struggled to interact with his peers. If Rowan had anything to do with it, Declan would know when people were laughing at him or with him.

*Or with each other,* he thought.

Rowan had spent the entirety of his life alone, not being invited to social situations when he'd been younger, avoiding them when he was older, and not learning the necessary skills to grow and maintain relationships. Maybe he wouldn't have been so taken aback by the whole thing with Ronald if he'd had those skills.

But he'd make sure Declan had them. If that meant he had to make up for lost time and learn how to socialize now, he would. For the sake of his son, he'd do anything. Even spend more time with Delilah.

As he thought it, his brain mocked him. So did his body. Because standing alone with her in this room, so close he could reach out and touch her, drove him insane.

He wanted her. Wanted to push her against the wall until there was no more space between them. Wanted to feel her heat, hear her moan.

He could see it so clearly: his mouth fused to hers, his hand down her panties, teasing her until his fingers were slicked with her wetness and he was so hard he could barely breathe.

And it was wrong. It was so wrong.

He'd shut down that side of him after Mckenna. It had been easy to do. He'd been too worried about being a father after she'd told him she was pregnant. Then, when he'd become a father, he'd been too tired to think of sex. So busy with diapers and feedings and ensuring that he gave Declan the best he could that thinking about it, fantasizing about it, never occurred to him.

His libido had been dead almost a year, and he'd been fine with it. Still would have been fine with it, if it weren't for Delilah. Now his imagination—and other parts of his body—was making up for lost time with enthusiasm.

The only comfort he had was that she'd acknowledged something was happening between them, too. It wasn't in his head.

It wasn't as comforting as he'd like.

"I can keep it together if you can," he said, resisting the urge to check whether she could see the consequences of him fantasizing about her.

"Of course. I'm the queen of self-control." She cleared her throat. "I'll help."

He stood. "Thank you."

"Okay, no. Nope." She shook her head vigorously. "No, I can't do this. When you stood right now? My heart skipped. It skipped."

She caught her bottom lip between her teeth and let go with a snap. Not an audible one, not a tangible one, but he felt it.

"Ha!" she exclaimed, pointing at him. "You can't do it either. You looked at me biting my lip, and your eyes . . . they flickered. And then something in my body flickered. No. No, Rowan, this is literally the worst idea."

The air had tightened, sucked in by her admissions.

"Why are you saying this?" he asked gruffly.

"Because you're ignoring it," she answered, steady despite the tension. "You're asking me to spend more time with you, and you're pretending like there isn't this thing between us that will follow."

"I didn't say that."

"No? Well, maybe it's not so bad for you. Maybe you can handle it. But I'm clearly in over my head, and—"

"Stop," he barked. "Stop talking about it."

"Don't you *dare* get angry at me! I'm doing the smart thing. Neither of us want—"

He stepped closer. He wasn't sure why, knew it was the bad idea she was making it out to be, but he couldn't help himself. It was the exact opposite of what he should have done, and he couldn't stop himself.

Still, he moved.

Now, so did she.

She straightened, stepping back until she was flush against the wall, her eyes defiant. Daring. She was daring him to make a move. To do *something*.

He narrowed his eyes and closed the distance between them.

"You're going to regret this," she breathed, her gaze on his lips.

"I don't care."

And then they were kissing, their mouths coming together in a rush of undeniable tension and simmering heat.

He groaned at the contact, at finally touching her, giving in to the desire he'd felt since that afternoon in the storeroom at the café. And he *was* touching her. His hands were on her hips, the lush curve of them, soft and full beneath his fingers. They slid up, over her waist, down and around, over her butt, pulling her closer.

He absorbed her inhale of air, tangling his tongue with her own, groaning again when it felt right and good. He was so hot, burning up from the inside. And she was kind. Pulling his shirt up, exposing his skin to the cool air, offering him relief.

Until her hands touched his body, exploring, claiming, and he turned into ash with each stroke.

She moaned into his mouth, and he drank that in, too, like he drank her in. Her scent, delicate and sweet, became a part of him. He'd never be able to enter a room she'd been in without smelling her first, without knowing that she'd been there, without wanting her.

The feel of her lips against his, the softness of them, their strength as they demanded his passion, as they made him worry that she would consume him whole with a stroke of her tongue.

And her tongue. Oh, her tongue. Its cleverness had him wondering if he'd ever really kissed before. If he'd ever really *been* kissed.

Every kiss before didn't matter anymore.

Every kiss after wouldn't matter.

Only this, with her, mattered.

Only she mattered.

"I want you," he whispered against her mouth. "I want you so much it hurts."

Her eyes went wide, her tongue darting out between her lips, as if she could taste him there. As if she wanted to.

Time slowed down. Everything became clear, sharp. The feel of her body against him. Her softness, her warmth. The weight of her butt in his hands.

His hardness, his need.

Her chest heaving. The small quick breaths that pushed her breasts against him.

"I want you, too," she whispered back, pulling his head forward so their lips met again with the same passion.

Someone moaned—him or her, he didn't know—and he deepened the kiss, barely aware of her hands moving, and then *only* aware of them when she undid his buckle and slid a hand into his underwear.

He drew back as her fingers closed around him, wanting to make sure she knew he didn't expect this. What he saw on her face made him impossibly harder. The raw lust. The knowledge of what she was doing, what she was feeling. The appreciation of it.

His head fell back when her hand began to move. Somehow, they'd ended up against the wall, like he'd fantasized about earlier, and he was grateful for the support.

Funny how, in that fantasy, he thought he'd be in charge. That he'd be the one torturing her, making her come.

Instead, here he was, precariously close to doing just that with each stroke of her hand.

*Exactly like you said you wouldn't.*

He froze.

So did she.

Their eyes met.

For the first time since they'd started kissing, rational thought returned. They had unlocked something. Something wonderful—and terrifying. Because now they knew what the other tasted like. What the other felt like.

Now they knew what they'd be sacrificing by staying apart.

She staggered back, went to stand on the opposite side of the room, as far away from him as possible.

And his heart cracked.

No, he told himself. Not his heart—his sense of self-respect. He should have been the one to move away from *her*. He shouldn't have kissed her at all.

It shouldn't have taken almost *coming* in his *pants* to realize that he was doing the very thing he'd told himself he wouldn't. The very thing he'd convinced himself he wouldn't. Not only with Delilah, with anyone.

Had he not learned his lesson with Mckenna? Had he not experienced how life changing the consequences of physical intimacy could be?

As if the universe decided he hadn't been embarrassed enough that day, the door opened. At least he'd managed to close his pants and retie his belt.

"Delilah? Are you here?"

It was the woman from the café. Her hair was different now, plaits or twists of some kind hanging around her face and making him realize, for the first time, that she was beautiful.

The woman saw Delilah first, and the smile on her face immediately disappeared. "What's wrong? What happened?"

Delilah's gaze was still on him, and the woman turned, saw him, and did a double take.

"Rowan," she said, as if his name, his presence, explained it all.

He looked at Delilah, too. Really looked at her. And cursed himself for not seeing how vulnerable she looked before now. For being so in his head he didn't think to check on her.

"Are you okay?" he asked, voice gruff.

At his words, her expression went blank. No, not blank—cold. Or was it controlled? He had no idea, but this wasn't the woman he'd been kissing minutes before.

"I'm fine."

He took a step toward her. "Delilah—"

"Fine, Rowan," she said, tone clipped, and he stopped.

He had no other choice.

"I'm . . . leaving," he said, willing it not to be a question but unable to keep it from coming out that way. If it was, though, he had his answer in her silence. He forced himself to move. Out the door, into the passage—where he almost walked into Matt.

*This must be some kind of punishment.*

The man steadied him with both hands. "Rowan."

"Matt," Rowan replied, fighting for composure. "Congratulations on your daughter's birthday."

"Thank you." Matt frowned. "Are you leaving already?"

"Yes."

"So soon?" he asked. "Is something wrong with Declan?"

No. Nothing was wrong with Declan. Rowan wouldn't allow there to be. But that meant making sure nothing was wrong with *him* either.

There could be no more slips of self-control. There could be no giving in to his baser desires. He wouldn't get distracted by a relationship, physical or otherwise. *Declan* deserved all his attention, all his love.

Rowan headed down the stairs and out the door without another goodbye.

# CHAPTER ELEVEN

Kirsten didn't say anything after Rowan left. It was as if she knew Delilah needed time to put herself together. Emotionally and mentally, she needed to put back the pieces she'd shattered into with that kiss.

He'd kissed her so thoroughly the veneer she'd encased herself in since moving to Sugarbush Bay had broken.

Yes, that was right. It wasn't that *she* had shattered. It was the person she wanted to be.

How was that any better?

But it was okay because she'd already put it back in place. Besides, Kirsten couldn't see any of the damage Rowan had caused. As ruffled as Delilah felt, she didn't actually look any worse for the wear.

Her clothing was straight, her hair likely still in place, and her lips . . . well, her lips were trouble. They felt bruised. Raw and swollen from the heat and intensity of a forbidden moment of passion.

She still felt the weight of him in her hand. The heat of giving him pleasure still simmered low in her belly.

And the fact that he'd stopped, completely stilled, while she'd been doing it sat like a rock on her chest.

"What was that?" Matt said, suddenly appearing in the doorway.

"What do you mean?" she replied calmly.

Because she'd put herself back together, damn it.

With a deep, deliberate breath, she shut down the part of her that was still spinning.

"Rowan ran out of here."

"Did he say anything?" Delilah asked.

"Something about his son needing him."

"So his son must need him."

She walked past her brother and made it all the way to the stairs before Matt said, "Were you doing something untoward in my office, Delilah?"

She snorted. "*Untoward?* How old are you? Seventy?"

"You know how old I am," he answered stiffly.

"It was a rhetorical question."

"Mine wasn't."

"No, Matt. I wasn't doing anything untoward in your office." *It wasn't untoward. It was definitely toward. Toward trouble.* "Can I go now? I'm sure Vanessa needs help making sure your party guests are happy and everything's going smoothly."

".That's why I came up here," Kirsten said finally.

Matt turned. He and Kirsten stared at one another for a moment; then, at the same time, almost as if they'd rehearsed it, they looked at her.

"The cake," Kirsten continued, her voice faint. "They want to cut the cake."

"We haven't even eaten yet," Delilah pointed out. "Cake is for after the food."

"That's what I told them, but they wouldn't listen to me."

"Vanessa?"

"She and Irene had an argument, and now she's doing damage control."

Delilah sighed. "Okay, let's go deal with that. If that's okay with you?" she asked her brother.

He glowered. She didn't flinch.

She wanted to, but she didn't.

She loved Matt. He was her big brother, and he'd helped her find her feet after the arrest without any judgment. Delilah had spent every day of the last eighteen months trying to thank him. But that meant she shied away from any conflict with him. At even the prospect of it, she pulled herself back so fast it caused whiplash.

The fact that she didn't now—despite how much she wanted to; despite her thumping heart and the clamminess of her skin—told her she hadn't quite succeeded in putting herself back together.

Or maybe she had, only the pieces weren't in the places they used to be.

"I'm fine," she told him with a nod. "It's fine."

She and Kirsten went to deal with the cake.

Delilah waited, but her friend said nothing about what she'd walked into upstairs. It didn't come after the cake situation had been sorted out and didn't come after they'd had lunch either. In fact, the entire day went on, and Kirsten said nothing at all.

It set her on edge. Her stomach had begun to twist in anticipation. She could barely focus on any conversation. So when Wendy, one of the town's council members and Delilah's friend, asked her about her plans for the rest of the weekend, Delilah didn't answer.

"Delilah?"

"Sorry," she said immediately. "Um, no plans. Just recovery, I guess."

Wendy gave her a sympathetic look. "Long day, huh?"

Delilah exhaled. "The longest."

"You should come by the salon tomorrow," Wendy said, slinging her bag over her shoulder. "I might have a therapist free to give you a manicure and pedicure."

Delilah smiled. "You *might*?"

"Yes," Wendy answered slyly. "Someone's appointment might get canceled, and boom, there you go!"

"Wendy!"

"Delilah! It happens!" She cackled. "Oh, don't worry. You know I'd never do that. No, I have a couple of free hours open in my schedule tomorrow. I'll do your hands and feet. If"—she paused—"you tell me more about Rowan."

Delilah made a concerted effort not to react. "Rowan? Why?"

"He's cute."

"He's not your type."

Wendy looked over at Jill, her expression softening. They'd been together for almost five years now, defying everyone who'd told them the ten-year age gap wouldn't work.

"No, he isn't. But he seems nice. Nervous, but nice."

"New town," Delilah said, as if that explained it all.

"Yeah, and if you tell me more about him, maybe we can figure out a way to make this new town a little less new for him."

Delilah smiled. This was how Wendy had embraced her, too. When she'd first moved to Sugarbush Bay, Wendy had shown Delilah around town, claiming that there were things Matt wouldn't show her that she had to know.

Those things turned out to be a hidden beach next to Wendy's apartment—and the male strip club one town over. The experience had been unpleasant—Delilah wasn't really a strip club kind of girl—but as soon as Wendy realized that, they'd bailed and gone to get food at a twenty-four-hour fast-food place.

It was exactly like Wendy to want to help Rowan settle in town. Delilah wanted to call him, tell him this was the community she knew. They didn't always get it right, obviously, but when they did, it was special.

The town would welcome him and Declan with open arms. Their hearts had more than enough space for everyone. Single fathers desperate to do right by their children—and ex-heiresses, desperate to do right by . . . everyone.

"Yeah, we can do that," she told Wendy. "I'll see you tomorrow."

It was late when everyone left. Kirsten had sent a text saying the babysitter had called and she needed to get home to Robbie. Delilah suspected this was a lie, but she didn't press. She replied that she hoped everyone was okay, and she saw the last of the guests out.

Vanessa was only in town for the weekend, and Matt was taking her and Irene to see a movie. It pained him to leave Delilah alone with the mess, she could see it, but she waved them away, saying cleanup would be her last gift for Irene's birthday.

The house was quiet for the first time since she'd arrived that morning, and she sank into one of the couches, promising herself she would clean as soon as she had a moment to think.

She was tired. Her feet hurt. There was the starting pulse of a headache at the base of her skull. And if she was being honest, her heart hurt a little, too.

He'd pulled away from her.

Rowan had asked for help, kissed her, told her he wanted her, and pulled away.

She could have forgiven him for it if he hadn't gotten her to admit that she wanted him, too. He'd said the words so reverently, his eyes boring into hers, that she'd been lured into an illusion. This, them, together. Him.

The ghost of his touch still lingered on her body. Her hips, where he'd rested his hands; her waist, where he'd traced her body; and her butt, where he'd pulled her closer, against him. Against his heat. His hardness.

The feel of him in her hand. The sound of his moans.

The memories of it, hot and intense, felt like she'd opened the oven door and been hit by that first wave of heat.

She got up, went to the kitchen, and put her hand in the sink. Most of the ice had dissolved, though the water was still cold, and her skin complained.

But she wasn't thinking about how the kiss had made her feel anymore. She was thinking about how unpleasant it was to show someone something of herself and have them pull away. How she'd tried to avoid that very thing since she'd moved to Sugarbush Bay. How right she'd been to worry about what Rowan made her feel.

She stuck her other hand in the water, letting it linger so long it went numb, too, and took both her hands out and rested them on her cheeks.

Indignation and embarrassment had made her hot, but now she was officially cooled down.

Officially logical.

She'd needed a reminder of what she had on the line, and Rowan had provided it. She could not indulge her attraction to him. She would not allow herself to feel as vulnerable as she did now. It too closely echoed how she'd felt when her brother had left, when her mother had been arrested, and she hated it as much now as she had then. She'd built her new life to keep from ever feeling it again.

And Rowan threatened it.

Not only that life but the deliberate steps she'd taken to turn herself into someone who gave more than they took.

Even if everything with Rowan wasn't so damn complicated, she didn't deserve romance. She'd hurt others. Unknowingly, yes, because she'd never suspected her lifestyle had been funded by dishonesty. By crime.

But what did that matter when the result was the same? Her mother had hurt people, and Delilah had reaped the rewards. She'd had everything she wanted. Her daily needs had been taken care of, often by professionals paid to feed her, dress her, see to her appearance. She had her fill of designer handbags, shoes. She'd gone to the best restaurants, mingled with the obscenely rich, the modestly wealthy.

All the while, people had been robbed. Their hard-earned money had been used by her, for things she hadn't even appreciated. Often for things she hadn't even wanted. They'd struggled to put food on the table for themselves and their loved ones, and she hadn't cared about what she'd eaten or what she'd wasted.

She'd looked up the victims of her mother's crimes. Donated the money from her bank account, money that was rightfully theirs, to the fundraising efforts hosted online. When that had felt good, right, she'd thought maybe helping others would feel that way, too.

She wanted to help them but knew none of them would want it. An excuse, perhaps, to save herself from the shame of what her mother had done, but one she heeded nonetheless.

She discovered that she liked to help. It gave her purpose. And it had given her a new life she was proud of, here in Sugarbush Bay.

Wouldn't it be the right thing to do to help Rowan have that, too?

Like Wendy had said, he was new in town, new to fatherhood. It was overwhelming, and if she didn't help because she was protecting herself from him, she'd be letting her own feelings get in the way. *That* would be selfish. And she wasn't selfish anymore.

But she also wasn't stupid. If she spent more time with Rowan than necessary, they'd be tempted to continue where they left off.

So—a compromise. She'd introduce him to Wendy. Wendy would take over, and it would be out of her hands. She'd be safe.

Satisfied, she began to tidy up.

His grandmother knew him too well.

As soon as she'd seen his face when he went to get Declan, she'd known something was wrong. He couldn't lie to her—she meant too much to him—so he gave her a half truth.

"There was a thing. At the party."

He told her about the situation with Ronald, Jill, and Dean. She listened, not reacting until the very end, when she put a hand on his face, sighing softly.

She knew him. She knew how much this meant to him, how much he wanted this, and how hard he found it. She'd understand how frustrating it was not to be able to give his son the life he'd never had.

"They handled that situation poorly," she said in a tone that made him think she'd tell them so herself. "You shouldn't have had to deal with family dynamics on your first try."

First try.

As if there'd be a second try.

"I'm so glad Delilah stepped in."

His body heated at the sound of her name.

At the *sound* of her *name*.

It had done the same thing when he'd said it while telling his grandmother the story. He'd been careful, saying it only once, using pronouns after. Still, she had power over him. Still, the sound of her name flushed him.

And the memory of how he'd handled it shamed him.

He didn't dwell on it. He changed the subject to Declan, who'd already been bathed and fed and was currently lying on a blanket on the floor, catching imaginary things in the sky. He ate the meal his grandmother prepared for him, said goodbye, and called Mckenna when he got home.

They'd spoken every night since she'd left and whenever she had a moment during the day. Which meant that, as much as he would have liked to avoid tonight's call, if he did so after near-constant communication for almost two weeks, Mckenna would worry.

Besides, neither Mckenna nor Declan deserved it.

"Hi, baby!" she squealed when she saw their son. Declan smiled, and Rowan's heart turned over. He'd been doing that for the last couple of weeks, since right after Mckenna had left. The first time she'd seen it, she'd screamed, then cried.

"Hi, baby! How are you? What have you been doing? Tell me everything!"

In typical fashion, he told her nothing but reached for the screen of the phone as if to touch her face.

"He's trying to reach for me, isn't he?" Mckenna asked Rowan. "I knew this would happen."

"That he'd touch the bright screen shining in his face?" Rowan asked. "Shocking. Hi, by the way."

She gave him an embarrassed smile. "Sorry. I get excited."

"I think I know that by now." He fought for an easy smile, though he wasn't sure he achieved it. "What did you know would happen?"

"He's reaching for me because I'm his mother and I'm not there."

"Maybe," Rowan allowed, "or maybe it's like I said. You're a bright, shiny screen."

"So you're saying he doesn't miss me?"

"No," he said quickly, skin itching.

There was no winning with a question like this. If he said yes, she'd freak out because she wasn't there and Declan missed her. If he said no, she'd freak out because she wasn't there and Declan had forgotten her.

"What I'm saying," he started slowly, "is that you're his mother, he loves you, and he'll respect the hell out of you for doing a job that's so important to so many people and you. And," he added, hoping he wouldn't regret it, "he probably won't remember that you weren't here for two weeks. You're coming back in the next couple of days. It'll be fine."

"Thanks," she said, her eyes on Declan.

She looked sad, and it kicked him in the gut. He cared about Mckenna. He respected her. He did not want a woman he respected and cared about to be sad.

"A couple of days," he repeated.

"No," she replied, looking at him now. "It's two more weeks. The conference is over, but there's an audit, and I need to be here to make sure . . ." She trailed off. "No, you know what? I don't have to stay. This isn't what we agreed to."

"Mckenna," he said, pressing pause on his inevitable freak-out. "Would it be better for you to stay?"

"Yes."

"So stay. Declan and I are fine."

"I . . . I don't want to."

"You do," he disagreed. "Which is fine. The NGO was your baby long before Declan."

"Yeah, but I don't want him to think it's more important than he is."

"He won't. We'll make sure of it."

She exhaled. "I'm sorry I sprang this on you. Thank you for taking it so well."

"You got it."

Her eyes sharpened. "You're taking this *too* well."

"Am I?" he asked dryly. "Must be because parenting is so easy without you."

"I'll come back."

"Wouldn't that make it harder?"

She snorted, and pride shimmered over him. He was having a normal conversation with Mckenna. A normal, mature conversation. There was no awkwardness, despite the topic, and he'd made her laugh. It was a balm after the sting of today. It was . . . it was progress.

The doorbell rang.

"Someone's at the door," he told Mckenna. "Same time tomorrow?"

"Please." She told Declan she loved and missed him and would be back before he knew it. Before saying goodbye, she said, "Rowan?"

He paused.

"Thank you."

"You don't have to keep thanking me for taking care of our son."

"I know. I'm thanking you for doing it so well."

With a small smile, she disconnected the call. He sat staring at the screen while his brain caught up.

Mckenna would be gone longer than either of them had anticipated.

He'd be parenting alone for two more weeks.

She thought he was doing a good job.

He wanted to believe he was. Maybe there was a part of him that did. But the rest of him knew it cost him. Parenting felt like an effort, a daily exercise in being present and being mindful. It exhausted him. Did that still qualify him as a good parent?

The doorbell rang again, and he shook his head, tapping his chest as if that would help ease the ache there. He scooped Declan into his arms and went to answer.

"Delilah."

She was still in the black-and-white summer dress she'd worn to the party. It swooped down to her ankles, had a sweetheart neckline, and had given him a clear idea of the curves of her body when he'd been touching her. She looked as beautiful in it now as she had then.

When his lips had been against hers.

When her hand had been stroking him.

When *his* hands had been exploring her.

When his brain had exploded from having her exactly where he wanted her. Exactly where he'd fantasize about having her, again and again, whether he liked it or not.

Some of her curls had escaped the tie at the top of her head, floating down to create a cute and frizzy frame around her face.

It kicked him in the gut. All of it. Her being here, the memory of kissing her. The reaction he'd had to her name had only been a shadow of his reaction to seeing her. It was why he'd gotten himself into the situation he had today. It was exactly why he couldn't afford to do it again.

He should explain that to her. How it had nothing to do with her and everything to do with him.

He took a fortifying breath.

"Hey," she said before he could speak. "I'm not here to talk about what happened today."

"Oh."

"Yeah. I guess I already know how you feel about that." She laughed. It wasn't mocking; it was sad, and he tightened his hold on Declan to keep from reaching out to her. "I'm here to tell you Wendy wants to help you."

"I don't know who that is." He paused. "Or what that means."

Her lips curved. "She's one of the most beloved people in this town. The unofficial chairperson of the 'welcome to Sugarbush Bay' club. And she's in charge of the festival. You know about that, right?"

He nodded.

"Well, getting involved with that will help you fully integrate with the townsfolk." She gave a wry smile. "It'll make things a lot easier for you, especially with Wendy. She'll take you under her wing."

"What are you saying?"

He knew exactly what she was saying, but he needed her to say it. He needed to hear it.

"You won't need me," she answered in the same quiet voice she'd been using since he opened the door. Her eyes flickered to Declan, softened, then looked up at him again.

She was doing it for the benefit of his baby. Keeping calm so that Declan didn't pick up any of the tension between them.

Good idea.

"She wants to help me?" he asked, mirroring her tone. "You told her I asked for help?"

"No! I'd never. She brought it up herself. She did it for me, too, when I moved here, so it's not because she's singling you out."

"I didn't ask for her help."

"No, you asked for mine, and you'll have it. I'll introduce you two, and you can—"

"She's not you."

Her eyes met his. "No, she's not, but maybe that's a good thing."

Neither of them said anything for a long time.

"You'll still see me," she said into the silence. "I'm on the planning committee."

That didn't surprise him.

"You can come with me to one of the meetings."

That did.

"What?"

"Come with me," she repeated, "to one of the planning sessions. There are a lot of people there. Good, kind people who will make you feel better about this town. The first half of the planning session is the planning, but the second half is chill. You can meet people without the pressure of having to socialize because no one is actually there to socialize."

He tried to wrap his head around it, but she didn't wait for him to.

"Think about it. The next session's this Wednesday. Bring Declan with. It's bound to get you points. Although . . ." She considered. "You might not want that much attention the first time round." She shrugged. "It's up to you. If you do decide to go, let me know. We can do it together."

With those words—and a small wave at Declan—she was gone.

# CHAPTER TWELVE

Delilah felt like she was on her way to take Rowan to the school dance. Nerves skipped in her stomach, doing intricate moves she'd never be able to replicate in real life. On principle, she thought that should mean her nerves couldn't do them either. But then, they'd had a mind of their own since she'd received Rowan's text.

I'm in

That was it. That was all he'd said. So of course, she'd been cool, too, and replied with:

Okay. Get you at six forty-five.

He'd sent her a thumbs-up emoji, which was even worse than two words. She hated that it bothered her, but it wasn't like she'd spent the three days following that message thinking about it.

She hadn't. She'd thought about other things. Like their kiss. And how awkward their last conversation had been.

And also, that message.

But it was okay. After tonight, she'd be off the hook. She'd already told Wendy she was bringing Rowan to the meeting. Wendy had been delighted, praising Delilah for thinking "out of the box" and picking a no-pressure situation.

Delilah knew the moment she and Rowan walked in, Wendy would take over, and Delilah would be able to hand the reins of social introductions to her friend.

Which was good. Dealing with the Rowan situation was making her tense. The day before, Delilah had all but shouted at Kirsten to share her opinion of what she'd walked into at Irene's birthday.

"What if I don't have an opinion?" Kirsten asked, frowning at the table she was cleaning.

"You always have an opinion."

"Not on this."

"Of course you do!"

"No," she insisted. "I don't. You're a grown woman who can make her own decisions—and one of the few people I've actually seen own up to the consequences of those decisions."

Delilah blinked at the unexpectedness of that. At the way her eyes filled a little, and how she had to turn away from Kirsten to catch her breath.

"I think we kind of mutually decided to not get involved with one another," she said, wiping her own tables clean, even though she'd already done them. "It's for the best. His situation is complicated, and so is mine."

"What's so complicated about yours?"

"I . . . you know. I have stuff to deal with. Emotional baggage."

"Yeah, and that's why you're seeing a therapist."

A true statement if ever there was one. But she knew as well as her therapist did that she was only going because she thought she should be going.

Witnessing her mother's arrest had been traumatic. Not to mention the whole *I grew up without the love of my parents, only my brother's, and when he left, I felt lost, so I acted like a spoiled rich girl because that's what the world expected from me* thing.

Except she never talked about any of it in any detail. Anne knew what had happened with Delilah's mother and the bare minimum of her childhood, but Delilah never shared her feelings about it. Mostly, she talked about her day.

In fact, it was a lot like her friendship with Kirsten, since she hadn't talked about what had happened with Kirsten either.

Then again, she never had to pay Kirsten to listen to her.

But that day, for the first time, Delilah wished she had been talking to her therapist like Kirsten said. If Delilah *had* told Anne about how it felt to grow up the way she did, how unsurprising it had actually been that her mother had been arrested, she'd have a place to talk about Rowan, too.

And if she'd told Kirsten the truth, Kirsten wouldn't have that frown of confusion on her face.

This was the price she paid for privacy.

After her world had imploded, she'd been written about in blogs, newspapers, magazines. Her name had trended on different social media platforms. People had speculated about how much she'd known, about what she'd used the money on, about who she was.

The last had been the hardest to swallow. Because the spoiled-selfish-rich-girl picture they'd painted had been right. Oh, she'd never gotten into much trouble herself, but her friends—she scoffed at that term now, knowing what it truly meant—had been rambunctious. And she'd been swept under the same umbrella because of it.

She'd promised herself her new life would be nothing like her old life. She'd deleted all her own social media, every trace of herself that she had control of on the internet, though she couldn't delete the news stories about her mother's crimes.

Couldn't remove any of the stories about her own life as a socialite, her trips around the world, and the company she'd kept.

It surprised her that no one in town ever talked about it. Had anyone done a single internet search on her name, they'd have uncovered it all. But no one did. Or if they had, they'd said nothing about it. Which was strange, in a town like this.

The only logical conclusion was that because she was Matt's sister, they trusted that she was a good person. So every day, she worked to become that person.

"We all have emotional baggage, you know," Kirsten told her. "It's okay to find someone willing to carry the load with us."

Delilah turned at that, at the sadness in Kirsten's voice. She'd forgotten that Kirsten had lived a whole different life before she'd met Delilah. And she could tell her friend was thinking about that life now, about the man she'd spent it with.

"I'm sorry."

Kirsten let out a small laugh. "For what?"

"That you lost your baggage partner."

"That sounds ridiculous."

"But you knew what I meant."

"I did. Thank you." She smiled, then tilted her head. "Are you sure Rowan isn't your baggage partner?"

"Yes," Delilah said firmly, as if doing so would convince herself, too. "I'm going to introduce him at the planning meeting tomorrow, and he'll be fine and I'll be fine. It'll all be fine."

Kirsten hummed in agreement but didn't look convinced. Which was fair. Delilah wasn't entirely convinced either. But she was doing her part for the community, putting others above herself, and it was all very altruistic and very *good Delilah* of her to do.

She was sure the universe approved of her plans—until the moment Rowan stepped out of his house.

He looked *good.*

*So. Good.*

She lifted her hand, tentatively checking her chin for drool.

He wore a green long-sleeved Henley, all three buttons tied. She wasn't sure why she expected that from him or why she found it so appealing. With black jeans, sneakers, and a black jacket thrown over his arm, he looked wholesome.

Except wholesome couldn't—*shouldn't*—provoke any of Delilah's pants feelings.

Her pants feelings were decidedly provoked.

Probably because he was her exact type. His body, broad and strong, soft and firm, had been the reason for many a celebrity crush. But with celebrities, Delilah could admire from a distance. They were unattainable; they were safe.

Rowan had been the same, once. When he'd first walked into the café with Declan, he'd been nice and unavailable. She should have known better.

His face was not the kind that allowed for a harmless crush. Those sharp angles above his beard were meant to slice through resistance. His thick, curly hair was designed to offer a safe place to land when falling in love. His mouth, warm and lush   and, she now knew, skilled—was the embodiment of temptation.

She could so easily imagine how much more passionate things could have gotten between them if they hadn't stopped. If *he* hadn't stopped.

But he had, and if that didn't tell her everything she needed to know, losing her mind simply because he was walking toward her did.

Rowan stopped in front of her, shoving his hands into his pockets despite the jacket over his arm. It was as if he'd forgotten about it, but still, it stayed there, obeying its master.

Could she blame it? She wanted to obey its master, too.

*And now you're finding things in common with an inanimate object. Great job!*

"Hey," he said.

"Hey." She ignored her strangled tone. "Ready?"

He nodded. She went to the driver's side and got in, put on her safety belt, and waited for him to do the same. When he had, she began the short drive to the café.

She could still remember her first festival meeting, when Kirsten had asked her to keep the café open for the planning committee. Looking back now, Delilah thought it might have been planned. Wendy had asked Delilah about Rowan; she might have asked Kirsten about Delilah, too.

Wendy invited her to stay at that meeting, after all, and before Delilah had known it, she'd ended up with tasks of her own and another invitation to the next meeting.

It had been the first real progress she'd felt in becoming part of the community. So if Kirsten *had* lied about her son being sick that night for Delilah's sake, Delilah would have to thank her. She'd thank Wendy someday, too.

"What are you thinking about?"

Rowan's voice was low. It traveled in the small space of the car, the rough rumble gliding over her skin.

She cleared her throat. "Why?"

"You're smiling."

"I am?" She touched her lips, and yep, there were her teeth. "Ah." She cleared her throat again. "I was thinking about my first meeting."

"It went well?"

"Yeah. It was . . . nice. Unexpected."

She told him about how Kirsten had looped her into it, about how she'd made coffee, tea, pastries. She'd cleaned every table and washed the floor— twice. And she'd waited with bated breath to see if they'd like her efforts.

"It didn't occur to me that night that maybe this was my way in. But it was. And after that, I was . . . in." She gave an embarrassed little laugh.

"*You* had to find a way in?"

"Everyone does. No matter how gracious a community is, they're a community. Fixed and whole and together. To become a part of that, you have to prove that you deserve to be there."

He made a gruff sound. She knew exactly what it meant.

"Look, when I got here . . ." How much should she say? How much did she want him to know? "When I got here, my life was in shambles."

She could feel his stare. She shrugged. "You think you're the only one life surprises?" She didn't wait for an answer. "I came here because my life in Cape Town imploded."

"What happened?"

"I . . . don't think I want to talk about it. Not because you asked," she added hurriedly. "I just haven't spoken about it since it happened. To anyone."

"Not even Matt?"

*Especially not Matt.*

"No."

Her brother had asked once, on the third night after she'd arrived in Sugarbush Bay. They'd been sitting outside in the garden. Irene had been at a school dance, and Delilah and Matt had been alone under that beautiful night sky. A dark, inky blue with bright stars and the thick and heavy weight of summer.

"You okay?" he'd asked.

"Yeah. Yeah, of course I am," she'd lied.

He'd stared at her for a long time. She hadn't looked at him.

"You're not."

"Matt, I don't want to talk about it."

"Okay." There was a long pause. He'd stared at her then, too. "I'll be here when you do."

He'd never brought it up again, and neither had she.

"I'm sorry," Rowan said softly. "For whatever happened. For whatever put that look on your face."

Her head whipped to the side. She took in his silhouette in the moonlight before turning back to the road.

"Thank you," she replied hoarsely—and cleared her throat yet again. "My point was that when I got here, I didn't have it all together either. I didn't think I belonged here. It was too . . . happy, I guess. I thought maybe I didn't deserve to be here, so I could hardly be upset if they thought I didn't."

Only they'd never treated her that way.

She thought back to those first six months. How she hadn't trusted it when people had been nice to her. How she'd kept waiting for someone to say something about her past. To out her as a fraud.

They hadn't excluded her from their community; she'd excluded herself. And once she'd figured that out, things had been easy.

"It took a long time for me to believe I belonged here. And it was only when I did—after months and months of building a life I could be proud of, one day at a time, deliberately—that I felt like this was my home. They'd welcomed me long before then, but what did that matter when I was the problem?" She softened her voice. "It'll happen for you, too, Rowan. Tonight is a good start."

Before she could stop herself, she reached out and squeezed his thigh. The muscles tensed beneath her touch. She was about to lift her hand, apologize, when he rested his own hand there, over hers.

The warmth of it soaked into her skin, into her blood, throbbing in her veins before it sank into her heart. From there, the heat pulsed with each beat, sending waves of *something* through her body.

She felt it in her face, as she blushed, as her ears reddened.

She felt it in her core: a low, forbidden place that welcomed this stranger with open arms despite what its owner wanted.

She felt it in her head, where rational thought told her this was impossible; this reaction to him was impossible.

A small seed buried itself within her. Delilah knew that every moment, every *second*, she spent with Rowan would feed that seed and it would grow, big and brash and beautiful, until it eclipsed all her doubts and silenced all her fears. Until there was only him, and them, and the future they could have.

The car swerved, and she snatched her hand back, clutching the steering wheel as if her life depended on it.

Her sanity, her *stability*, certainly did.

"I'm sorry," she said. "I'm a good driver, I promise."

"I didn't think otherwise."

"You should have," she breathed, her heart rate still accelerated for some annoying reason. "I almost killed you."

He chuckled. "There were no cars in the other lane."

"And that makes what I did safe?"

"No, but it wasn't dangerous either."

"I'm glad you think so," she muttered.

Because to her, everything about this car ride had been dangerous.

# CHAPTER THIRTEEN

Rowan had been worried from the moment Delilah invited him to the planning session. He wasn't sure whether it *was* a good place to meet people. Wouldn't they think him rude for just appearing? Wouldn't they think him lazy for not contributing?

And what about after? Should he stay to socialize? He'd contribute nothing to the meeting, but he'd be eating their food and drinking their beverages?

Would Delilah be a good buffer? They hadn't sorted things out after their . . . kiss. He was stubbornly calling it that because he couldn't think of a word that encompassed "a kind of hand job, too."

Because he didn't want to examine what had caused him to pull away beyond knowing that things had gone too far, too quickly.

He didn't want to think about how he'd treated Delilah in that moment either.

He wouldn't blame her if she left him to fend for himself tonight. But more than likely, she wouldn't leave his side. She'd be perfect, and he would want to convince her to help him for more than one night.

He was right.

From the moment they arrived, people were warm and welcoming. But they always greeted Delilah first, before letting her introduce him. They'd acknowledge him then, smile, shake his hand. They'd mention his grandmother, his son, and express how much they were looking forward to getting to know them both.

After which they'd turn back to Delilah and talk to her about something or the other.

Only half the time, it had something to do with the festival. Still, it sounded like they were going all out. The celebration would start with a bonfire and movie on Friday night. The food and snacks that would be offered was a spirited topic of debate. Surprisingly, the movie was not. Apparently the town had voted—literally voted through an online questionnaire—for what they wanted to watch.

He hadn't wanted to ask why they hadn't done the same thing with the food. He'd barely been there half an hour.

Saturday was a full day, with a carnival-type atmosphere. There would be a Ferris wheel. Games. A petting zoo. Children's entertainment. Karaoke. Professionals—photographers and chefs and other local business owners—had offered to teach people their craft and donated their services.

That night, there'd be a town dance. Delilah had secured a local band to perform, and when she'd announced that, she'd received a round of applause and a hoot from one of the younger volunteers.

Festivities would wrap up with a food festival on Sunday. Professional and amateur cooks could partake and sell their goods. The day would conclude with a prize-giving for the competitions held throughout the festival that afternoon.

They hadn't worked through the festival from point A to point B for his benefit, but doing it that way had helped him understand the magnitude of the event. It wasn't an attempt at making money, gaining popularity, or putting the town on the map for tourists.

It was a celebration, pure and simple. A celebration of the town's heritage, of its people and their strengths. It was an opportunity to be thankful for the community in which they lived.

For the first time since he'd moved here, Rowan felt the faint shimmer of comfort. Maybe Sugarbush Bay was always where he was meant to be. Suddenly, he couldn't imagine raising his son anywhere else.

"I'm so glad you came tonight," a voice said from beside him.

He'd been standing at one of the craft tables—the one with almost no food on, since it ensured no one would bother him—while Delilah talked to some people. Obviously his strategy hadn't worked.

But it wouldn't have worked. Not with this woman. Delilah had introduced him to Wendy within the first five minutes of their arrival. She was short, with long, sleek hair tucked behind her ears, the result of a habit he'd noted when she'd been running the meeting.

Despite her stature, or perhaps because of it, she commanded the attention in the room. When she wanted people's attention, she got it. And now, she had his.

"I didn't have much to offer, but I appreciate that."

Wendy waved a hand. "You're not here to offer anything. You might have to, once things start moving forward. We have about a month, and things still feel a little abstract at this point. But I'm pretty sure that once things start rolling, someone will find a use for you." She smiled. "Tonight, though, is for us to welcome you. So do you feel welcomed?"

He laughed a little, both at her assumption that he'd be of use and at her forwardness in asking. He wanted to say yes, that he did, but the truth wasn't that simple. Only—wasn't socializing lying? People offering a version of themselves that wasn't really themselves but who they pretended to be?

He opened his mouth to socialize, to lie, when he felt Delilah looking at him. He didn't know how he knew it was her or how he could track her gaze to across the room on the left, where she was talking to a man he didn't recognize.

He met her look, held it. And saw there that he shouldn't lie, that he should be himself, and it would all be okay.

"I'm not sure," he told Wendy. "It feels new. I think . . . I think maybe once I have more time, maybe to get to know everyone, I'll feel differently."

Wendy nodded, as if that made complete sense. "It's a lot to take in, isn't it? All the coziness from this small town. You said you're from Cape Town, right?"

"Born and raised," he replied, easily. He'd said it *easily*. "And you? Did you grow up here?"

He was asking her a question back! Who *was* this person speaking?

"Yeah. My parents grew up here, too, and my grandparents. I'm third-generation Sugarbush Bay."

"That's great."

"It is. It's not often we have a history that long. Not looking like us, and not in this country."

She winked at him, but it was a knowing wink, a sad wink. The kind that people of color in South Africa, with its divided history and racial disparity, shared with one another too often—and understood immediately.

"My family grew up in Cape Town. Different parts of the city, but my parents and theirs, which of course you know, since you know my grandmother. Thank you for that, by the way."

"For what?"

"For welcoming her when she first moved here."

"Well, you don't have to thank me personally," she said with a huff of laughter. "I wasn't the one who welcomed her."

"Since you're spearheading my welcome, I'll have to check with her before I believe that."

Wendy looked at him, eyes twinkling, and Rowan felt another shift in his body. Another . . . easing. As if there'd been something inside of him tense, tight, and finally, *finally*, it was relaxing.

Was this what it felt like to be normal? To have normal conversations with strangers? No. No, it couldn't be. He'd done that before. Had those before. But this felt different. He felt different.

And it had only taken one look from Delilah.

"I can't take credit for welcoming you either," Wendy told him with those twinkling eyes. "We both know Delilah's taken you under her wing. Lot of people respect her and her wing."

"You make her sound like an animal."

She snorted. "I do, don't I? You know what I mean."

"I do."

It was why he'd asked for Delilah's help in the first place. Although if he was being honest with himself, he only needed to spend time with her to get that help. He watched her interact with people then. Saw her kindness, her ease around them. It made him wonder what would happen if he relaxed.

He hadn't been relaxed at Irene's party. He'd been tense and worried, and it had turned out exactly as he feared. But one look at Delilah tonight had given him the confidence to be himself. And because of it, this conversation with Wendy had been fine.

"She's a good person," he said softly.

"She is. Still beating herself up over her mother's arrest, but she'll let go of that eventually."

Wendy didn't give him a chance to comment or process his surprise before she patted his shoulder and went to speak with someone else.

He stared after her.

Delilah's mother had been arrested? So that was what she'd been referring to in the car—and every other time she'd talked about her life before Sugarbush Bay.

She closed in on herself when she talked about her past. In the car, her shoulders had been hunched over, her grip on the steering wheel tight, as if somehow, she could keep the hurt from spilling out her body.

He'd hated seeing that. Hated knowing that something had caused her so much pain.

Still, alarm unfurled inside him.

"Hey," Delilah said, stopping next to him. "Your conversation with Wendy looked like it was going well. Did it?"

Her eyes swept over his face anxiously, like she was checking for any signs of distress. He knew she'd find it. Not because things had gone poorly with Wendy but because now all he could think about was that she was related to someone the police had enough evidence on to arrest.

It shouldn't matter. Whatever her mother had done had nothing to do with Delilah. But did he want Declan to have someone with those ties in his life?

Panic vibrated in his body. He could recognize the emotion. Understood that it was panic that shook all rational thought out his brain.

It made no sense for him to worry about Declan with Delilah. She'd been nothing but good to him—to both of them. It was unfair to suddenly believe the worst of her because her mother had been arrested. Only he couldn't really tell if that was what was happening.

He didn't understand it. Not when he knew better than anyone that a parent's actions didn't have anything to do with their child. If that were true, it would mean his parents' neglect, their uninterest in him . . . that would be on him, wouldn't it?

He'd rejected that premise his entire adult life.

But should he have?

"Yeah," he said gruffly. "She was . . . we were . . . fine."

She lifted her brows. "Really? You don't look fine."

"I'm fine."

The words were curt. She blinked. Studied him.

And swiftly shut down.

"Well, I guess I believe you." She offered him a small smile. A fake smile. He instantly despised it. "Do you want me to give you a lift home? Or are you too upset with me to ride in the same car?"

"I'm not upset with you."

"No?" She lifted a brow. "What is this, then? Acting? Are you trying out for a role where you take out your emotions on innocent bystanders? Do you want me to run lines with you?"

She barreled on, using a hand to gesture between them. "Shall we go back and forth where I keep asking you what's wrong, and you keep telling me nothing, but you're obviously upset, so we do that for a while, and eventually, I punch you in the face because *why* are you so *frustrating!*"

Her voice rose at the end. Not so high that people looked at them but enough for Rowan to turn and face her, angling his body to give them some semblance of privacy.

"You'd punch me?"

"Yeah!" She exhaled. "Well, no. It just came out. Even if I really wanted to, I wouldn't."

The look she gave him told him she really wanted to.

He refused the smile tugging at his lips.

"I think I could take you, if I had to."

"You clearly don't know about my brother's self-defense classes. He's been forcing me to learn since I moved here. I could immobilize you and steal your wallet before you even knew it happened."

He stared. "Could you really?"

"No, Rowan. Stop being so cute and gullible, damn it."

He didn't have a reply for that. He did, however, notice how the insistent throbbing in his veins had eased. His brain felt clearer. The tension had been defused.

She'd managed to calm him with one confusing exchange, and she'd been annoyed with him during most of it.

"You really should find a lift with someone else," she said, hands on her hips. "I said I'd lock up after the meeting."

"I can wait."

"Do you want to wait?"

"Yes," he said without hesitation.

"You confuse me, Rowan," she replied with a shake of her head.

"I know. I . . . *I'm* confused."

It was an embarrassing confession, one that had taken a lot to admit, but Delilah didn't seem to care.

"So it's confusing. But we can deal with it like adults, or we can do whatever you're doing. I'd prefer the first option, but you let me know if we're going to be children, and I'll act accordingly."

She stomped past him, as if proving her point.

And damn it, it made him smile—even though he knew she was right.

# CHAPTER FOURTEEN

Rowan spent three days after the planning meeting entirely in his house.

He took care of his son. When his grandmother took Declan, he worked. He called Mckenna. Ordered groceries. Cooked. Did the laundry. Slept.

It was familiar. He'd spent many days like this before Declan. His work had taken up most of his time. In his spare moments, he'd done the admin and chores that had kept him alive.

It had never felt unfulfilling. No, staying in his house and focusing on what he'd deemed important had felt like the only possible purpose of his life.

The fact that these three days when he'd isolated himself had killed his soul, slowly and steadily, told him how drastically he'd changed in less than a year.

And how much he'd changed in a matter of weeks.

He longed for Delilah to visit him. To stop by unexpectedly. To be his neighbor, damn it.

He knew she wouldn't. No, it was his turn to make a move. The only problem was that he couldn't. He couldn't admit that he'd been an idiot, that he'd treated her unfairly, that he wanted her so much it hurt. It was better for the both of them if he stayed away.

If he maintained a healthy distance, they wouldn't get sucked into the vortex their attraction created. He wouldn't let anything but his son preoccupy his time. He wouldn't disappoint Delilah with his clumsiness in relationships. He wouldn't have to consider how he felt about her mother's arrest.

Thinking about it was exhausting. Feeling it was exhausting.

So the distraction of the men currently standing in his doorway was greatly appreciated.

They looked to be holding containers of food. Corey definitely had beer in that cooler box, and . . . was that a plant in Lucas's hands?

"What are you doing here?" he asked.

"Helping you with your kid," Corey said. "Can we come in? Or should I eat this doughnut on the patio?"

Rowan stood aside, his movements feeling disjointed. Turned out appreciation didn't make their presence as easy as he'd have liked.

"Did someone tell you I needed help with my kid?" he asked when the last of them was in.

He closed the door and went back to Declan, who he'd left in a bouncer trying to figure out what to do with a set of toy keys.

Corey bent down, ignoring Rowan completely. "Hey, little guy. My name's Uncle Corey; this is Uncle Matt, and that's Uncle Lucas. I know, I know, we're a handsome bunch of fellows. Some more handsome than others." He looked up at Matt and winked. Matt grunted. "But we're your dad's friends, so we'll be around awhile."

His . . . friends. Had Corey really said that? That they were friends? That they were *Rowan's* friends?

He had friends.

He had *friends.*

A thick lump formed in his throat. It made him feel like an idiot, but what could he do? It meant something to him.

"You killed him," Lucas pointed out, unapologetically staring at Rowan.

"No," Rowan said immediately, but the sound came out strangled. "I'm fine."

"Really?" Lucas asked, eyes narrowing. "Your face is a weird color."

"Lucas," Corey said, straightening. "How many times do we have to tell you not to make inane observations?"

"About as many times as we have to tell you to speak like a normal human being."

"Normal human beings use complicated words!" Corey exclaimed. He looked over his shoulder at Rowan. "Mind if we put this in the kitchen?" Without waiting for a reply, Corey went to the kitchen, Lucas trailing behind him. They were still arguing.

Matt stayed behind.

"We wanted to help," he offered after a bit.

"With what?" Rowan asked.

"We know how it goes," Matt said, stuffing his hands into his pockets. "You keep taking care of your kid, get little to no sleep, spend zero time with other adults, go out of your mind." He shrugged. "We're here to help."

Rowan waited a beat. "Did my grandmother send you?"

Matt shrugged again. "She might have told me she was worried."

Another point to the interfering grandmother. This time, she'd sent the other Huntington sibling.

"But really, it was my sister who told me to come here."

Rowan's head shot up. It took him seconds to realize Matt was lying, that he'd been trying to get a reaction out of Rowan, and that he'd gotten the reaction he'd been expecting.

"She's an adult," Matt said after a long, uncomfortable silence. "She makes her own decisions. But"—his voice deepened to a growl—"hurt her, and we'll have words. Now, you want pancakes?"

"What?"

"I brought pancakes. You want some?"

Rowan nodded wordlessly and followed Matt to the kitchen.

He tried to think of something to say, but in the kitchen, Corey asked him a question, Lucas asked him another, and he didn't get the chance to reply at all.

Small mercies. He had no idea what he'd say. So he let himself be pulled into the conversation while Matt heated pancakes and put them in front of him.

Lucas disappeared into the living room and returned with Declan. Corey started talking to the baby. Matt pinched his cheek. All of them filed out of the kitchen, headed back to the living room, and left Rowan sitting alone at the kitchen table.

Rowan stared after them, his pancakes untouched. His kitchen smelled like cinnamon and sugar and cologne. There was laughter and gurgling and the faint sound of sports coming from his living room. His house felt full, for the first time in . . .

In forever.

Deliberately, he picked up a pancake and stuffed it in his mouth. He groaned at the taste. It was room temperature, the sugar crunching between his teeth, and it was delicious. The best thing he'd ever eaten.

And that thought made him remember he'd forgotten to eat breakfast. Declan had had a blowout, and Rowan had washed him and changed him before taking care of the clothing and sheets, and he'd forgotten about food for himself.

But now he was in his kitchen, eating alone, quietly, without a baby to fuss over, because his friends had come over to help.

He wished he could go back in time and tell his younger self about this day. He doubted he'd believe it—not when experiencing it even in the present was hard to wrap his head around.

He was pretty sure his parents hadn't intended on messing him up. They'd had him because they loved one another. But they'd quickly discovered that loving one another wasn't enough to raise a child.

Yes, the child was a part of both of them. Yes, it might have been some symbol of their love. But that child needed to eat. To sleep. To have a routine, structure. And giving that to a child required time.

His parents' time had been spent on the jobs they enjoyed, on their relationship. They'd had none to spare for Rowan. As he'd grown older, he'd put up layer after layer of protection. Anything to keep the fact that he'd needed love and attention from his parents and hadn't gotten it from hurting him.

It had helped him deal with not having friends. It had convinced him that succeeding at tangible things like school and work rather than relationships was enough. As an adult, he'd successfully shut everyone out—and convinced himself he was happy to do it.

Then came the news that he was going to be a father. He'd never wanted to be a father. Never wanted the opportunity to screw up a kid so badly it affected them for the rest of their life.

But he *was* a father now. It was the most important thing he'd ever do. He didn't want Declan to have the same childhood he'd had. Somehow, in his quest to keep that from happening, Rowan was finding out more about himself than he'd ever considered before.

He wanted the joy coming from his living room. The support of having friends. The comfort of knowing he could call up his grand-mother and she'd be there within minutes. That she'd call the people who cared about him when she was worried.

And he wanted Delilah.

Only he couldn't have her.

He knew that. He kept telling himself that. The internet search he'd done on her after the festival meeting only emphasized how much he couldn't have her.

He'd read about her life before Sugarbush Bay. The parties she'd attended, the rumors of her misbehaving at them. He'd seen the pictures of her on gossip sites. Pictures that looked like her but somehow didn't.

She was dressed differently: short skirts, tight tops, high heels. Her posture had always been stiff, her expression always haughty. Beneath it, she looked . . . fragile. Like the facade she presented could shatter at any point.

And based on the photos taken after her mother's arrest, it had.

Still, he didn't know who the real Delilah was. Her mother's crimes had nothing to do with her, of that he was sure, but she'd cultivated her image before the arrest. Had she cultivated the one after? Was the person he thought he knew really who she was, or was she hiding yet again?

It shamed him that he couldn't figure it out. That he even wondered. And it was why he didn't want to think about it too much.

He was going to mess it up. He already had, based on how she'd called him out Wednesday night. And now with Matt's warning in the mix, Rowan knew the situation required more care than he had time or energy to give.

So he would sacrifice this one thing so he and Declan could have the life he wanted for them.

Even if the mere thought of it made him ache.

Delilah refused to think about Rowan. Refused to acknowledge that the way he'd treated her the night of the planning meeting had hurt, badly. He'd looked at her differently that night. With a distance she hadn't liked. And then he'd teased her, confused her, and admitted to being confused himself.

What was she supposed to do with that?

Nothing. She would do nothing. She wouldn't even think about it.

If she did, she would wonder why things had changed. Whether he'd seen something in her that he hadn't liked. And she'd be tempted, so tempted, to change whatever it was so he *would* like her again.

So—she wouldn't think about it.

It was easy to do today, when she was with Kirsten at Robbie's school concert. Delilah had been delighted to be invited. Watching a bunch of small children run around the stage, chaos reigning, as teachers desperately tried to figure out how to establish order? It sounded like a Saturday well spent.

She met Kirsten in front of the school. Robbie looked adorable in a yellow-and-black tracksuit that Delilah knew Kirsten had searched for for weeks. He was a bumblebee in the production, using his toddler superpower of running around for no reason for the good of something bigger than himself.

Kirsten couldn't make his outfit like some of the other parents had, and Delilah saw her judging herself because of the elaborate outfits around her.

"Don't you dare," Delilah said. "You're an amazing mother, and you're juggling a job, a kid, and . . ." She paused. "I wanted to say studies, but I'm not sure if that would be helpful or not."

"Neither," Kirsten informed her, "because I'm not talking about it. You know, most of these mothers have a job and a kid, too. But only my one is in a tracksuit I took embarrassingly long to find."

"Yeah, but those mothers have partners," Delilah replied gently. "And they likely have money, too. Do you know how much easier having money makes things?"

"No." Kirsten shot her a look. "Do you?"

She wasn't sure what made her tell the truth. For almost two years, she'd been avoiding talking about her past, about her privilege, because she'd been ashamed. But she could handle her own shame if it mitigated Kirsten's.

And maybe, just maybe, she was tired of hiding.

"Yeah," she said. "When Matt and I grew up, we had money. A lot of it."

Kirsten's eyes narrowed. "Define *a lot*."

"Birthday parties on a yacht, a lot."

"Wow. And that's just because you made it rhyme."

"Unintentional."

"So you don't have any of that money now?"

"No. We didn't get it . . . legally."

"Drugs?" Kirsten breathed.

"What? No. Why would your mind even go there?"

"It's been there since Wendy asked me if I knew about your past."

"Wendy did *what* now?"

"She knows. Said she looked you up? Asked me if I wanted to know, to which I said no." She shrugged when Delilah looked at her. "If you wanted me to know, you would have told me. And I guess I was waiting for you to tell me."

Delilah swallowed down the lump in her throat. "You resisted Wendy . . . for me?"

"I did," Kirsten said solemnly. "And it was hard."

"Which is why you've been speculating about my drug past."

"Not yours, necessarily. Maybe like . . . your father's. Or your grandfather's."

There was a pause. Delilah laughed when she realized Kirsten was waiting for confirmation.

"No, no drugs." And then she kept talking, because she wanted Kirsten to know. "My mother owned a brokerage, and she was really successful. But she'd been defrauding her clients for years. She was arrested before I got here."

There was a part of her that was almost wistful for a drug bust.

"I donated the money I had to some of the people she stole from. I live off what I earn at the café, which is easy to do when Matt refuses to let me pay for staying at the cottage and basically takes care of every meal I eat."

There was another pause this time. It was longer, and every second of it killed Delilah. A wave of shame crashed over her, dragging her under, and it took herculean strength to climb out from under it.

To stick out her head, so that she could breathe, so that she could get oxygen to her brain and think. Remind herself that she was no longer the person who'd taken advantage of other people's suffering, intentional or not.

It didn't seem to matter that she worked hard to prove she wasn't that person. Why would it when she *felt* it? Deep in her bones, beneath her desires to help, to make up for her naivety, she felt the judgment. The fear that she could go back to being someone she despised.

As she sank beneath the surface of that shame again, she felt a warm hand around hers. Kirsten. Her friend was holding her hand, facing her, and looking at her with the kindest expression Delilah had ever seen.

Before the whispers could start in her head—whispers that told her she didn't deserve kindness—Kirsten said, "That must have been awful."

"It was worse for the people it happened to."

"It happened to you, my darling."

Kirsten leaned forward and brushed Delilah's forehead with a kiss. It didn't matter that they were basically the same age; in that moment, Kirsten's gesture felt almost maternal.

Delilah hadn't known until now how much she'd wanted maternal comfort.

"There is nothing I can say to make what happened better," Kirsten murmured as she leaned back. "But maybe *I* don't have to. Because there are a bunch of toddlers about to run around a stage pretending to be parts of nature, screaming and shouting and giving everyone watching enough joy for the next decade. Would you like to see that?"

"Yes," Delilah said on an exhale. "I'd like that very much."

# CHAPTER FIFTEEN

Delilah was still riding the high of Robbie's concert when she arrived in Sugarbush Park the next day. With the festival drawing closer, planning meetings tended to be more frequent, though still as casual.

Everyone who'd volunteered to help with the more hands-on aspects of the festival after Wednesday's meeting had agreed to meet in the park Sunday evening, and it was the perfect venue for it.

The park overlooked the ocean, with a pathway for cyclists and pedestrians and a play area for kids. The rest of the space was open, the grass green and yellow, withered by the heat, yet somehow still full. Volunteers stood all over the place, grouped according to each day of the festival, with a leader for each day to delegate what needed to be done.

According to Wendy's emails, Delilah was the leader for Friday night. The first time Delilah had read that email, she'd been thrilled. This was only her second festival. She'd worked hard the first time around, doing anything anyone asked of her, jumping at the opportunity to do the things no one wanted to.

It hadn't been to suck up; she'd only wanted to prove herself. Wendy's email had been the ultimate acknowledgment that she had.

So seeing everyone there, looking pretty deep in discussion when she'd only now arrived, was . . . confusing.

She walked over to Wendy, who was sitting on one of the park benches. The older woman watched the people in front of her with the same expression Delilah had seen on grandmothers watching their grandchildren play.

"Hey," she asked. "What's all this?"

Wendy beamed up at her. "We're planning."

"I can see that." She shifted her weight from one leg to the other. "Was I not supposed to be planning, too?"

"Oh yes."

She waited for more. Didn't get it. "My team is—"

"Talking to Carmen. I thought it would be better since you weren't here when the meeting started."

Delilah blinked. "It's six p.m. You told me this thing starts at six thirty."

"I know," Wendy said with a smile. "It started half an hour ago. I lied."

"You—"

"Because," she continued, "I have another task for you."

Stunned, Delilah didn't reply, only listened.

"We're thinking of adding a lake cruise to Saturday evening's festivities. Before the dance. This one will be for the romantics, since it'll take place at sunset, and Gordon has graciously offered his yacht."

Gordon was the town's resident millionaire. He lived on a hill at the top of the town, literally looking down on them, and seldomly interacted with the regular townsfolk.

Delilah had seen him often enough—the man still had to come into town to eat—but they'd never spoken. All she knew about him was what people told her, and that was pretty unflattering.

"How did you manage that?"

Wendy smirked. "We got into a little disagreement about the state of the lake."

Technically, Sugarbush Lake formed part of Gordon's property. People had to drive by it—and the house on the hill—on their way in to Sugarbush Bay.

Despite it having always been private property, the town's municipality took care of the lake, ensuring it was cleaned regularly. But over

171

the last few months, Delilah had noticed how rough it looked. She'd assumed they hadn't had enough volunteers to clean up, had considered volunteering herself, but now that Wendy was saying this . . .

"You blackmailed him."

"*Blackmail* is so harsh." Wendy waved a hand. "As a part of the town's council, I have some say over which projects we direct manpower to. I told him I might be persuaded to help with this one."

"After persuading everyone to stop helping in the first place."

"Why would I risk the town's image that way?" Wendy asked, eyes twinkling. "Anyway, he agreed to let us use that gorgeous yacht that always sits at the bottom of the hill. But"—her voice dropped—"none of us actually know whether the boat is in working condition."

"And you think I do?"

"Don't you?" Wendy replied, not unkindly.

Delilah could have pretended that she didn't know what Wendy was talking about. She considered it. She wouldn't have to acknowledge her past. Wouldn't have to deal with the inevitable wave of emotion that came with the memories of that time. Wouldn't have to deal with her friend looking at her differently.

Though she supposed that last one was unlikely. Wendy had known about her mother's arrest most of the time Delilah had been in Sugarbush Bay, and she hadn't treated Delilah the way people back home had, after they found out.

Her so-called friends had posted about how terrible a person she was, how she should be ashamed of herself. As if she hadn't felt terrible, as if she hadn't been ashamed.

Those who recognized her in those brief weeks before she moved ignored her, sneered at her, or shouted obscene things.

*I deserve this,* she'd thought. She'd believed. Still did.

But there was something else now, too. Something that came from the kindness Kirsten had treated her with when Delilah had shared what had happened.

Maybe she didn't have to carry the weight of the secret in addition to the burden of her mother's arrest. Maybe she could face the people in her life knowing.

It wouldn't help with the shame. Wouldn't make her feel any better about her mother's actions and their consequences. But it would free her from the worry that someone would find out. Someone *had* found out, and the world hadn't ended. Things hadn't changed, at least not in any perceptible way.

If she acknowledged this now, she wouldn't have to pretend with one more person. She had no doubt Wendy would share that Delilah *had* acknowledged it with everyone the woman had told about Delilah's life, and that would mean even less pretense.

Delilah could move forward. Probably not as smoothly as she would have if no one knew, but more authentically.

It would mean everything to her if she could live more authentically.

"Yes," she said, tilting her chin up. "I know a few things about yachts." It was true. Her father had bought one, and they'd traveled on it often enough. "Very rudimentary knowledge, but I could probably coax some answers out of the captain."

Delilah didn't miss the approval she saw on Wendy's face. "Great." They both stood there for a moment. "What are you waiting for?"

"Oh, you want me to go right now?"

"It was the only time we could get Gordon to agree to."

"So this whole different-time ruse was because of that?"

A muscle jumped in the corner of Wendy's otherwise-neutral expression. "Yep."

"Why not tell me? Or ask me? Did you think I wouldn't say yes?"

"I wasn't sure. You have been keeping this a secret for almost two years." There was chiding in the tone but not too much. "Although I suppose I didn't have to be so manipulative."

"No," Delilah agreed. "But I get it. I think . . . I think next time I'd like you to talk to me, okay?"

"Okay!"

The agreement was too jovial and came too quickly, but Delilah didn't have the energy to worry about it. The conversation had taken a lot out of her. Pretending like she wasn't shaken by acknowledging her past, even covertly, took a lot from her.

So she was more than happy for this task that would leave her pretty much alone for the next hour.

If interfering in someone's life were a competition, Rowan's grandmother would without a doubt be in the finals.

And then she would win, because she was *exceptionally* good at it.

He couldn't get annoyed, not really, when that interference usually improved his life. He'd seen his friends again that morning. They'd forced him to sit down, to rest, while they fed Declan and burped him, taking turns so, as Corey had put it, no one would feel out.

They'd fed Rowan and forced him to take a nap, and that . . . had been a miracle. Firstly that he'd fallen asleep at all, and secondly that he'd slept long and deep and had woken up three hours later to food, a sleeping baby, and no judgment. Not from them and not from himself.

They'd left with promises of another visit, when they'd all take their kids to the park. Well, everyone but Matt, since his daughter would rather die than spend time with her father and his friends. A direct quote, Matt had told him.

Rowan was looking forward to it. When he spent time with his friends—would he ever get sick of saying that?—the spinning inside his head eased. And in those moments, he realized how much he owed Delilah, how grateful he was to her for the introduction.

After which he would promptly move his thoughts on, because thinking about Delilah was in direct opposition to his newly made promise to forget about her.

So yes, he was thankful to his grandmother for interfering a little bit. But the social media updates were getting a bit much:

GRANDSON IS STILL MOPING AT HOME. HOW DO I GET
HIM OUT TO THE TOWN?

The fact that people had responded to this status, earnestly, too,
irritated and softened him. One of them had asked why Rowan wasn't
yet involved with the town's festival planning. His grandmother had
replied that he was, and somehow, that had resulted in him standing in
front of Wendy because apparently, she'd specifically requested his help.

His grandmother clearly wasn't the only one invested in his life.

But he hadn't said no, because she'd been kind to him, and because
despite all his protests, the small taste of community he'd gotten in the
last three weeks meant something to him.

If he wanted to maintain the relationships he was building, it would
require effort. And so he'd gone and obeyed Wendy's request to take
some paperwork to the owner of a yacht near the lake.

He'd driven past the lake on his way into town, though he hadn't
paid much attention to it then. Now, he did. It was surrounded by
thick, plush grass, the greenest he'd ever seen in his life, despite the
heat. The grass rose and fell in small hills, some with trees, others with
bushes, and more with nothing.

On the far end was the tallest hill, not as high as he'd expected but
big enough to be noticed. And on that hill, between trees and bushes,
stood a house. It was white and stately, the grass around it cut short,
hedges sharp and neat, with one single car in front of it.

He was supposed to meet the captain of the yacht at the dock,
which was nestled at the base of the hill the house was on. It was a pity
they'd built a road on such a beautiful piece of land, but Rowan couldn't
deny that the drive had been breathtaking.

He'd been in the middle of the trees, the bushes, and if the wind
blew too hard, he was half-sure his car would fall into the lake.

He parked near the dock and grabbed the folder Wendy had given
him. Carefully, he navigated the steep steps down and walked to the
small wooden structure. No one was there.

After ten minutes, he considered going up to the house, but one look told him that option would be his last resort. The climb would be torture on his legs, and he didn't want to be in pain when he took care of his kid the next day.

His only other option was the boat.

It was simple enough to get on, since the ladder had already been set up. It was sleek, everything white and expensive, and he worried that he might have tracked dirt on it. He had, after all, found baby vomit on the shirt he'd been wearing that morning. He hadn't known where it had come from or how long it had been there.

But none of that mattered when he saw a figure through the window to the cabin. When he got inside, a woman stood with her back to him.

He recognized her instantly.

"Delilah? What are you doing here?"

# CHAPTER SIXTEEN

Delilah turned at his voice, her polite smile fading as recognition flashed through her eyes.

"Rowan."

She greeted him coolly, exactly like he'd expect an heiress to. But she wasn't an heiress anymore, was she? Her mother had been arrested, her family had lost everything, and the news about her had stopped for the most part.

There'd been an article a few months ago, speculating on where the ex-heiress was now, but the author clearly hadn't cared that much. The writing had been lackluster, the piece desperately looking for some link to past scandals since another heiress had recently lost her money.

But it wasn't the facts of the case that told Rowan she wasn't an heiress anymore. It was the fact that she was a waitress. A job in service required a level of humility people with money often didn't have.

It was the fact that she'd taken time out of her day to help him with his son. She'd introduced him to friends, brought him food, invited and driven him to the festival planning session . . .

He'd been foolish to even consider that she still might be the person she'd presented to the press.

"I was supposed to be meeting someone here," he said, clearing his throat.

She frowned. "Me, too."

"The captain?"

"Yeah."

Something was off, but before he could articulate it, a man walked in.

"Good afternoon. You must be Delilah and Rowan?" He walked to the windows on either side of the cabin, opening the curtains. "We've lifted the anchor. We'll be ready to go in . . ." He looked down at the watch. "Five minutes."

"To go?"

"The anchor?"

They spoke at the same time, not daring to look at one another. At least Rowan didn't dare look at Delilah. He had no idea what was going on, but since the captain had their names, they'd clearly been expected. Together.

Rowan wanted to say it disturbed him, but it didn't. Which was exactly why it should. He'd made up his mind about what he would do about Delilah. He couldn't go back on it the first time he saw her.

But there was no memory of that promise, no *logic*, when he saw her. Only his body's reaction to her. The heat, yes, but also a feeling of rightness. As if she'd been the last piece to his intricate puzzle and had quietly clicked into place.

Was that what his parents had felt? This overwhelming connection that had everything else fading?

He couldn't be a part of that. He didn't want to be a part of that.

But that wasn't Delilah's fault. She didn't deserve that he take it out on her.

"Yes," the captain said, ignorant to Rowan's internal battle. "I was told to expect the both of you, to give you a chance to see what the sunset cruise would be."

Rowan only then noticed the engine was already on beneath them. Had it been on when he'd walked onto the yacht? Surely he would have realized that?

Or had seeing Delilah left him oblivious to everything but her?

"No, that's not why I'm here," Delilah said, her tone stiff. "We're supposed to have a conversation about the yacht. Its condition, the number of passengers it can take, that kind of thing."

"It's in excellent condition," the man offered. "I'll talk you through the daily routine to assure you of this, and you'll be able to gauge quite a bit from the ride itself."

"I've never seen this yacht move. How can it be in excellent condition?"

"I do a four a.m. ride around the lake once a week." The man shrugged. "Mr. Pillay doesn't want to be ostentatious about the yacht, so we try to keep as inconspicuous as possible. As for the number of passengers," he went on, "I'd recommend twelve. Are there any other questions?"

Delilah opened her mouth, closed it, and opened it again. She managed a sound before the yacht started to move.

The man smiled again, pleasant and polite.

"If you'll go out onto the deck, I'll be able to show you exactly what passengers can expect."

Delilah looked at Rowan then, mild panic in her eyes.

Was she afraid of boats? Did she get seasick? Or was she afraid of being stuck on a boat with him?

"We don't have a choice." His words were sharp, but he couldn't help it. He wasn't *that* bad. "Might as well go along with the ruse."

"Excuse me," the man interjected. "I apologize for the interruption. You both seem quite surprised for people whose task is to enjoy this. And now you're describing this as a ruse. Am I correct in assuming you two have been . . . duped?"

Delilah's head whipped in the direction of the man, who was now regarding them with the first genuine expression Rowan had seen on him. A pity it was amusement—at their expense.

At their faces, the man grinned. "I have my answer."

Delilah sighed. "Yes, you do . . . I'm sorry, I don't think I got your name?"

"Judd."

"Yes, you do, Judd. Apparently, Rowan and I have been the victims of the nosy people in town." She narrowed her eyes at Judd. "Hey, how is it that this is the first time I've seen you? If you're on this boat once a week, you must be living here?"

"I do," Judd confirmed, relaxing now that, apparently, they weren't there to judge him. "I live on Mr. Pillay's estate. I don't need anything living there. In fact, I need far less." He grimaced. "I'm used to living on—and with—much less. So there's no need for me to go to town."

"But . . . never?" Delilah shook her head. "Don't you get lonely?"

Judd offered her a soft smile, and jealousy punched Rowan in the gut. His fingers clenched in response, as if somehow, he could trap the emotion in his fist.

*And hit Judd in the face with it.*

He ignored the thought. It clearly came from a wayward part of himself. He needed to find that part, rehabilitate it, so he could focus on other, more important emotions. Like his guilt at treating Delilah like she was someone he didn't know. And his duty to his son.

Oh yes, remember that fear? The anxiety that he might turn out like his parents and mess up his son? Yeah, those were the good old *familiar* emotions. He needed to deal with those, not jealousy because some guy smiled at Delilah.

Although Judd had smiled softly, as if her question had amused him.

He was probably amused because she was cute.

Which she was.

Today, she wore another summer dress that was designed to torture him. It was a muted yellow, almost eggshell color, which made the golden brown of her skin seem sharper, more striking. She wore a gold necklace and gold hoops in her ears, and her hair had a matching yellow bow in it.

She looked like the sun itself, and if he stared too long, he knew he'd find himself burning. He had no protection from her, no SPF.

He'd spent a lifetime protecting himself from everyone, and barely two months of knowing her, a month of which he'd actually spent speaking to her, and he was powerless.

"Not lonely, no," Judd answered Delilah's question. "I'm used to long periods on the ocean. I used to work on a ship before I came here."

"Why did you come here?" Delilah asked.

Judd's mouth twisted. "As a favor to Mr. Pillay. He's my . . ." Judd paused. "He's family."

Delilah's eyes widened. "Oh. Well, it's good I didn't say something bad about him, then."

Judd laughed. Rowan got that desire to hit him again.

"No, I probably would have agreed with you. Now," he said, his tone effortlessly switching to professionalism, "if you come out on the deck, I'll show you both what we have in mind for the festival."

Unfortunately, Judd was actually good at his job. He explained the mechanics of the boat to Delilah, making good on his promise to go through his routine. For her sake, Rowan thought, and not because he believed it was necessary.

Most of it went over Rowan's head—what did he know about yachts?—but Delilah seemed to understand and asked the right questions.

Once they got through that, Judd told them the guests would be treated to a selection of drinks and canapés and that they'd be prepared for a variety of diets and preferences. After some back-and-forth with that, which Delilah took care of, Judd told them to sit down and enjoy the boat ride.

He disappeared into the cabin before either of them could reply and, moments later, reappeared with two glasses of champagne and what looked like a charcuterie board.

"Enjoy," he said. "It's about a ninety-minute round trip, so you have time."

"Join us!" Delilah said quickly, when he turned to leave. "Please."

Everyone heard the desperation in her tone.

"I can't." Judd's smile was apologetic. "I have to check on the crew downstairs."

"There's a whole crew?" Rowan asked. How had they missed that?

"Not many," Judd allowed, "but I'm their captain."

He left after that. Neither Delilah nor Rowan spoke.

"For all he knows," Delilah finally ventured, "you're a serial killer. He left me with a serial killer."

"For all he knows, *you* could be the killer."

"Do killers wear dresses like this?" she asked, aghast.

"Do they wear jeans and a T-shirt?"

Her eyes roamed over him, and he forced himself not to react. In any way.

"Yeah, actually," she said after a moment. "I'm pretty sure this is the kind of outfit a serial killer would wear exactly."

He looked down at himself, at his jeans and T-shirt, and saw her point immediately. He'd watched enough documentaries to know serial killers faded into the ordinary, and he certainly nailed *that* look.

"Maybe Judd's the serial killer. Or his crew," Delilah said with a gasp. "How did he manage to hide a whole bunch of people? What if they're *dead*?"

She hissed the last word, looking so appropriately scandalized he almost laughed.

"Look, if it makes you feel any better, if there's a murderer on board, I'll protect you."

"How?" she asked.

"I don't know. Throw them overboard?"

"But . . . you could hurt yourself."

He shrugged. "I like you alive."

She stared, then gave a small laugh. "I think that's the most romantic thing you've ever said to me, Rowan."

He wasn't sure how he felt about that. Firstly, because he shouldn't be saying anything romantic to her. Secondly, if it was true . . . it was

tragic. They'd made out quite heatedly, and while it had been spontaneous, it should have meant he'd done better than *I like you alive.*

"Great, I've put that look on your face again," she muttered, cutting
through his thoughts. "Honestly, Rowan, you'd think by now you'd
know not to listen to me."

Her words were harsh, as if she really believed she wasn't worth
listening to. He hated that he'd caused her to react that way. But with
the kind of certainty he didn't feel very often, he knew it wasn't because
of him.

"Why would you say that?" he asked quietly.

"It's true, isn't it?"

"Not at all. You've given me great advice."

She nodded, as if this pleased her. "Thank you for saying that."

"Why? Why are you acting as if you shouldn't be the most confident person in the world?"

She scoffed. "Great advice doesn't translate to confidence."

He stared and shook his head. "You really are different to the person
from those pictures."

Delilah's eyes widened.

Right. He wasn't supposed to know about those pictures.

*Rowan, you idiot.*

Rowan's face looked the same as it had during his conversation with
Ronald the day of Irene's party. The lines at his eyes pulled tight, his
mouth thinned, and she could tell he was berating himself. Clearly, he
hadn't meant to tell her about the pictures.

She was pretty sure she knew what pictures he was talking about.

"You looked me up."

"Yes," he replied cautiously. "Wendy mentioned something about
your mother, and I looked you up."

"Wendy again," she muttered.

But it made sense. Rowan had begun to act even more strange after that meeting. *During* that meeting, after his conversation with Wendy. It was exactly what she'd feared would happen when someone looked her up.

Not that she was upset he'd looked her up. She'd looked *him* up. After their kiss, she'd done an internet search on him.

She'd gone through his company's website, knew how highly his customers and peers regarded him based on comments and reviews. Knew from a few human-interest articles about him online that he was a successful businessman who'd built his business from scratch.

So while she'd come out of her search having a better opinion of him, his had resulted in the exact opposite. He'd seen the stories written about her and assumed the worst—because those stories had wanted their readers to assume the worst.

She was beginning to think that perhaps it was better if people around her found out what had happened through *her*, not what had been written about her.

"I didn't mean to invade your privacy," Rowan said quietly.

She shook her head. "No, you didn't. Well, you did, but I don't think privacy exists in the time of the internet. Why didn't you ask me about it?"

"I was afraid to. I wanted to know what happened. I didn't think you'd tell me."

"I want to say that I would have, but that's not true." She looked at the water ripples caused by the boat, considering her options. "But I think . . . I think I'd rather you have found out from me than people who don't know what really happened."

It caused a flutter in her chest, that thought. Only . . . what was the point of hiding it anymore? Now that she'd started talking about it, everyone would know soon enough.

She wanted them to know her side of the story. That way, if they looked at her differently, at least she'd know she'd been honest. That way, if they responded like Kirsten had, like Wendy had, she could embrace how good it felt to share this burden she'd been carrying for such a long time.

Maybe she could take solace in telling people who cared about her the truth. She could feel . . . comforted. When she'd told Kirsten, she had felt comforted. She wanted to keep feeling that way.

She took a deep breath.

"What happened with my mother is the worst thing that's ever happened to me. And that's saying a lot, because my entire life changed when Matt moved out." She looked at Rowan. "Did he tell you what happened after they found out about Irene?"

He shook his head.

"Well, it was a scandal, of course. If you look Matt up," she said dryly, "you'll find articles about the 'Huntington teen father.' They'd only found out about Irene after she was born because both Vanessa, Irene's mother, and Matt wanted to keep things under wrap. It worked for my parents to do that, and so we did."

She flicked at her skirt with her finger.

"Anyway, my parents weren't happy that he'd 'brought shame to the family'"—she used finger quotes—"and they treated him that way. Didn't care about their grandchild, so Matt was over at Vanessa's a lot. I think I realized I was losing him then already." She let out a shaky breath. "He moved to Sugarbush Bay when he turned eighteen."

"How old were you?"

"Twelve."

"Must have been hard," he commented.

"Yeah, it was. He was the only person in my house who cared about me. And then he was gone, and I . . . did a lot of stupid shit." She laughed a little. "That's what you see in those pictures, by the way. I pretended to be this person who didn't care about anything. I *wanted* to be that person. If I didn't care, it wouldn't hurt so much that he'd left. It wouldn't hurt that my parents didn't give a damn about me."

He didn't speak for a long time.

"It was *a lot* of stupid shit," he said eventually.

Her laugh was more natural this time. "Are you referring to any-thing specific?"

"You vandalized an art museum?"

"Oh, no." She shook her head. "I wasn't even there that night. Thank goodness, or I might have done exactly what those idiots I called my friends did. The media only speculated about my presence."

"Walking out of a restaurant without paying?"

She wrinkled her nose. "I did that. In the moment. And then, when the night was over, I went back and paid for everyone, including a fat tip because that was awful of us."

"You demanded every dress at a fashion show be made in your size?"

"Yes. But I stand by that one. Most women aren't sample size."

"This is a lot less stupid the more we talk about it," Rowan pointed out.

"Nope! Pretty much all stupid. I wanted to fit in so badly, I did whatever I could to make that happen. All while pretending not to care." She rolled her eyes.

"I get it," he said after a moment. "I built a wall around me so my parents wouldn't hurt me."

She looked at him. He was staring out at the water now, too, but she could still make out the pain.

"They left me alone a lot. They loved their careers and one another, and that didn't translate to me. I was a burden."

Did he know he was clenching his fist?

"I'm sorry, Rowan."

He shrugged. "It doesn't hurt as much anymore."

*Yes, it does,* she thought but didn't say it.

"So I get protecting yourself from being hurt by the people who are meant to love you."

"And that's before they get arrested," she joked.

But he didn't laugh. Only looked at her with a piercing gaze. She felt something collapse inside her.

"It's okay," she said quickly. "It really is! Do I hate what she did? Of course. She let down so many people who depended on her."

"Including you."

Her throat thickened, but she forced herself to say, "I didn't have my livelihood stolen from me."

"Only your life."

"Rowan! Stop that!"

"What?"

"Stop being so *kind* about this."

His eyes narrowed, searched her face. Then he looked out at the water, the hills and trees they were passing. His expression was thoughtful, as if he was trying to reconcile what he'd seen on her face with what he knew about her.

Nerves settled in her chest. Before she knew it, she was speaking again.

"I've always worried about people finding out the truth. I knew it was a possibility, though. Anyone can do an internet search." She bit her lip. "I mean, I figured they'd ask me about it if they knew. Or treat me differently. *See* me differently. I thought I'd know the minute people knew. But I didn't. I'm not even sure who knows at this point, because no one has treated me differently."

Her stomach rolled, a faint swell of nausea going through it like a wave across the shore before high tide.

"You did, though. That's what happened at the meeting, right? Wendy mentioned it, and you thought about all the ways I'd be a bad influence on Declan? How I'd probably destroy your life in some way or the other, like my mother did with those people?"

His gaze settled on her. She could see the truth in his eyes but also the shame. He didn't try to hide it. She had to respect that.

"I'd be lying if I said I didn't think about all those things," he said. "And I'm ashamed of it now. Not because I thought them—I should think them. It's my job to protect my child, from a perceived threat as much as an actual threat. If that's because someone's family member is untrustworthy, I need to evaluate that, figure out if they are, too."

The respect went up another notch, though there were some holes in that theory.

"When you found out, did you think that about Matt, too?"

He blinked.

"Didn't even occur to you, did it?" she asked. "Why do you think that is? Because Matt's a man? Because there weren't any dramatic stories written about him? Which is bullshit, by the way. Matt did stupid things before he pulled himself together to be a father. Some of it was public knowledge, but only the story about Vanessa's pregnancy ever got published."

"Maybe," he allowed. "I don't know. I didn't think about Matt because Wendy told me about *your* mother. I didn't put it together." He took a deep breath. "But I also didn't think about it because Matt isn't as great a threat as you."

"Of course he is! He's stronger and could totally—"

"Because I don't have feelings for Matt."

Her jaw dropped, but she snapped her mouth shut. "Oh."

His mouth twisted into a small smile. "That's what I was going to say earlier. I'm not ashamed that I thought about whether Declan needed protection. I'm ashamed I thought Declan needed protection from *you*."

"That's . . . okay, I guess."

He laughed quietly. "I guess. Except I don't know what to do about them. The feelings or the fact that I've admitted them to you. This is hard for me."

"Honesty?"

"Vulnerability."

"They're the same thing in a lot of ways," she said. "Being honest about my past would give people the opportunity to judge me. Why would I do that?"

"Being honest about my parents would give people the opportunity to judge me. As a father. They'd be able to see my desperation not to repeat the mistakes my parents made."

The anguish in his voice had her reaching out, gripping his hand. For a moment, he did nothing. Then he held on to her hand as if he were hanging from a cliff and his only chance at survival was if she pulled him up.

"I don't want Declan to feel the way I did. Like I wasn't a person but a . . . a role. Child. Take care of child by feeding, cleaning, and ensuring sleep." His voice had become robotic. "But they treated one another with a love and care I could only—"

He broke off. She tightened her hold, even though she could barely feel her fingers at this point.

"I don't want Declan to see me care more about someone than I do him."

"That won't happen."

"It could," he said, looking at her. "It could with you."

She inhaled sharply. Swallowed.

Oh, this man. This man with his honesty and his vulnerability. He'd slipped underneath all those walls she'd put up when she'd moved to Sugarbush Bay. He'd been a thief, deft and clever, and she'd barely noticed.

Well—no. She had noticed. But she'd been in denial. No one, not even her best friend, not even her brother, had gotten past those defenses. Although she supposed they'd chipped away at them.

With each day that passed when Kirsten had confided in her or treated her with kindness, she'd knocked down a brick of that defensive wall. With every meal, every generous gesture, every moment of laughter and family with Matt, he'd plowed directly into that wall.

Every moment she'd spent with Irene, Wendy and Jill, Linda, Lucas and Corey, and every other person in this town who'd made her feel welcome had created the suspicion that she could be herself and still be loved.

How terrifying.

More so was this admission from Rowan.

She'd worked so hard to deserve the goodness of her life now, but accepting it was something else entirely.

"I can't even be mad at it," Rowan continued, so softly she had to lean forward to hear him over the buzz of the engine. "You've always been more than I could imagine."

"Oh, you're sneaky!"

"What?"

"You know what you're doing."

She pulled her hands from his, reached desperately for her champagne. Downed it, then pointed the empty glass at him.

"You're all, 'I want to be a good father to my son, and I'm worried my feelings for you will get in the way of that, but you're so amazing I can't help but want to be with you.' You know what you're doing."

"I . . . do not."

"Yes, you do. How am I supposed to resist that? It's selfless. And that's so sexy I'm dying. Even though I agree," she went on quickly so he couldn't dwell on what she'd said—and neither could she, "that we're a mess. We both have parental-neglect issues. That's not something you want to have in common with your partner. Like, we want to balance it out, right? You have parental abandonment, I have overprotective parents, and we meet in the middle."

He coughed. She narrowed her eyes.

"Was that . . . are you *laughing* at me?"

"No," he said quickly. *Too* quickly. "No. I just didn't realize that was how it worked."

"I know that's not how it works," she snapped. "But it would be a much easier relationship."

"Relationship," he repeated.

As if testing the word out.

As if testing the word out for *them.*

"We don't have to let them affect this," he said, looking at her now. "Us."

"Don't we? Because I think that's the rule about being a child. Your parents automatically mess you up."

"I guess." He took a breath. "But I don't want to mess Declan up in the same way my parents messed me up."

"Oh, no, I didn't mean—"

"No, it's true," he interrupted. "Your parents mess you up. But if you're lucky, they mess you up differently to how they were messed up. In new and exciting ways."

She laughed at that, easing back against the boat seat. Sobered.

"I refuse to repeat my mother's mistakes. I refuse to use people."

"I refuse to become my parents. I won't neglect Declan."

"Great," she said, offering him a wry smile. "I guess that's dealt with. Since we said it."

"Should we say it again?" he deadpanned. "Twice more. The power of three in the universe and all that."

"Hmm. Maybe we should declare it. I think that makes it binding to the powers of the universe."

"What would be our sacrifice? To seal the deal?"

"Our sanity?"

"Not enough."

"You're right," she said and stood. Walked to the edge of the boat. She turned back to Rowan. "Please tell Matt and Irene I love them."

And she curled herself over the railing.

# CHAPTER SEVENTEEN

Rowan knew she was joking. He could see her hands tight on the railing, her feet planted on the yacht's floor, and she'd only curved slightly.

Still, panic had him up, striding toward her, his arms around her waist, as if it were all real. As if she really planned to sacrifice herself to some sea god so that he could keep from becoming his parents.

No matter how much he wanted that, it wasn't worth losing Delilah.

The thought struck him as she laughed in his face, her eyes wild and dancing.

"I wasn't going to jump."

"I know."

"You're holding me as if I was about to do exactly that," she pointed out.

"I can't help it," he said hoarsely.

The laughter died on her face, but the wildness in her eyes remained. This time, it danced with danger, with the knowledge that whatever was to come was forbidden.

Their honesty over the last half an hour was finally catching up to them.

It was impossible to remain unaffected by the admissions. Now that he knew she felt something for him, wanted to be in a relationship with him, despite the complications, a screw had loosened inside him.

Clearly, it had been keeping his inhibitions in control, because they ran away now, wishing him all the best as his and Delilah's lips drew closer. As the heat of her breath tangled with his, a sharp contrast to the cool mist of the water.

Somehow, that combination heightened the arousal, the sensuality. It was intimate. It was *romantic*. The faint buzz of the boat beneath them. The fact that it was only the two of them on that deck. The sun was lowering behind the hills, casting a glow over their bodies.

But the heat he felt had nothing to do with the sun and everything to do with the spark of fire he held in his arms.

When their lips touched, he swore something shifted in his body. Slotted right into place with a strong and firm click. It hadn't been like this at Matt's house. That had been desperate and edgy, as if they'd been rock stars making a final attempt at dying careers.

But this . . . this was a creative finally finding their calling. A painter finally putting paint on a canvas; a writer finally finding their muse.

It felt as if he'd been searching for this, for her, for too long, and now he'd found her.

He crushed her mouth when the thought brought a deep and terrifying longing to his chest. She moaned, opened her arms, and circled them around his neck. Their bodies were now touching. He could feel the mounds of her breasts against him. He could feel his hardness pressed against her.

It all felt so right, and he couldn't, he wouldn't, take a moment to doubt it.

His hands couldn't get their fill of her. They roamed, kneaded, and skimmed, fingers digging into luxurious curves, hoping they'd leave indents to find later.

At the thought of later, anxiety pulsed through him. But he pushed it aside, focusing only on her mouth opening, angling, drawing him deeper in. Their tongues danced and retreated: a game or a duel, he couldn't quite figure out which.

He didn't want to. Not when each stroke made his blood pulse in his ears. Not when her hips pressed against his and she rocked forward, a small, inquiring movement that almost sent him into the water himself.

Instead, he pulled away from her mouth, pressing his lips to the nape of her neck. She angled, giving him full access. He nibbled and licked, taking note of where and what made her shudder. He lifted a hand, cupped her breast through her dress.

She made no sound of protest, said nothing to make him think he'd crossed a line. Still, he drew back so he could see her face.

She opened her eyes the moment he pulled away. They were unfocused, desire a sea inside them. He smiled, and she smiled back and gave him a slight nod, and he knew it was permission. That she was telling him his hand on her breast was exactly what she wanted.

Good. It was exactly what he wanted, too.

He squeezed the soft curve of her breast, testing its weight in his hands, memorizing it so he could come back to it later and torture himself every moment he didn't get to feel it.

Full, it was full.

He could already imagine how her breasts would taste—sweet and sharp, like the tang of lemonade on a summer's day, quenching his thirst. He wanted to pull down the neckline of her dress, check what bra she was wearing.

Cotton or lace?

Would he be able to see her nipple beneath the material? How would it look teased beneath his fingers, his tongue?

What color was her bra? Yellow, like her dress, or blue, like the water around them? Maybe some seductive color like red or black or anything because *anything* would be seductive on her.

She shuddered beneath his touch, his exploration, harder when he turned his attention to the peak beneath his thumb. He teased it, nibbling on the part of her neck that she'd liked earlier, and got a breathy, tangled sound for his efforts.

"You're terrible," she said, the remnants of her breathlessness imbued in her tone.

*I'd be worse if we were truly alone,* he thought, shocking himself. He didn't react to it. Forced himself to keep doing what he'd been doing and ignore the fear that thought had brought.

He still couldn't figure it out. Still didn't know how he could want her so much, how he could be swept into heated moments with her— and be afraid of them. Of her. Of what she made him feel. What she made him want to do.

"If we were alone," she whispered, her hand slipping between their bodies, trailing down his chest, over his stomach, hooking into his belt, "I'd show you why my teachers called me curious."

A finger dug into the front of his pants. He was trembling now, as much from the knowledge of how close she was to the tip of his penis as from the restraint he was exerting to keep from giving in to his desires completely.

"Although they would say it as if it were a bad thing. As if figuring out how something worked, its likes and dislikes, its desires"—her finger was now right next to his erection—"was a bad thing."

She looked at him as she stroked him. He jerked from the arousal her words, her touch, shot through him.

The stroke was teasing, up and down, slowly, steadily, still with that single finger.

"I don't think this is a bad thing. Do you?"

The question was more genuine than he expected. Than either of them expected.

Had she somehow heard what he'd been thinking?

He tensed and cursed himself when it made her tense, too. She removed her hand from his pants but didn't step away. He dropped his hand from her breast, gripping the railing instead.

He should tell her now. Tell her how he'd put away the physical part of himself. Put away the man who'd taken care of his needs in careless, efficient ways.

It had been those desires that had led him down the path to Declan. Not that he regretted his son—not a single part of him did—but the unexpectedness of it? The less-than-ideal circumstances surrounding Declan's conception, his existence? Rowan regretted that.

What would he say when Declan asked how Rowan and Mckenna had met? What would he say when Declan asked about why they weren't together?

Both times he and Delilah had kissed, the complication of sex faded to the background. That told him how powerful this . . . this thing was between them.

But it wasn't all-powerful. It didn't eradicate all his fears, his concerns. The reality of it sneaked up on him. It had back at Matt's house. It had today. Every time it did, he risked hurting her. He *had* hurt her. He didn't want to do it again.

So how could he tell her any of this? Let alone now, when she looked up at him with eyes wide and open and so desperate for reassurance?

"It's not a bad thing, no," he lied, gently pressing a finger into the dent in her cheek.

She gave him a relieved smile, her arms curling around his waist.

*You're doing the right thing,* a voice in his head said.

Why did he feel so uncomfortable, then?

"It is a bad idea, though, isn't it?" Her smile turned into a bemused expression. "Getting here has been a disaster, and is this even a 'here'?"

"Yes," he said immediately and hated himself for it. He had no right to give her assurances. No right when he could barely kiss her without thinking about all the reasons he shouldn't.

"We'll figure it out," she replied quietly, resting her head on his chest.

They stood like that for a long time. The sun lowered as they did, dipping beneath the hills, the slopes, turning the sky from a bright orange to a paler one.

Rowan wanted to believe Delilah. Wanted to believe that they would figure things out.

He didn't know if that was true.

But he would take this moment with her. As he stood with her in his arms, her head on his chest, his thoughts quieted. His worries eased. He felt full and light. It was a uniquely Delilah effect, and for this moment, for this one moment, he'd enjoy it.

She turned, facing out to the sunset, his arms falling to hold her. She wrapped her own arms around his, and so they stood. Minutes, hours, he didn't know. Didn't care.

It was only when the sun finally disappeared, when the boat reached the edge of the lake and made the wide turn to head back to the dock, that they finally broke apart.

Delilah walked to their table, lowering to the seat but only perching at the end of it. She reached out a hand to him, but her other gripped the edge of the cushion tightly.

He took the hand and sat down beside her. "What's wrong?"

"I know Declan's your first priority. I also know that you have a relationship to maintain with Mckenna."

"You know there's nothing romantic between me and Mckenna."

"That's not what I meant. She's . . . the mother of your child. I will always respect that. Especially now. I can't imagine she'd be happy with you seeing someone else when your baby is so young."

"I don't know. She'll only be back next week. And I don't . . . know her very well."

"You said you two weren't a couple when you found out about Declan. You weren't in a relationship before either?"

His face heated. "No. She and I . . . we went to school together."

"Okay . . . ?"

"And we met up again about a year ago."

"Yes, that math sounds correct," she teased.

He almost smiled. Except he was about to tell the truth surrounding Declan's conception. It was awkward.

Practice, he supposed. For one day, when he had to tell his son the truth.

"We hooked up," he said in a rush. "Once. And we used protection. Only something went wrong, because she found me a few months later and told me she was pregnant."

"Oh."

She went silent.

*Tell her,* his heart said in direct opposition to what his head had told him minutes ago. *Tell her how it's affected the way you feel about sex. Tell her how it might affect your relationship.*

"What happened?" Delilah asked. He blinked, and she gave him a sympathetic smile. "Between you and Mckenna after you found out she was pregnant."

He couldn't tell her the truth now. He had to answer her question.

*Coward,* his heart accused.

He couldn't deny it.

Rowan cleared his throat. "We tried to date. Realized pretty quickly that we didn't have all that much in common. The chemistry of that one night had been . . . a fluke."

"Uh-huh." She angled her head toward him. "Okay, so you had a one-night stand with someone you knew at school, and now you're a father."

"I . . . yeah."

She nodded. "Still, I think she might appreciate a conversation about you dating someone else."

That matter-of-fact comment shifted his focus from his cowardice. "Wait, that's it?"

"What's it?"

"You're not going to give me a hard time?"

"About what?" Her confusion was genuine, before it cleared. "Oh, you want me to judge you. I mean, if that's what you *want*."

"No! No," he repeated, calmer, his own lips twitching at her chuckle. "I thought you might, that's all."

She shrugged. "I'm hardly in the position to judge."

"You didn't make a baby with someone you barely know."

"Have you ever heard of self-flagellation?"

He narrowed his eyes at her. "Where are you going with this?"

"You know where I'm going with this," she told him with a smirk. "You're so hard on yourself."

"As if you aren't."

"I . . . don't appreciate that." But she laughed. "You're probably right. I guess I'm not in the position to give advice about giving yourself a break."

"No."

"You had to agree so quickly, huh?"

"When it's true, it's true."

She hummed.

"Thank you," he said after a beat. "For being so kind about Mckenna. For understanding."

"Of course."

"It's . . . not a deal breaker?"

"Mckenna?"

"Mckenna. Declan," he forced himself to say. "Things would be a lot easier for you if you didn't have feelings for a co-parenting single father."

"Probably." His heart fell. "Except I *do* have feelings for a co-parenting single father. Whose baby is the sweetest, cutest little guy. I mean, I'm basically signing up for infinite baby cuddles. Sounds like a pretty good deal to me."

And just like that, his heart climbed back into place.

"I don't know Mckenna," she added softly, "but I'll respect boundaries. I'll put Declan's welfare first."

He swallowed. "You sound serious about this. Me."

"Shit, I'm sorry. I'm coming on too strong."

"I like it," he said, gripping her hand. Letting his heart speak, even though he didn't deserve it. "I don't want to play games. I can't afford to. These kinds of discussions are . . . necessary. For me, at least."

"Me, too. I . . . I don't want to play games either." She looked at him. "And you're not put off by it? By me? My past?"

He tugged her hand, bringing her closer. Leaned in. "No."

He pressed a kiss to her lips.

She was smiling when he pulled back. "I like this. It's easy."

No, it wasn't. Not for him. Only the more they talked, the easier he thought it could be. If he told her how he felt, all of how he felt, maybe the doubts would go away. Things might no longer creep in and out of his thoughts, casting shadows, planting questions.

He opened his mouth, tried to talk, but his inability to open up about this felt almost physical.

"For the record," she said into the quiet, and once again, he saw his opportunity drift away, "I think it's pretty sexy that you're such a dedicated father."

He fought for steadiness. Won.

He didn't know how he won, but he did.

"Yeah?" he said.

"Yeah."

"In that case, I might as well admit that those pictures of you during your heiress years were hot." He shrugged at her laugh of shock. "What? You expect me not to like what I saw? Tell me, did you own a dress that went past your thighs?"

"Oh, no. Legally, an heiress can be sued if she wears anything below midthigh. It's in the handbook," she said. "Along with wearing a bag on your inner elbow and always, always being meticulously groomed."

"That makes you sound like a dog."

"Accurate." She tilted her head. "You have to look a certain way, behave a certain way. And if you do it right, you win best in show."

She grinned, and he laughed.

Despite the discomfort shimmering in his chest, Rowan thought he might have just had the most magical night of his life.

# CHAPTER EIGHTEEN

"Your boyfriend's here," Kirsten said, clearing the table next to the one Delilah was clearing.

Delilah looked up, directly at Rowan, and smiled.

"Hmm."

She tore her gaze away from the man—he was wearing his glasses again! And he had Declan with him!—and turned to her friend. "What?"

"You usually tell me he isn't your boyfriend."

"He's not."

"Okay." Kirsten gave her an unconvinced smile. "You're on lunch in an hour, right? Take it now. With him. I'll take care of stuff around here."

She walked away before Delilah could protest.

Rowan stopped in front of Delilah, Declan gurgling contently in the carrier Rowan wore.

"Hey," he said, offering her a finger wave. The finger in question was wrapped in a tiny baby fist. Could they get any cuter?

"Hi. Hi," she said again, this time to Declan. He looked at her with eyes wide open, kicking his legs. She straightened and smiled. "Can I get you your regular order?"

"Yeah," Rowan said. "Yeah, that would be nice. If . . ." He trailed off, cleared his throat. "If you get one for yourself, too, and come with me."

She narrowed her eyes playfully. "Are you asking me out?"

"No." His reply was quick. "Why would I do that?"

"No idea. But you know what? I could do with some coffee. I'll go get it, and we can go for a walk."

He grinned. "Great."

She laughed softly as she turned away. She'd agreed to take a walk with him, and he was grinning ear to ear. Two days ago, they'd made out at sunset, admitted their feelings for one another, yet something as simple as her agreement to go for a walk had brought him so much joy.

It had for her, too.

Simple was a refreshing change to the chaos of the last weeks. The uncertainty between them had settled, and they were in this space of . . . comfort.

*It won't last.*

She ignored the thought, even though she worried it might be right. Something made her think Rowan wasn't being completely honest with her, but she was pretty sure it came from her conscience sabotaging her.

It had, after all, been weaving a web of guilt since things had gotten more serious with him, telling her she didn't deserve it.

She wouldn't get tangled in that web today.

She busied herself with getting their coffees ready, gestured to Rowan to grab them, and ducked into the back room to remove her apron. She hung it up. Took a deep breath as she tried to smooth her clothing.

If she'd known they'd be going on a date, she'd have put on some-thing nicer. Her T-shirt and jeans felt wholly inadequate, though they were perfect for work. But . . . it wasn't a date, right? So for a stroll in the park with a friend and his baby, this was more than adequate.

More than adequate. The way every girl wanted to feel in front of the man she liked.

It still made her feel weird to admit it. Her skin felt too tight. She felt . . . vulnerable. She was well acquainted with the concept. She'd spent most of her childhood feeling it. The hours she'd gone without seeing anyone.

Not her nannies, who'd left her to deal with homework, bathing, and anything else they thought she should handle herself. Not her mother, who she didn't see until after work, or her father, who honestly couldn't be bothered with her.

Matt had been the only presence in her life that had been substantial. And then he'd left, too, and she'd felt even more alone and, yes, vulnerable.

Each of those instances, those moments when she could pinpoint how it had overwhelmed her, had hardened something inside her. And now . . . now she didn't let herself feel vulnerable if she could manage it.

That had changed when she'd told Kirsten the truth. When she'd admitted it to Wendy. She'd been open, raw. But only a little. Only enough for her to still feel like she had it under control.

She hadn't felt that way when she'd told Rowan about her feelings for him. There had been no control, only vulnerability. And here he was, showing up for her. Asking her out.

Maybe letting someone see the real her could be a good thing.

But that didn't make the doubts disappear. There had been a moment on the boat, when she'd had her finger in Rowan's pants, when she'd felt . . . something. Rowan pulling back.

It was similar to what had happened at Matt's house, only this time, he hadn't run. They'd talked. And he was here, now. Surely that meant it was in her head? She must have been projecting her own fears onto him.

Yes, that was it.

That must have been it.

She walked out of the storeroom then, because her thoughts were too much for such a small space. She grabbed two sandwiches from the fridge, told Kirsten she'd pay when she got back, got two chocolate chip cookies, stuffed them all into the brown bags they used for takeaways, and headed to the table where Rowan was waiting.

"I'm sorry that took so long," she said brightly. "But I brought things to make up for it." She gestured to the bag. "Can we put this in the backpack?"

"Sure," he replied, offering it to her. She made quick work of it, and when she was done, his eyes searched her face. "Do you want to do this? I won't be upset if you say no."

"No. No, I don't mean no, I don't want to do this. Only no to you saying no." She shook her head. "Can we get out of here? My brain clearly needs fresh air."

He studied her awhile longer. Nodded. Gestured for her to head out first. She did, holding the door open for him and Declan.

They made their way down the sidewalk, dodging people with their pets, lamps that stretched to the sky at every few meters, benches, postboxes.

The town never failed to charm Delilah. Cape Town hadn't been like this. Not that the town wasn't wonderful; it was. But people were busy there. They were strangers. Unless it was a neighborhood or a specific public space, places were designed for efficiency, not community.

But in Sugarbush Bay, it felt different. People were busy, but never too busy for a chat. If there was a stranger, they were embraced, greeted, drawn into sometimes awkward but never unfriendly conversations.

The sidewalk, with its lamps and benches and postboxes, was designed for leisure, for waiting, for a much slower pace than a metropolis like Cape Town.

It was exactly what Delilah had needed when she'd moved here. She could hear the crash of the ocean as she walked, swore that when she needed it most, she felt the familiar sound soothe the aches in her soul.

The shops on the main road were painted in pastel colors: pinks and blues and greens that made this part of town seem like a delightful snippet from a movie or a children's book.

It wasn't busy, despite being the main place people shopped, did their daily chores, went to the dentist or the doctor, or got their cars fixed. There were other places, of course. Shops and restaurants and medical facilities scattered around town, but this was the hub, and most people treated it as such.

Delilah sneaked a glance at Rowan, trying to figure out what he thought of it. Her breath stumbled on the way out as she looked at him. As she admired his profile: all sharp bones, furrowed brows, pursed lips—and those *glasses*.

A part of her bemoaned the fact that he hadn't worn them on the boat. They awoke something fiercely primal in her, heaven only knew why. If he *had* worn them on the boat, she might have lost all control.

She could still feel his body against hers. Could still remember what it felt like when she'd been enveloped in heat and softness, strength and cushion, with the most spectacular hardness at the core of her . . .

She'd kissed him twice now, and both times, they'd been unexpected. Both times, they'd gone further than she was prepared for, but not far enough. She wanted Rowan, more than she'd wanted any person before him.

Which explained why she lost herself with him. Touching him more intimately, more boldly, than their relationship invited. Than she'd ever done with anyone else without intending to.

But then, she'd never felt the way she felt about Rowan with anyone else. She *wanted* to touch him intimately, boldly. And she wanted him to touch her. He'd been tentative when he had before, as if she were precious cargo he needed to handle with care.

It was early days, still, and they hadn't defined what was happening between them. Maybe he was tentative because he was learning. Maybe he wanted to go slow. Maybe he was shy.

Luckily, shyness couldn't hide his desire.

His very *impressive* desire.

She stumbled, and Rowan caught her, his fingers curled around her bicep, keeping her from falling to the ground in a somewhat inelegant fashion. But it worked, and she was able to save the coffees from spilling too much.

"Sorry," he said. "That was the only way I could help with Declan in the carrier."

"Of course."

Her voice was breathy. Of course it was. Her thoughts had caused her to *stumble*. He'd caught her. Touched her. And though the contact was so far from intimate it had entered a different time zone, her body still felt alarmingly alert.

Distance. She needed distance. It was the best way to combat horniness.

She stepped back. "You don't have to apologize for saving me from my own clumsiness."

He studied her. "You aren't clumsy."

"What? Yes, I am."

"I've seen you carry trays with dishes stacked in impossible ways. You maneuvered through a bunch of people at the party, at the meeting, and at your job without ever dropping anything. You also managed to stop those coffees from landing on the ground. You've never been clumsy. What happened?"

"A real asshole move of you to be that observant, Rowan."

He gave her an innocent smile.

Her stomach looped.

Fell.

Down, down, down, until it found the special pathway to her vagina, who'd suddenly decided to log on for this conversation.

Yeah, there was no way she was telling him the truth.

"I didn't see it," she said quickly, moving the coffee holder to one hand. "The thing on the path. And I tripped over it."

He very deliberately looked down behind them. "Are you talking about that stone?"

"Sure."

"That *tiny* stone over there?"

"Did I sign up for an inquisition and forget?"

He laughed and held up his hands in front of him. Declan reached out his pudgy little fingers to try to grab one of Rowan's.

"No, no. I can see how that stone I made up had no right being in a path for humans."

She narrowed her eyes. "Listen, I'm not sure I like this new attitude of yours."

He laughed again and reached for her free hand. It happened so normally, so naturally. He'd simply reached out—*and taken her hand.*

She almost froze. Almost didn't accept the gesture because of the surprise.

This was something couples did. They weren't a couple. She liked him, wanted him, and she was pretty confident he felt the same way. But they weren't together. Not in any official capacity. This? This felt official.

She took his hand.

"I know you're joking," he said as they started walking again, "but I do feel different."

"Different how?"

He shrugged, color dancing over his cheeks—which was, damn it, endearing—as he offered Declan his free hand again. The baby immediately wrapped his fingers around Rowan's index finger. Delilah thought she heard a chorus of angels sigh.

"I don't know. More . . . comfortable, I guess. The last couple of weeks I've stopped thinking it might have been a bad idea to move my entire life to this town I hadn't heard of before my grandmother moved here."

"You worried about that?"

"Didn't you?"

They'd reached the T junction that led to Beach Road. Once they crossed, they'd be at Sugarbush Park.

Today, kids were playing at the play area, and the primary school's girls' soccer team was running drills. There were a few food trucks down the way, an ice cream truck in the parking lot, and benches right in front of the sand that sloped down and led to Sugarbush Beach.

It was a disgustingly gorgeous picture—the bright-blue sky, the green grass, the dark-blue ocean—with the children playing and screaming and adults relaxing.

Delilah turned to Rowan with a smile.

"No, I never did. But then, this"—she gestured around them— "is far beyond anything I imagined I could have after what happened with my mother. Beyond what I thought I deserved. So yeah, it's a big change, and I completely get why you felt the way you did. But when you don't think you get a second chance and you get Sugarbush Bay?" She let out a happy sigh. "It's a miracle."

Rowan would have felt chastised by Delilah's declaration if he weren't so fascinated by her passion. Her fierceness. Color had flooded her face; her eyes were bright, expression determined; and he wanted to pull her in, kiss her. Put all the emotion crashing into him at the mere look of her into that kiss until they were breathless and wanting.

This woman.

She had a power over him that he'd never experienced before. It scared him—especially because it didn't scare him. Not as much as it should have.

It was a kind of sorcery, one he'd seen in his parents' relationship. Their days had begun with one another, ended with one another. And he'd woken up that morning thinking of Delilah; he'd gone to sleep thinking of her, too.

But he'd taken care of Declan.

He'd called his grandmother that morning, told her not to come, and he'd taken care of his son. By himself.

It had been a point of pride—or perhaps an opportunity to prove himself. He could feel this way about someone and still function. He could fall for someone without neglecting his son.

He didn't know what it meant that he was trying.

Then again, here he was, holding her hand, walking with her to the beach, his son with him.

Did he really not know what it meant?

"Sorry," Delilah said with a wince. "That was a little intense, wasn't it?"

"No," he lied. Laughed at her expression. "Fine, it was. But I liked it."

She laughed, too. "You did not."

"I really did. You don't see people getting intense about things any-more. Well—not good things."

"This *is* a good thing, isn't it?"

"A place for second chances? Absolutely. And you do deserve it." He lifted her hand, bringing it to his lips, not caring that they were in public. "Everyone deserves a second chance."

Her blush deepened. Rowan wished he were a painter so he could capture the color.

"I should offer a course," she muttered. "How to make shy guys charming. I have a one hundred percent success rate. I should capitalize on it."

He laughed and tugged on her hand. They started walking again, across the road to the park that spread out in front of the ocean.

There was no mountain in the distance, not like in Cape Town, but the water was gorgeous. The sky had puffy white clouds in it, and Rowan dropped Delilah's hand so he could point them out to Declan.

They found an empty patch of grass to sit on, and he held out a hand. "Could you help me get the backpack off first?"

"Sure."

She set the coffees down and helped him. He took out the bag she'd put there earlier and handed it to her before taking out the blanket he'd stuffed in when he'd left home.

She looked impressed. "Did you plan this?"

"I came all the way to the café, didn't I?"

"Sure did," she said with a smile. "Why don't I take Declan, and you can set up?"

He hesitated. Not because it was her but because . . . shouldn't he be able to do it all? Only he'd already established he couldn't. He'd moved all the way to Sugarbush Bay because he couldn't. On top of his grandmother's help, he now had friends to make his life easier. And he had Delilah.

Maybe getting help wasn't the failure he worried it would be.

He undid the baby carrier and handed Declan to Delilah.

Handed a very *smelly* Declan to Delilah.

"I am so sorry," he said, almost taking Declan back when he got the first whiff of it. "I didn't smell that until right now."

"Sure," she said dryly but winked. "It's not a problem. I've dealt with baby poop before. Doesn't change how cute they are," she cooed to Declan as she began bouncing him on her hip. "A little baby poop never hurt anyone, did it?"

The image hit him square in the chest.

Delilah holding his baby, the grass around them, the sea behind them. It was like they'd come here for a family shoot and they'd taken the perfect picture.

His heart clenched, his head hurt, and he worried again that letting Delilah hold Declan might be encroaching on Mckenna's territory. Or was it because seeing Mckenna hold Declan had never elicited such a powerful response in him?

He shook his head, trying to shake out the thoughts, and did what he needed to with the blanket, coffee, and food. Delilah had gotten them both sandwiches and cookies, and he laid them out before reaching for Declan.

"Don't you want me to change him?" Delilah asked.

"I don't expect that of you."

"Oh, I know."

She dropped to her knees and put Declan down on the blanket. Then she took the backpack from Rowan and searched for everything she needed to change his baby.

It shouldn't have surprised Rowan. Delilah had been Declan's babysitter once, and at the rate his son pooped, she'd definitely changed him at least a couple of times.

But this time, things felt different. More intimate. He watched her go about this task with his heart growing larger, filling more, and he was glad when she was done, because he didn't think he had any more space inside himself.

"All done!" she announced, lifting Declan and kissing his belly before gently placing him on his stomach and sanitizing her hands.

"I have to say, if you've got to change a baby, you should do it outside on the grass. Well"—she wrinkled her nose—"I guess maybe that isn't the best idea, all things considered, but it does take the edge off."

She reached out for the coffee, saw his face, frowned. "What's up?"

"Nothing," he replied gruffly. "Nothing. I . . ." *Am amazed at you.* "Nothing."

She gave him a strange look but shrugged. "I would try to figure out what this nothing is, but I'm actually really hungry."

She took a sandwich, unwrapped it, and started eating. Rowan had to force himself to stop staring at her. The more he stared, the more he tried to understand what she was doing to him.

But there was no understanding it. Not unless he wanted to take a hard look at those feelings he had for her. Feelings that were deep and real and—

"Are you going to eat?" she asked, interrupting his thoughts.

"Yeah. Yes."

He took a sandwich and started eating.

And tried not to think about how content he was sitting with her and his son in the sunshine in the middle of Sugarbush Bay.

# CHAPTER NINETEEN

It became a routine of sorts. Each day that week, Rowan took Declan to the café around lunchtime, and the two of them and Delilah had lunch in the park.

He didn't tell his grandmother where he was going. Only that he was heading out for lunch, and he'd be back in an hour.

She hadn't been surprised. Had begun giving him knowing looks— which turned into bemused looks when, on Thursday and Friday, he'd taken meals he'd prepared with him.

He had no doubt someone had told his grandmother where he was disappearing to, so he didn't feel the need to share what she already knew.

This was very likely an excuse to keep from speaking about Delilah. About the strange and wonderful thing that was happening between them as they met each day. As they talked about their lives. As they cared for Declan.

Rowan hadn't wanted Delilah to keep taking sandwiches from the café, so he'd begun to cook for them. Now, his skills were limited to what he could put together quickly, but she'd been so happy that he'd made lunch for her, had groaned with delight as she'd eaten it, that he didn't care.

"You don't have to do this," she told him on Friday, as they took a seat on the park bench. Rowan had taken the stroller today, and Declan had fallen asleep on their way from the café. "I know you barely have time for yourself, let alone to make me food."

"I want to," he answered honestly. "It makes you happy."

*And I want to make you happy.*

He might not have used those exact words, but she'd heard them nevertheless. She blushed, a secret smile playing on her lips.

He wanted to kiss her. A light and gentle kiss, like a butterfly flitting from one flower to the next. He wanted the raw, passion-filled kisses, too. He wanted them all.

Which was exactly why he couldn't have any of them. Innocent kisses would turn into desperate need, and need would turn into hurt. Whether it was now or later, it would happen. It always did in relationships. It always did with him.

But he could make it happen later. Even if he couldn't stay away from her completely—and he'd tried—he could limit how often he saw her. At these lunches. Never outside those times. Never without Declan as a buffer.

She'd hinted about coming by his house, made jokes about being neighborly, but he'd brushed them off as gently as he could.

He pretended not to notice her disappointment. It was too early for her to push, and Rowan was taking advantage of that. He hated himself for it, knew it wouldn't last, but he wanted it, her, for as long as possible.

Before she realized he was broken.

Maybe he could figure out how to fix himself.

"I like to cook," she said, her voice soft and warm and untainted by his torment. "It's one of the things I discovered about myself when I left home. Before everything happened, so many things got done for me. When I started to take care of myself, there was a kind of joy in that, you know?"

He looked over, and she blushed.

"It sounds silly, I know. Especially . . ." Her voice faltered. "Especially since I really like that you've started taking care of me, too."

"I only bring lunch," he replied sheepishly.

He didn't know why her words embarrassed him. It wasn't a bad embarrassment either. Rather like how it felt when he'd tried his best at something and someone acknowledged his efforts.

*It's because you want her to notice.*

He supposed that was true. Only it wasn't the entire truth. The entire truth was . . . was that he wanted to take care of her in more ways than simply bringing her lunch.

"You say that as if it's a small thing," she said, rolling her eyes. "I know it's huge. Matt brings me food, too. I think acts of service is his love language."

Rowan silently thanked her for bringing Matt up. It gave him something other than his uncomfortable realization to think about.

She talked about her brother a lot, which did nothing to assuage Rowan's guilt. He knew he wasn't doing anything wrong. Still, he felt guilty. Maybe because Matt had brought him food twice since last week, too, and Rowan had said nothing to the man about dating his sister.

Rowan didn't want to mess up the friendship they'd only just begun, and Delilah was already a point of tension between them. Besides, with how close the siblings were, Rowan would have to get Matt's approval eventually. No, not his approval, his respect. Not as a man, friend, or father but as Delilah's boyfriend.

Yet another thing he was trying to delay for as long as possible.

"He's protective of you," Rowan said through the knot in his throat.

Delilah inclined her head. "He feels bad about what happened with our parents."

"Did he say that?"

"He doesn't have to." She braced her hands on the edge of the bench, leaning forward as her fingers gripped the wood. "I know he feels bad for leaving me behind when he moved here with Irene. We didn't keep in touch that much before. My fault," she said, lips twisting, "but he feels like it's his."

"Maybe he realizes that maintaining a relationship is a two-person job."

"Not when one person isn't interested."

"Delilah," he said after a moment. "Do you realize that whenever something happens to someone you care about, you take responsibility for it?"

She turned. "I don't know what you mean."

"You do," he replied gently. "You told me your therapist would love to hear you admit it."

"Yeah, and I pay her. Do you think I'm going to admit it to you for free?"

He laughed, but it faded when he realized what she was doing. Deflecting. Using humor to ignore that she took too much on herself, even when the weight wasn't hers to carry.

At least he was carrying his own weight. He was trying to work through his stuff before he told her about it. Before she took responsibility for his problems.

*This* was the real reason he hadn't been honest with her about how conceiving Declan had affected him. It was so clear now; he didn't know why he hadn't seen it before.

"It can't be easy. To keep blaming yourself for everything."

She sat back on the bench. "You tell me. Do you feel like the way your parents treated you was your fault?"

"Yeah, sometimes," he answered honestly. "I carried it with me for a long time. Hell, I still carry it with me. We have no relationship now. They don't contact me; I don't contact them. I doubt they know I have a kid, unless my grandmother told them. But she barely has a relationship with them, either, so maybe not."

Saying it out loud confirmed how terrible the situation with his parents was. As soon as he'd gone off to university, he'd stopped pretending that they hadn't hurt him. With a full scholarship for academics and residence, he hadn't needed them financially. And without that tether, he'd begun the process of letting go.

They hadn't wanted him, and frankly, he could think of nothing he wanted less than a relationship with the two people who'd made him feel inadequate his entire life. The fact that they hadn't tried to get in touch with him since then proved it had been the best choice for everyone involved.

It was sad that Declan wouldn't have Rowan's parents as grandparents. But then, considering the damage they'd done to Rowan, perhaps that was for the best.

Besides, Declan had Mckenna's parents, who, despite living across the world, had promised to make it to Sugarbush Bay for Christmas to meet their grandson. Declan had his grandmother. Delilah. Matt, Lucas, Corey.

Most importantly, he had two parents who wanted and adored him.

"I want Declan to feel the way I never felt. Loved, supported. That desire comes almost entirely from never feeling that way myself," he admitted quietly. "Of course my parents' actions affected me. I've asked myself what more I could have done. I've thought about reaching out to them to apologize for not being whoever they thought I'd be when they had a son. But logically? I know none of that matters. This was about my parents and never about me."

He took her hand. She immediately turned hers over, entangling their fingers, and pleasure spun through him, round and round until he felt dizzy.

"Can you say the same?"

"Sure," she replied, her grip tightening. "I know Matt's decision to move here had nothing to do with me."

Not quite what he'd been asking, but it was something.

"How did it make you feel?"

"Betrayed."

Such a simple answer, such heavy emotion.

"I had no right to feel that way, though. I should have escaped, too. But I never had Matt's courage. His . . . steadiness. It was easy to take Matt's lead when he was around, and when he was gone, it took me a long time to figure out I often let the people around me dictate how I should live my life."

There was a long pause.

"I think that's why I did the stupid things you read about. At first, it was asserting independence. Then it became about discovering who I was. I didn't know until after my mother's arrest." She gave a sharp laugh. "I was twenty-five years old, and I didn't have the slightest idea of who I was. It was only when I came here that I started figuring that out."

Rowan was beginning to see an even clearer picture of Delilah. She'd been lost, eager for something to anchor her, and she'd only found it when the foundation of the life she'd been lost in disappeared.

Everything she did now was an active choice. She chose to help people. She chose to put them above herself. And as she did, she sank lower and lower beneath the surface.

"Matt kept in touch, you know," she said. "He promised he would, and he did, for a long time. But I couldn't . . . I didn't . . ." She shook her head. "*I* stopped. My mother told me his life was so difficult and that I was lucky I'd listened to her. None of what I'd done had been as serious as what Matt had done in her eyes."

Delilah blew out a breath. "I believed her. I felt guilty for being lucky. I never questioned it."

"You didn't have to."

"Didn't I? He's my brother. I love him."

"And he left you. Abandoned you."

"No, that isn't—"

"That's how you felt, Delilah," he insisted in a voice he hoped conveyed compassion. "Matt might not have intended to, but he hurt you. Mix that in with the guilt about apparently living a life easier than his . . . it's a lot."

"You're giving me too much grace."

"You're not giving yourself enough."

She exhaled and peeked inside Declan's stroller. Satisfied by whatever she saw, she leaned back again.

"He's more than made up for it. Not that he had to, but he has. He invited me here. He gave me a place to stay—he gave me a *life*. I can never thank him enough."

Rowan thought about how utterly devoted Delilah was to Matt, to Irene, and thought maybe she *had* thanked him enough.

"You're incredible."

"What?"

"You've done it. You're doing it."

"I still have no idea what you're talking about."

"You want to prove that you're a good person. That you're worthy of this new life. And you have. You are." He couldn't resist kissing her hand. "You've always deserved this life, even when you didn't know who you were."

She blinked rapidly, biting her lip. She looked up at the sky. "Damn you."

He knew exactly what she meant.

"How dare I say your deepest, darkest fears out loud?"

"How dare you?" she repeated on a hiccup. "I wish . . . I wish I could see the world the way you do."

"Not the world," he replied. "Only you."

When he thought back to this moment, he'd probably think that Cupid must have pointed an arrow in their direction and hit them. A bubble had formed around them, secluding them from the world.

Rowan didn't hear anything, didn't see anything. There was only Delilah and Declan, two of the people he cared about most in the world.

That bubble kept him from becoming alarmed. From panicking. From remembering the caution he'd been working with since things had changed between them.

He leaned forward and kissed her.

She sighed into his mouth, a soft, arousing sound that settled in his blood. The taste of her was sweet, the feel of her enticing, and he tried to think of another moment when he'd ever felt this way.

But there was no other moment.

He hadn't known her until now.

The thought had him deepening the kiss, slipping his tongue into her mouth. She gasped, opened, meeting his tongue with her own, making him drop the hand he kept on the stroller so it could land on her thigh, squeeze her flesh.

It was so despairingly far from and so enticingly near to where he wanted to touch her.

But they were in public. And this wasn't what he wanted for the first time.

The thought punctured the bubble.

He pulled back.

Stared.

"Wow," she said, lifting a shaking hand to her lips. "I was not expecting that."

"No, neither was I."

The world spun. He looked at Declan, wishing with all his might his son were awake. That he could channel all this sudden nervous energy in his body into taking care of his child.

But no. As usual, Declan worked on his own schedule and didn't care for his father's needs whatsoever. With no small amount of will-power, Rowan looked back to Delilah.

"It's okay," she said, eyes searching his face. "It doesn't have to mean anything."

It meant everything.

They both knew it.

"Do you think your grandmother could look after Declan tomorrow night?" she asked suddenly.

"Why?"

"We haven't been on a nighttime date. I thought I could make *you* something nice for a change."

He should say no. After this conversation, after that kiss . . . it proved that he'd been right keeping her at a distance. He'd been protecting her. He *had* to protect her. She was too good, too sweet, too *everything*, for him.

For the brokenness still rolling around him.

For the brokenness still rolling around her.

He would say no.

Instead, he said, "I'll ask."

# CHAPTER TWENTY

When Delilah got home from the grocery store, the first thing she did to prepare for her date was take care of Teddy.

"He's got a kid, Ted," she told the plant as she watered him, stroking his leaves. "And you're mine, right? Kind of."

She thought about what Matt would say if he'd heard her, and laughed. But then she thought that she didn't want to think about Matt at all. If she did, she'd remember how raw she still felt after her conversation with Rowan about Matt leaving. About everything, really.

One conversation had turned her inside out. Made her think about her worth, her value. About whether the person she'd chosen to be was who she was or who she wanted people to see her as.

It might have been the same thing. She didn't know. Thinking about it made her head hurt. Thinking about how open she'd been with Rowan made her heart hurt, too. But in a good way. A . . . a necessary way.

This was what she needed to do, to feel, to be in a healthy relationship, right? Being completely honest, feeling uncomfortable. She was showing Rowan who she really was: the good, the bad, and the ugly.

It terrified her.

It thrilled her.

Because Rowan hadn't run from her truth. He'd validated her feelings. This thing with him . . . it was good. Real.

And she'd have him all to herself tonight.

Which was probably why she'd gone a little overboard with the menu.

She stared at the groceries she'd brought in only a few moments ago. She'd bought every ingredient to the best entrées she could cook: lasagna and a delicious caramelized-walnut-and-strawberry salad; steak fillet with roasted vegetables and freshly baked bread; pork belly with a potato bake and greens.

If anything went wrong while she was cooking, she'd have a backup.

Maybe—definitely—not enough time to make the backup, but a backup nonetheless.

She'd bought the ingredients for her famous chocolate brownies and also the ingredients for her equally famous sago pudding. The scorcher of a day would lend itself to brownies and ice cream, but she loved the idea of giving him something she'd learned to cook because it was perfectly South African.

Decisions, decisions.

When making those decisions took more time than she liked, Delilah went with instinct. She'd use the steak as an appetizer and whip up a mushroom sauce to go with it; the lasagna and salad would be the entrée; and they'd have the brownies for dessert.

She put the pork in the freezer, stashed the sago-pudding ingredients in the cupboard and fridge, and told herself she'd use them the next time Rowan came over.

She hoped there'd be a next time. She'd even suffer through more of Kirsten's knowing looks to secure it.

She'd asked her friend to cover her shift for the day, with the vaguest explanation about why. Kirsten didn't ask, only shot Delilah that look, because of course she already knew why Delilah needed her first day off in the eighteen months she'd worked at the café.

Delilah appreciated Kirsten's discretion. She was still figuring things out with Rowan. Rowan was, too, she thought. Why else would they be taking things so slow?

They'd already admitted to feeling something for each other, and they clearly had chemistry, but he'd made no move to ask her out beyond their lunch dates.

She understood. And she didn't mind it! He was a single father. He didn't have time to plan a date or think about making out with her.

She, however, had plenty of time to think about both.

She had never been as aware of another person as she was of Rowan. The man kissed as if he'd been trained to do so. As if he'd gone to a kissing academy that taught technique and skill and he'd graduated at the top of his class.

He knew what he was doing. His intensity filtered into his actions, his tongue and hands working in tandem with one another, heating her from the inside out.

Delilah rarely allowed herself the space to fantasize, but sometimes she found herself wondering what it would be like to make love with him.

They'd never had privacy before to explore it. Real privacy. That was probably why Rowan always seemed so . . . restrained every time they kissed, touched. She could sense the passion in him, though. The almost physical vibration of him holding himself back.

She wanted him to lose control. She hoped it would happen tonight.

Not that she would do anything without his express interest and consent. No matter how much she wanted to tell him to put his tongue on her body, kiss her between her thighs, *devour* her, she wouldn't.

She would respect his desire to take things slow. They had time to figure it out. That was what they'd said, hadn't they?

Besides, she already felt so vulnerable with him. She'd told him things she'd kept in a safe deep inside herself. And he'd seen so much more than what she'd said. As if he'd wrenched that safe open and all her secrets had spilled out.

But it made sense that he'd understand her better than anyone else. They had so many—too many—things in common. Unstable childhoods. The lack of love and devotion from their parents. A desire to prove that they were different to the people who'd raised them.

She wanted to believe that she was succeeding in that. Rowan had told her she was. Only it didn't feel that simple. It felt . . . murky. And because she didn't want to wade into that water, didn't want to discover how deep it was beneath the surface, she focused on getting ready for the night.

She showered, shaved, did her hair and makeup. She put on a summer dress; bright and long, it flowed down to her ankles, opening in a slit up to her knee. She prepared the appetizer, checked on the lasagna in the oven, and took one last look at the house she'd spent the entire morning cleaning.

Good. It was good.

Right then, as if he knew she was ready for him, Rowan rang the doorbell.

Rowan slowed to a stroll as he approached Delilah's house. Even though they were neighbors—even though she'd been at his house several times now—he'd never been to hers. Never taken the time to really look at it either.

It was more cottage than house, a quaint little building that wasn't too different from where he and Mckenna were living at the moment.

When he'd looked into long-term rentals, their place had seemed perfect for a lot of reasons. It had enough space for him, Mckenna, and the baby; it was close to his grandmother's house; and they'd have easy access to the amenities in town, too.

He and Mckenna had agreed to live in Sugarbush Bay for a year so they'd have his grandmother's support and reevaluate after that. Mckenna could work from anywhere, though she'd have to travel for conferences and certain meetings. Rowan could work from anywhere, too, and he'd already begun to delegate anything that required him to be in Cape Town.

He'd travel when he had to, but the sense of belonging he felt in Sugarbush Bay? The fact that he could take Declan to the beach whenever he wanted? He didn't need to reevaluate after a year. He already knew he wanted to stay.

Exactly where he was, too. Because now the house he'd rented seemed perfect for entirely different reasons: it was close to Delilah.

Her cottage house felt warm with its bright flowers bursting from beds below yellow windowpanes against the white exterior. Next to the front door—yellow as well, unsurprisingly—was a sign that said **YOU'RE WELCOME HERE**.

It was very Delilah, although he couldn't figure out who she was trying to convince more: her guests or herself. Either way, it calmed some of the nerves fluttering around his body.

They were similar to—but not quite the same as—the nerves he'd felt before the dates he'd had a lifetime ago. He'd hated those nerves, how they'd almost always affected the way he'd behaved, and they had been a huge part of why he'd stopped dating years ago.

With Mckenna, things had been different. Physical. There had been no nerves then, only lust, and the consequences of that lust had turned his life upside down.

Yes, his nerves might have been different tonight than before, more anticipation than dread, but he welcomed them. They reminded him that, despite the fact that he'd agreed to see her in private, he couldn't lose sight of what was important.

He wanted to see Delilah, wanted to spend time with her.

He was looking forward to it.

But he would always, always protect her. Even from himself.

Approximately thirty seconds after he'd rung the bell, Delilah opened the door. His eyes swept over her.

She was magnificent.

She wore a red dress that fell down to her feet, cinched beneath her breasts, and had a slit up to her knee. The color glowed against her brown skin, the simple gold chain she wore dipping to the barest cleavage she showed.

With her earrings—gold, too—she looked as if she'd dressed for a dinner on the beach rather than a date with him.

"You're beautiful," he said in lieu of a greeting.

She smiled, her simple pleasure making both his brain and heart go warm. "Thank you. I spent almost the entire time since you said yes thinking about what I was going to wear to get that exact reaction from you."

His lips curved. "Mission accomplished."

"Yeah, you, too." She looked him over, as if his perusal had given her permission. "I'm sure you didn't spend as much time deciding what you wanted to wear today. Not because you don't look great," she added in a rush. "I just know I spend too much time thinking about everything." She wrinkled her nose. "Sorry. What I mean to say is, you look great, too."

He smiled and wondered if he should tell her that he had, in fact, spent an embarrassingly long time deciding what to wear. A blue shirt— linen, thin enough for this hot summer's night, but formal enough that it didn't seem like he wasn't trying—and jeans. He'd thought about wearing shorts, but that seemed disrespectful.

*Yes, because showing your knees is a crime.*

Damn. This date truly had unsettled him.

But seeing her in that dress and hearing how much thought she'd put into wearing it, he was glad he'd made an effort to look nice for her. He was also pleased he'd succeeded.

"Why are you still standing out here?" she asked. "Come in, come in."

He walked in and stopped as she closed the door behind him. Because in front of him stood the most peculiar-looking plant. Not the plant itself but its . . . presentation.

It was on a pedestal. A literal pedestal. There was a candle next to it. On the other side stood a photo of Delilah holding a smaller version of what he assumed was the same plant. It was in a bigger pot now and looked taller, though he could barely say that. It had probably doubled its size, which didn't mean much, considering it peeked out of the pot in the photo.

Rowan turned to find Delilah looking at him expectantly. He opened his mouth to ask but reconsidered. She had a potted plant on a pedestal. A candle. A picture of herself with the potted plant when it was . . . a baby?

And then there was this look. This expectant look, threaded with hope and something else. Something like concern.

Was she worried he wouldn't like her plant?

"This is . . . special," he settled on. "How long have you had it?"

"Him," she corrected. "This is Theodore Huntington, also known as Teddy. I got him when I first moved to Sugarbush Bay, so about a year and a half ago? He's the best."

She grinned at him now, worry forgotten, and kept telling him about the plant. She didn't know what it was, because she wanted to be surprised, but some lady along the side of the road had given it to her when she'd stopped to give the woman a lift.

Rowan wanted to ask her why she'd stopped for a hitchhiker, let alone accepted a gift like a plant from a hitchhiker, but then he remembered who she was. She helped strangers.

He'd been one, once upon a time, hadn't he? And she'd have accepted the gift to not be rude. So even if it was, say, a marijuana plant, Delilah would have loved and nurtured it. Because that was who she was.

"I know it's over the top," she said with a laugh, "but he was the first thing that needed me after everything with my mother. It felt good. And I want to honor how he gave me back my purpose. Which I know doesn't make sense, but—"

It had only been a few minutes, but he'd already lost his mind.

He slid an arm around her waist and kissed her.

She went pliant in his arms the moment their lips touched, her own arms wrapping around his neck and pulling him close as she molded herself to his body.

Selfish. He was so selfish. He knew better than to give in to this . . . this *need* around her. But he was helpless against it. Against her. Her sweetness, her earnestness, her goodness. He wanted it all, and she was giving it to him, and so he took.

Took, and took, and took.

A buzzer went off in the distance. They pulled away from one another, panting.

Delilah blinked. "The oven," she said, dazed. Then her eyes sharpened. "The *oven*. Shit!"

She sprinted past him, leaving him behind as she went to take care of whatever was in the oven.

*Get a grip, Rowan.*

Yes, his conscience was right. He needed to get a grip. Control himself. If he couldn't, he needed to leave.

But it would be okay now. He'd gotten it out of his system.

Now he only had to get the part of himself that told him yes, this was it, this was the person he'd been waiting for his entire life, to quiet.

It was an impossible voice, an impossible thought. He hadn't been waiting to find Delilah. He'd never had any desire to feel the way he felt now. Consumed, utterly and completely consumed, by this woman.

But then, he hadn't been waiting for Declan either. And his son . . . his son filled a part of him he'd never known existed. So maybe it was the same with Delilah. Maybe . . . maybe she *was* the person he'd been waiting for, only he hadn't known he'd been waiting.

Maybe he didn't have to protect her. Maybe he could tell her the truth.

He would tell her the truth.

He took a breath, unsteadied by more than the kiss.

"Okay," she announced from behind him, and he turned. "It's fine. The top of the lasagna is a little crisp, but that adds to the fun, right?"

"I've always liked a bit of burnt cheese," he replied gruffly.

"You're going to regret indulging me," she said, rolling her eyes, but that sweet smile on her face, the light flush? They undid him. Strengthened his resolve to be honest with her. He spent the rest of the night looking for an opportunity to do that.

Instead, he was distracted by her.

She was nervous. So nervous it was sweet—and a little intimidating. Because the more time he spent with her, the more enamored he became. The more he observed of her, the more she captivated him.

She put a hand in front of her mouth when she laughed.

She rolled her eyes when she talked about being an heiress.

She rubbed her chest whenever her family came up.

When she spoke of Matt, that rub was accompanied by a smile. When she spoke about her parents, it came with a frown. With the slightest heartbreak in her eyes.

She was so vulnerable, so open about it, too, that he couldn't help but share about his own life. The way his parents had never seen him the way they'd seen one another. How devastating it had been to witness their capacity for love but to never feel it directed toward him.

He told her about the simple things: the parent-teacher conferences they'd never attended; the birthdays they'd missed; the special holidays they hadn't cared to make special.

He told her about the harder things.

How when he'd stopped trying to make them proud, he'd felt lost, because trying, no matter how unfair it had been, had defined him. He cared about his family. And then he'd stopped caring about anyone except his grandmother. He'd pulled away from the world, built a business in which interaction with the outside world was limited, and protected himself.

When Mckenna had told him about Declan, everything had changed, and he'd hated it. At first.

But Delilah didn't judge him. She only watched him with empathy, nodding in understanding, murmuring in support. At the end of the night, when she brought the dessert out and was dishing them the most enticing-looking brownies, she said, "I get it now. Why it's so important for you to be a good father."

His lips turned up. "You didn't before?"

"I don't know." She handed him a bowl, then snatched it back before he could take it. "Sorry, I didn't add the ice cream." She walked to the freezer. "No, I think before . . . I thought it was a matter of integrity. Now I see it's a matter . . . well," she said as she turned with the ice cream in her hands, "I suppose it's a matter of love."

He stared.

It *had* been a matter of integrity to him. It was the right thing to do to raise a child properly. The reason the child existed at all had nothing to do with the choices of that child, and they deserved to have the freedom to make their own choices someday.

Freedom was heavily determined by environment—and it was the parent's responsibility to create a safe and supportive environment for those decisions to occur.

But now he saw that it could be as simple as love. He loved Declan more than he thought possible. He wanted Declan to have more than he ever dreamed of for himself.

It was that simple in many, many ways, and he'd been too blinded by the integrity of it all, the righteousness of doing it better than his parents had, to see it.

Delilah handed him his bowl again. "Eat. It'll make you feel better."

"What's wrong with the way I feel?"

"Sugar helps with surprise." She leaned back in her chair across from him and put her feet up on the one next to her. The fabric of her dress fell down the chair, exposing the skin of one of her legs. He might as well have been a Victorian male based on the shudder of desire he felt. "You seem surprised."

"I . . . am." He dug into the brownie, chocolate exploding in his mouth and, to his utter surprise—oh, the irony—helping him process his emotions. "I never thought of it as love. It felt like an obsession."

"And it might be," she said between bites of her own, "but why does that mean it's bad?"

"How can an obsession be good?"

"Hmm." She licked the spoon, and if he thought the skin of her leg aroused him, he was utterly unprepared for the way that made him feel. "I guess the reason obsessions are wrong are because they take over your life, don't they?"

He laughed softly. "That sounds about right. My life has entirely been about Declan since he was born."

"No," she replied, pushing her bowl aside. "You're here, aren't you? With me. You have friends. I assume," she clarified with a roll of her eyes, "since my brother still refuses to talk about you. But I know you guys have been getting together more regularly. And you work. So I hardly think Declan is your obsession, Rowan. He hasn't taken over your life. If anything, he's helped you find more balance."

It was true. And the overwhelming emotion he felt about it was . . . guilt.

He and Mckenna had had long and difficult conversations about her pregnancy. Neither of them wanted an abortion. Mckenna had always wanted children, and Rowan . . . well, he hadn't wanted Mckenna to do anything that she hadn't wanted to. As time had gone by, he'd realized he wanted his baby.

He'd chosen to have a child, and that child deserved to be the center of his life. Deserved to be his obsession. Somehow, his goal of being a good parent had given him the life he'd always wanted. Friends. A community. Love.

Wasn't it selfish? Wasn't it another form of what his parents had done?

"You're still a human being," Delilah said, as if she'd heard his self-admonishments. "Your life can't be about one thing, even if that thing is your kid."

"Isn't making up for your past what your life is about now?"

She stuck her tongue in her cheek, not replying.

Rowan drew in a breath. "I'm sorry. That was uncalled for."

"But was it wrong?" she asked quietly. "I don't think so. Our talks this week . . . it's made me think about why I do what I do. Who I'm doing it for. Myself? Other people?" She shook her head. "I don't have an answer."

"I . . . I didn't mean to make you feel that way."

"It's okay. I am fully aware of who I'm dating."

His brows lifted. "Oh?"

"Yeah. You're basically a porcupine." She shrugged, as if this were the most normal announcement. "If I corner you with feelings, you're going to shoot me with your quills. But I'm the one cornering you. I know the risks."

"I'm trying to figure out how I feel about you comparing me to an animal."

"An adorable animal."

"A prickly animal."

"Would you rather I compare you to another animal?"

"I'd rather you not compare me to an animal at all."

"Well, now, that's just unreasonable."

She grinned at him, and his head confirmed what his heart had known for a while now: He loved her. He was in love with Delilah Huntington.

There was a distant part of him panicking, but he couldn't pay attention to it when the reasons for his love were flitting through his head.

She made him smile. She said sweet and quirky things to describe him. Not in the same way mothers spoke about their misbehaving kids but as if he were unique, interesting. She saw him like no one else did, like no one else had, and she didn't mind it.

Didn't mind that he was prickly.

Didn't mind that he shot his quills at her.

Didn't care that he went from self-recrimination to lashing out to adoration of her within minutes.

She accepted his apologies when he offered them, accepted that he was human. It should have helped *him* accept that he was human. But he couldn't do it. Not in the way he wanted to.

Because now, he could see the countless opportunities he'd had to tell her how much of a mess he was. Hell, even tonight, when he'd been looking for them, he hadn't taken them. And now he was in too deep.

What would happen if he told her that he didn't want to have sex with her *now*? No, not that he didn't want to—that he couldn't.

Because he wanted to, damn it. He wanted to take all the feelings he had for her, the *love* he had for her, and make them physical.

Why the hell couldn't he?

He'd been the one to make the rules about abstaining. Surely he could unmake them for the woman he loved?

*The woman he loved.*

The panic began to grow, eating at the glow of realizing he was in love with the perfect woman for him. Eating at . . . eating at the love.

Before it could devour it completely, he'd take this moment.

*Stupid,* a voice in his head whispered.

He acknowledged its wisdom.

Then he got up, walked over to her side of the table, and hauled her up against him to kiss her.

# CHAPTER
# TWENTY-ONE

Delilah had never, ever been pulled out of her seat, and she had to say, if it was going to happen, it should happen for a kiss.

A *spectacular* kiss.

She was pressed against Rowan's body, his mouth claiming hers. His passion, his desire, his intensity, rippling through her. Into her.

She moaned, opening her mouth, letting him taste her, tasting him. Sweet, he tasted sweet, like the brownie he'd eaten, the hint of vanilla ice cream still coating his tongue.

He did magical things with that tongue. Licking her lips, into her mouth, an intricate dance with her own tongue that she somehow knew all the moves to.

Each movement turned her legs into jelly, her blood to lava, her core into some heady combination of the two.

She pushed him back, against the wall that divided the kitchen from her living room. The space was small, but it did its job, supporting Rowan's body as she slid her hands under his shirt.

She touched his stomach, the muscles jumping beneath her touch, and she smiled against his mouth. At the power she had in doing such a simple thing. At the knowledge that finally, finally this was happening.

She tried to slide her hands higher, to his chest, but the shirt restricted her, and she was annoyed at the audacity, so she began to undo his buttons.

"You're taking too long," Rowan complained after a moment.

"Whose fault is that?" she shot back.

His hands had come out of their stupor and were touching her. Her hips, her butt, her waist. Up, over the sides of her breasts. Her nipples strained against her bra, aching to be caressed, to be kissed, and she didn't know if she should be thankful or resigned that she'd worn a bra.

The dress didn't need her to, and since she hadn't been as blessed in that department as others, she wouldn't have worn one if it weren't for him.

She hadn't wanted him to think her presumptuous, even though she wanted, very much, to be.

"You undo them," she said as she fumbled yet again. "My hands aren't steady."

"You think mine are?" he asked in a choked voice.

She laughed but didn't move any closer. In fact, she took a step back. "Take your shirt off."

His eyes darkened—and so did his cheeks. A flush that had nothing to do with passion and everything to do with self-consciousness. But he didn't look away. He only furrowed his brows in concentration, as if she'd given him a particularly consuming task, and slowly began to unbutton his shirt.

He didn't do it without faltering. She could see his fingers shaking from where she was. But there was determination lighting his eyes, and desire, which turned into a fire driving his actions.

The smoke of it reached across the room to her. She sucked in her breath, breathing it in, letting herself become intoxicated by him. By his want. His need.

It was working.

She watched as he pulled off his shirt, as he threw it to the floor. As he exposed that glorious chest she'd seen in the storeroom so long ago now and never again.

His brown skin was smooth except around his nipples, where there was a spattering of hair, and down the base of his stomach, leading into his pants.

He was beautiful, real, and so perfect her fingers itched to dig into his skin. To draw patterns, trails she could retrace later.

She hoped there'd be a later. That there would be a now *and* a later.

His hands moved to his pants. To his belt—and stopped.

She narrowed her eyes. "What are you waiting for?"

"You," he said simply.

Hungrily.

And she realized what he meant.

"Unfair. I only have one item on. If I take it off, I'll pretty much be naked."

His eyes flashed. "Who wears only one item of clothing to a date?"

"How was I supposed to know we were going to strip? But fine. If that's how you want to play it."

She kicked off her shoes. Cocked her head.

"Your turn."

He kicked off his shoes. Stared at her.

"Socks, too," she said.

He smirked but took off the socks.

She took off her jewelry.

He took off his belt.

There was nothing else to hedge with, so she reached for the back of her dress. She turned so he could see her hands as they undid the zip. He didn't think it was an invitation, as she was worried he would. No, his labored breathing on the other side of the room told her he was watching.

Her zipper slid down. She lowered the straps of her dress. When she reached her waist, she stopped. Wanting the thin red lines of her lace bra to entice him. Wanting the slope of her back, her rolls and curves, to drive him mad.

Unable to resist anymore, she looked over her shoulder.

It had worked.

There was pure greed on his face. Greed and need. Her stomach twisted in response. In anticipation. She'd wanted him to devour her, hadn't she? Seemed she'd get her wish.

She turned to face him. His gaze lowered to her breasts. Stayed there.

"They're underwhelming, I know."

"They're perfect," he growled.

"I don't think . . ." She tilted her head. "I don't care that they're underwhelming, but I wouldn't go that far."

"Then you aren't going far enough."

He quirked a brow, telling her he'd meant the words both literally and figuratively.

She laughed. Obeyed. Shimmied the dress over her hips, letting go of the material and watching as it fell to the floor. He did, too, and then he studied her. All of her. Her bare feet, her calves, her knees. He lingered at her thighs.

She swallowed, because it really did seem like he wanted to eat the flesh off her body. She was ready. Ready to be sacrificed in some cannibalistic ritual. Ready to be consumed. To be eaten.

"You're . . ." He paused.

She shook her head. "I don't want to hear it." Was that breathy voice hers? "I want to see you."

He undid his pants without the delicacy or grace they'd been using until now. Roughly, he lowered them to his feet, then kicked them aside. His erection strained against his black underwear. Her stomach did a loop, then another, and somehow, it ended with a pulsing between her legs.

"You want me."

It wasn't a question.

"No," he replied, walking toward her. The pulse intensified. "Where would you get that idea?"

Her laugh was swallowed by his mouth as he kissed her. Lifted her so that she wrapped her legs around his waist, settling against the hardness she'd admired barely a minute ago, letting it tease and soothe and torture the ache of her arousal.

"Bedroom?" he asked against her mouth.

"Through the passage, on the left."

He nodded and kept kissing her, and she thought she might die at the sensation of his mouth against hers as the rest of his body was, too.

The journey to the bed wasn't easy. He knocked her against the doorframe; she dropped to her feet in response. He reached for her, she reached for him, and they came together too forcefully.

She laughed. "This is the stuff they don't put in movies."

He tried to smile, but it didn't work.

"What? What is it?" she asked.

"I want it to be perfect."

"That's really sweet of you," she whispered, her heart melting. "But I don't expect perfect. I don't expect any of this, of you, to be perfect. I prefer real and honest. When I think back to this moment, I want to remember . . . us."

He studied her, eyes full of something she didn't understand, and his mouth crashed into hers. It was different than his other kisses. Deeper. Emotional. As if he were pouring himself into her. She drank her fill gratefully. Opened herself up to him, took his emotions, and cherished them.

When they got to the bed, he wrenched his mouth away from hers, peppering kisses down her neck, over her collarbone, and finally, finally, to her breasts. She arched into his mouth, the torture of it, of him, thundering through her body, creating a storm that built and built.

Unaware, he continued. Took his time. Repeated any action that made her moan. Looked up at her with a teasing smile when she gasped, when she writhed, when she cried out for him.

With each second, the storm grew, drowning out the light and sound so that when he slid a finger inside her, then another, slow and sure, it took her less time than it ever had to orgasm.

She shuddered in his arms, *shattered* in his arms, every wall and defense crumbling down as her body enjoyed him, as her heart told her it loved him.

She loved him.

This man she was sharing her body with had her heart, too.

He lifted his head from her breast when she was done shaking, pressing a kiss to her lips. She cupped his face and looked at him. He looked at her.

There was something in his eyes. Something that had discomfort rippling through her.

She ignored it. Brushed it off.

It wasn't important. What was important was him.

She took his hardness in her hand, relishing his low groan. And she began to move. Slowly, so slowly it tortured her as much as it tortured him. She'd already come once, but if he touched her, she would come apart again.

Because of his pleasure. Because she was giving him pleasure.

His hips thrust up, pumping into her hand, and she let him move. She still gripped him firmly, but he controlled the pace. Faster and faster and faster. She was ready for him to spill over, was ready to take him into her mouth, if he wanted her to.

But that didn't happen.

Nothing happened.

Because one moment he was moving, and the next, he'd stopped.

Before she knew it, he was standing on the other side of the room.

"I'm sorry," he said with a heaving chest. "I can't."

What she'd seen in his eyes after she'd come finally made sense: he didn't want this.

He didn't want her.

He walked toward her. "This isn't about you."

She didn't reply.

"I . . . I just . . . it's me."

"What is?" she asked.

"This." He gestured between them. "Not being able to"—he cringed—"finish."

"Why?"

He ran a hand over his mouth. "I don't know how to say it. I've been trying to figure it out, but . . . I didn't know how to tell you."

So he'd known. He'd known there was something keeping him from letting go completely, and he hadn't told her. And she . . . she'd been a fool.

She'd suspected he was holding something back, had even identified it when they'd kissed, but she'd never, ever linked the two. Why hadn't she linked the two?

*Because you're a fool.*

"When Mckenna and I . . . when we were together," he said through clenched teeth, as if the words caused him pain, "we used a condom. It didn't work. Sex . . . sex is always going to have the potential for conception to me, and I need to be sure that if it happens, it's with the right person."

Each word out of his mouth felt like a physical stab. To the body that he'd commanded only minutes ago. To the heart that had given itself so completely to him. And to the soul that had surrendered to him.

The worst thing Delilah had ever been through was her mother's arrest. When she'd felt so utterly alone as her world had fallen apart in front of her eyes. As her father left her. As her mother was taken away in handcuffs.

Her heart had broken into pieces. Since then, Delilah had done the work to pick those pieces up. She'd found new ways to put them back together. Ways that would make her proud.

It didn't matter. Because this moment . . . this was now the worst moment of her life.

The man she loved didn't know if she was the right person for him. She'd known he was right for her for a very long time.

She'd bared her soul to him in a way she never had with anyone else. She'd shown him the best of her, the worst of her, and she thought he had, too. He hadn't. He'd hidden his uncertainty about her from her. He'd let her believe that they were vulnerable equals when they weren't.

Her brain understood this was on him. Agreed that this was on him.

Her heart told her she'd given him everything and it wasn't good enough.

He'd let her open up to him, emotionally, physically, and he'd pulled away from her. Abandoned her, just like her parents had. Just like Matt had.

She was the common denominator here. She *must* not have been good enough.

She wanted to fall apart. She wanted to sob and scream and cry out. But she wouldn't. If her childhood had taught her anything, it was restraint. It was poise. She hadn't used these skills when her mother had been arrested. She'd cried then, afraid and overwhelmed. She knew better now. Her dignity would remain intact.

Her decorum, however, would not.

"You're an asshole, Rowan."

He blinked. "What?"

"You heard me." Calmly, oh so calmly, she got up and grabbed a robe. "You couldn't figure out that you didn't think I was right for you before we got naked?"

"No! Delilah, no, that's not what I meant."

"That's what you said."

"It was clumsy." His voice had gone deep and gruff. She hated that it thrilled her. "I'm sorry. What I meant was that sex is . . . it's complicated."

"I realize that," she replied, still calm even though she wanted to scream. "I even realized that your feelings on it were more complicated than mine. I didn't get offended when you all but ran away from me at Matt's house. I didn't get upset when you pulled away from me on the boat. No, I . . . I waited for you to make the first move."

She took a fortifying breath.

"I think . . . I think I would have been okay with that move being an honest conversation about how complicated sex is for you. Maybe then we could have talked about how beautiful it can be, too. How sharing your body with someone you care about can be incredibly impactful. Meaningful. Fun, and sexy, and wonderful, and not that complicated at all.

"But," she continued, "I guess it *is* complicated, since you don't think I'm—*we* are—worth discovering that."

"No! No!" He swore. "It's not that. It's not that at all. You're worth it. Of course you're worth it. We *are*. This is . . . it's me. It's not you. Please, please understand . . ."

She waited. Waited for understanding to magically pulse through her. It didn't.

Huh.

"You kissed me, Rowan," she said, still composed by some miracle. "Made me come. *That* was your move. And it was amazing. For me. Right until the moment you pulled away. Rejected me." Her voice wavered on that word, but she ignored it. She would *not* fall apart in front of him. "So I think we're done here, don't you?"

Distress rippled over his face, and the magic almost happened then. She almost understood, almost forgave, almost embraced him.

But she didn't. Couldn't. Not when all her energy had gone into cocooning herself from the hurt exploding inside her.

"Shut the door when you're gone," she said softly.

# CHAPTER
# TWENTY-TWO

The universe must have had it in for him. Because when Rowan got home after the mess at Delilah's, Mckenna opened the door before he could even use his key.

"Mckenna? You're not supposed to be home until Monday."

"That's it?" She quirked a brow. "No 'Welcome home, Mckenna. So nice to see you. I'm thrilled you're here. What a lovely surprise that you've come home early'?"

"Do you actually want me to say that?"

"It would have been nice," she answered, narrowing her eyes. But she stepped aside and let him through the door.

The house was quiet, which he'd expected. Declan had started sleeping for longer stretches at night the last week or so. Sometimes it was three hours at a time, sometimes four, but either way, it was late enough that he'd be at least an hour into it.

Which meant his grandmother would be sleeping in his bed . . . only now that he thought about it, he hadn't seen her car.

"Where's Gran?"

"I told her she could go home," she said with a shrug. "I'm here. I'm his mother, and I'm here."

Rowan had no idea how he'd already stuck his foot into it. "I didn't mean that . . . however you took it."

She studied him. So intently, so thoroughly, he had to resist the desire to shift. To deny whatever she saw on his face, his body, his hands.

But no—Mckenna didn't have the power to see what had happened at Delilah's house. She wouldn't know he'd gone mad with desire as he'd watched Delilah strip. Her full body in that red lace was the kind of fantasy he'd always wanted but didn't have the imagination for.

So touching her? Touching her had driven him out of his mind. The memory of it had his heart racing, his blood rushing south. He couldn't think of it now, couldn't remember it, or else Mckenna *would* see through him.

Instead, he thought about how he'd ruined the most intimate, most erotic experience of his life by speaking carelessly.

Yep. That cooled him all the way down.

Delilah had come apart in his arms. She'd come apart, and he'd held her together. He'd known it as she'd shuddered against him. Known it when he'd looked in her face after.

After, she'd hid nothing from him. Not that he'd satisfied her, which had stroked his ego. Not that she wanted him, which had tortured his body.

Not that she loved him, which had scared the living shit out of him.

Man, he'd messed up.

He'd almost come apart, too. Thrown caution to the wind and let her hold him together in the same way he'd done for her. But he hadn't. He'd gotten it together right before he'd come—only it felt like he hadn't gotten it together at all.

And then he'd spoken. Like an idiot, he'd let all the panic, fears, and doubts rush out his mouth at the worst time.

He'd done the very thing he'd wanted not to do since the beginning: hurt her.

*Inevitable,* a familiar voice said in his head. It had quieted over the weeks as his life had shifted, changed. As *he'd* shifted, changed. Only he hadn't changed that much. Maybe he hadn't changed at all.

Beneath the validation his grandmother, his friends, and even Delilah herself had offered him was the same insecure boy who'd sought his parents' love. That boy had done everything in his power to make his parents care for him. They never had, not in the way he needed them to.

And he was supposed to believe Delilah could? That she loved him, flaws and all? That a simple conversation about his fears would have prevented all this?

No.

The panic, the fears, the doubts? Those were familiar. That nagging voice that told him he wasn't good enough, that he didn't deserve nice things? That was familiar. But this? Feeling worthy, feeling loved, feeling accepted? Those were . . . too good to believe. They felt too good to believe. He'd never survive if they disappeared.

So he'd stopped them before they could.

It had never entirely been about the sex. It had been . . . him.

He'd sabotaged himself.

He hadn't been protecting Delilah at all. He'd been protecting *himself*. Damn it.

"Your grandmother said you're seeing someone," Mckenna said at last.

He took a breath and tilted his head to the kitchen. It was still whirling, and he needed a break before . . . whatever this was happened.

Mckenna followed him, waiting as he poured himself a glass of water. He downed it and poured himself another.

Water was a parent's liquor.

"What do you want to know?"

"Who is she?"

Right. So he *was* about to have the most awkward conversation of his life. "Do you remember the woman who babysat for us before you left? The waitress? Delilah?"

Something fluttered in her eyes. "Yes."

"Well." He nodded. "Her."

"The babysitter," she repeated. "How unoriginal of you, Rowan."

"What is this reaction?" he asked quietly. "I thought we agreed we're not together."

She ignored the question. "How often did you have the babysitter here? Was she taking care of our son while I was away? Were the two of you being *inappropriate* in front of my son?"

"No! No, there was none of that." He hated this. He hated this with a passion. "She hasn't babysat since that first day. We . . . got to know one another when I got our coffees."

"And here I thought that was out of the goodness of your heart." She was twisting everything he said.

"Nothing happened. Not until—" No. No, he wouldn't tell her any more than he felt comfortable with. "Why are you so angry?"

"I moved here, Rowan. I moved to the middle of nowhere for our family. And you . . ." She lifted a hand. "You come home with a hickey."

He almost slapped a hand over his neck. Almost.

"What are you saying?"

"One of those things is not like the other."

"We talked about moving here. Went through every pro and con. And you were always the deciding vote. If you'd said no, we would have stayed in Cape Town. You know that," he emphasized. "As for making it seem like I'm not as devoted to this family as you are . . ." He shook his head. It hurt, more than he could say, that she'd believe that. "It's unfair of you."

She bit her lip, put her hands on her hips, looked to the sky. As she did, a tear rolled down her face.

"Mckenna."

"No," she said, taking a step back. "You're right. I'm being unfair. I just . . . I thought we were in this together, you know?" The words were thick. "My life completely changed after I found out I was pregnant. But yours did, too, so it felt . . . it felt okay. And here you are now, moving on without me."

What did he say to this? What did he do?

"I'm sorry," Mckenna said, as if reading his thoughts. "I'm tired. I got home excited to see you all, and you weren't here. And Declan . . ."

"And Declan?"

"He didn't recognize me," she said on a sob.

He walked to her then, pulling her into his arms, holding her as she cried. It would have killed him, too, if Declan hadn't recognized him after he'd been away for work, something he had no control over.

And if he'd made the same effort Mckenna had to stay in touch? To make sure Declan had known Rowan was thinking about him?

Yeah, he understood.

"Sorry," she said again as she pulled away. "I really am tired."

"And hurt that you came back to a different home than the one you left."

"Yeah." She offered him a small smile. Puffed out her cheeks and blew out the air. "Look, I didn't mean to make you feel bad about dating. I'm surprised."

"That's my fault." He shoved his hands into his pockets. "Delilah told me I should talk to you about it, but honestly, I couldn't think of anything worse."

"Bet you wish you listened to her now."

"Oh yeah."

"She really said that, huh?" Mckenna asked after a while. "She told you to tell me?"

He angled his head. "Said it might be difficult for you to see me dating so soon after Declan was born."

"Hmm." She twisted her mouth. "She sounds wise."

"She is. Wise and caring. She wouldn't want you upset over this. I think . . . I think she might have suggested we take a break so you can get used to the idea."

"Wow. That's . . . a little weird."

He chuckled. "Her generosity can get weird."

"She makes you happy," Mckenna noted. "I've only ever seen you smile this way with Declan."

He had no idea what to say to that.

"I can't deny I'm jealous," she continued, seemingly not noticing his silence. "I think I would have liked to be the person you loved."

"I don't . . . I . . ." He frowned. "Mckenna, are you saying you want to be together?"

"Oh." She laughed a little. "You're a good man, Rowan, and you're the father of my child. I'd be lying if I said I didn't wish we were compatible enough for a romantic relationship. But no, I meant I would have liked to be in a relationship with a man who looked that way when he talked about me."

"You say that as if it won't happen."

She shrugged. "I'm being realistic. Single mothers aren't exactly hot property."

"I wouldn't have cared."

"And that's why I said I wished I was into you."

He laughed. Marveled at how they'd gone from the tension to this. And had to acknowledge that it was growth. His growth.

If this had happened before Mckenna had gone away, he would have felt guilty. For not being home when she got here, for not wanting to be with her and give Declan the traditional nuclear family.

And sure, there was still a part of Rowan that felt that way. But he hadn't let it overwhelm him. He hadn't let it guide the conversation.

It sat with him over the next week. If he could have a mature conversation with Mckenna, he could have had one with Delilah. Only he hadn't been ready.

He hadn't been ready to face that his feelings about sex were so closely linked to his insecurities, his fears about accepting Delilah's love. He *still* wasn't ready.

Until he was, he couldn't contact Delilah.

He didn't call, didn't text. He didn't get coffee at the café or visit her house. He didn't go outside in case they bumped into one another either. No, he would give her space until he could give her certainty.

"I'm worried about you," his grandmother told him one morning.

247

Mckenna had taken Declan to get coffee, so Rowan and Linda were alone. Mckenna had promised not to get coffee at the café, since he'd told her at one point that he and Delilah were having some problems, which had garnered him a lot of sympathy.

From not only his baby's mother, it seemed.

"You don't have to be," he replied. "I'm fine."

"You're moping."

"I am . . ." Had it been that obvious? "Not," he finished weakly.

"As reassuring as you made that sound, dear," Linda said dryly, "you haven't been outside in a week. Not since your date with Delilah."

"Mckenna told you."

"No." The answer was too quick. She obviously realized this. "Told me what?"

He snorted. "It's fine, Gran. I don't mind."

"What happened?"

"Nothing I want to talk about."

"But . . . you're sad, darling. I hate that you're sad."

"It's my problem."

"It's not," she said gently. "I know the way you grew up meant you had to depend on yourself for a good many things, Rowan, but that is no longer true. I'm here for you. In the ways I couldn't be when you were younger."

Something about the way she said it made him narrow his eyes.

"I was not your responsibility then. Nor am I now."

"Do you feel that way about me? No, I didn't think so," she said when he didn't answer. "We care about one another, which means we feel responsible for one another. I can't say if it's right or wrong; it simply is."

"Very wise."

"Thank you. Now, why don't you want to be happy?"

He laughed at the abrupt change. "When did I say I didn't want to be happy?"

"You don't have to say it. You do it. You're still punishing yourself for having Declan unexpectedly. You haven't been in touch with your friends, and you've obviously pushed Delilah away."

"No, I—"

"Declan wouldn't want his father to be unhappy because of him," Linda told him, sternly now. "He deserves more than that. He deserves a full life. And he'll only know that if he sees his parents with one."

Rowan opened his mouth, but she left him in the kitchen before he could reply.

Just as well. She'd robbed him of his thoughts, his words. But she hadn't robbed him of his emotions: a strange mixture of guilt and hope that he had no idea how to manage.

# CHAPTER

# TWENTY-THREE

"Right, we've sorted out most of the responsibilities for the day. Now, we only need someone to put up the lights and the signage. I'll do those," Delilah said, crossing them off the list of duties she'd made for Friday night of the Founder's Day festival.

"I'll help with the setup for the movie and make sure the food trucks are okay, since I'll already be here." She gave Wendy a smile. "Everything will be up and running by the time people start rolling in for the bonfire."

Wendy's brow furrowed.

"What?" Delilah asked. "What's the problem?"

"No problem," Wendy answered slowly. "I'm only wondering if one person can do all of this."

"Oh, it's not even an issue." Delilah waved her hand. "I like this."

It wasn't a lie. Since she'd joined the committee as a full-time member, she'd found herself enjoying the planning. She loved it when things went right. She appreciated the challenge when they went wrong.

A wave of pleasure crashed inside her every time she succeeded with a task, big or small, and maybe that was important.

But it wasn't for now.

"Let's move on to Saturday. What do you need?"

Wendy studied her but thankfully started talking. Delilah didn't get off scot-free, though. There were some very pointed comments about "delegation" and "sharing the load," but Delilah ignored them.

She didn't mind the load. In fact, keeping busy had saved her from dwelling on what had happened between her and Rowan. She'd picked up more shifts at the café and more babysitting shifts, and the last week had gone by so quickly she'd barely had time to think, let alone think about Rowan.

About how he hadn't called.

About how he hadn't come by.

About how he'd given her the most intimate night of her life and broken her heart.

But even with the work, she struggled against him. His presence took up too much space in her mind. When she stumbled into her house at night, the place smelled like him.

It was impossible. She'd cleaned the house from top to bottom the moment he'd left, determined to erase all traces of him. Her bedding had been washed, the table cleared, the food put into containers and dropped off at the community center for whatever club was meeting that day.

And when she was done with that, the only thing left of him was her. But as she showered beneath the hot water, scrubbing her body, which still ached from the pleasure he'd given her, she knew there was no point.

He was inside her. In her heart and her soul and her mind. Erasing him there would take more than a night, more than a scalding shower.

Still, she tried. And when it became clear that she was only punishing herself, her skin red and sensitive from the loofah, she swore she wouldn't let him do this to her.

Work was her best defense, even if sometimes he still slipped through. So she kept busy. Only people were starting to notice.

Therese Beharrie

The first day she hadn't gone out for lunch with Rowan—she hated that it had disappointed her, that she'd still hoped he'd come, even after what had happened—Kirsten had swooped down on her like a bird of prey.

"What happened?" she demanded.

"Nothing."

"Nothing? *Nothing?*" She frowned. "You're lying."

"Of course I'm lying," Delilah said impatiently. "I don't want to talk about it. It's"—her throat tightened—"over."

She quickly moved on because she couldn't bear Kirsten's platitudes or her judgment. Her friend had backed off, hadn't questioned how much Delilah was working, despite giving her the same worried looks Wendy had tonight.

Before long, one of them would tell Matt; she had no doubts about that. Or about how her brother would react when he found out the truth, for that matter. It was exactly why she'd been avoiding Matt for the past week.

He'd made his opinion on her dating Rowan clear enough—by not talking about it at all. She knew someone had told him she and Rowan had been on lunch dates. That they'd held hands and kissed. No one in this town could resist a good piece of gossip.

But her brother had said nothing about it. Maybe he was waiting on her to tell him. If so, it was a good thing she hadn't. Because then she'd have to tell him that they were no longer together. Now . . . now she wouldn't have to say anything at all.

Delilah shook her head. It was feeling foggy, but she blamed that on the fact that it was almost 10:00 p.m. on the Friday of a very long week.

Wendy had come to the café to talk through the last of the plans for the following week, and she'd left a while ago. Delilah just hadn't mustered up the strength to do the last of the cleaning before she could lock the café yet.

But she should. She needed to get home and into bed so she could open the café the next morning.

After a quick pep talk, Delilah managed to stand. The fogginess turned into a spinning. She must have stood too quickly. She gripped the back of her chair and waited as her head calmed. Seconds turned into minutes, maybe more, before she felt like she could move again.

And when she did, her limbs felt heavy. Her whole body did. Which was probably the reason her legs couldn't hold it up.

Falling didn't hurt. She'd dropped more than fallen anyway. If it had been a movie, she would have placed a hand on her forehead and delicately crumpled to the floor. Only it wasn't a movie, and she'd half slumped onto the chair, ribs first.

It had knocked some of the breath out of her, and since she didn't have any to spare, she stayed there until her lungs started to work again.

She used the time to do inventory of her body. Her butt was on the floor, but her arms were draped over the seat of the chair she'd knocked against, her forehead between them. Her head still swam, and her ribs ached a bit, but she was okay.

Except—what was that noise she heard? A sharp sound. A shaky sound. Almost as if . . . almost as if someone was crying. There was no one else here, only her, and so—

Oh. It was her. The sound was coming from her. She was crying.

Oh no.

Surely the fact that she hadn't realized she was crying didn't reflect well on her emotional well-being? Neither did knowing that once she started, she wouldn't stop. Not for a while. All the suppressed emotion had to go *somewhere*.

Apparently, that was the seat of this unassuming chair.

She cried and cried. About her life, which had seemed so simple, so straightforward, before Rowan. She'd been making progress on being a good person. She'd *been* a good person. Now she wondered if that was true.

Did good people want to be good people? Or were they simply good? Did trying so hard to be good mean it didn't come naturally to her? And if that was true, was there a point in trying?

Every decision in her life since her mother's arrest had been with the purpose of making up for her past. For what her mother had done, for who Delilah had been. For what Delilah had enjoyed when there'd been so many people suffering as a result of her family's actions.

If she didn't have to make up for it, what was the point of her life? What was the point of any of it?

She heard another sound then. The bell indicating that the door had opened. She didn't lift her head. Held in her whimpers.

Crime was basically nonexistent in Sugarbush Bay, and if it was one of the townspeople, as she suspected, she didn't want them to see her crying. Sure, they'd see her on the floor, but she'd tell them she'd fallen asleep. No one would know.

Shoes came into her view. Black trainers with small flecks of cement. She knew those shoes. Knew the abnormally large feet that fit into them.

Her brother didn't say anything. Only sat down beside her on the floor and pulled her into his arms. Of course, that made her cry more. She was tired; she had no defenses against kindness.

More importantly, her heart had been broken. She let her big brother comfort her, because that was the only thing that would help.

And maybe she'd known that all along, so she'd avoided him. So she could avoid this. The emotion that wouldn't go away, no matter how hard she worked or how busy she kept.

"What did you eat for supper?" Matt asked when she finally stopped crying.

Her head felt like lead, but she lifted it. "What?"

"Did you have supper?" His eyes took in her face, hardening at whatever he saw there. "When's the last time you ate anything?"

"I . . . I don't know. This afternoon? Lunch?"

No, that wasn't right. She hadn't eaten during lunch because she'd offered to get groceries for some of the people at the retirement village.

"Breakfast?" she offered more tentatively and more to herself. But she hadn't had breakfast. She'd thought she'd get an early start and grab something at the café. She hadn't. Why hadn't she?

"I ate a brownie today."

Of that, she was sure. But she didn't know when, exactly, that had happened.

"Also, I had coffee."

Matt's lips thinned. "I'm going to make you an omelet." Gently, he pulled her up from the floor until she was once again sitting on the chair, not using it like a buoy. "And a smoothie. With fruit. And vegetables."

"A *vegetable* smoothie?"

He folded over the sleeves of his top until his forearms were visible. "Yes."

"You hate that stuff."

"Yes." His gaze flickered to hers. "You do, too. But you'll drink it. You're starving." He studied her. "Possibly dehydrated."

"If I were dehydrated, I'd need to go to the hospital."

"I found you on the floor," he growled. "You're going to the hospital anyway. But first, you need to eat."

She didn't have the energy to argue, so she waited. He disappeared into the back, and after a few clatters and clangs, she heard the soothing sound of cooking.

She complained a lot about Matt cooking for her, but mostly it was for show. She loved that he did. It reminded her of how he'd made pancakes and eggs for her when she was little. About how, during that hour in the kitchen, she'd felt like she'd had family.

She'd get the chocolate spread out, cut up the berries, and put some bread in the toaster, and they'd talk.

Well, she'd talk. Even then, Matt was quiet. But he'd laugh when she'd tell him about whatever stupid thing a kid at school did. He'd ask about her day, her friends, and he'd answer her own questions, even though they were silly and immature.

She smiled at him when he came out with the food and smoothie and set it down in front of her. And immediately stopped when he put a hand on her forehead.

"What are you doing?"

"Checking for a fever. I think you're delirious."

She rolled her eyes. "I'm not. I was thinking about home. When we'd cook together."

She picked up her fork, stared at the plate. A strange mixture of nausea and hunger rolled through her stomach. She wouldn't get away with letting the nausea win, so she took a tentative bite. Chewed. Swallowed.

With supervision, she did it again, and again, until she was halfway through and Matt finally sat down.

His brow knit. "I still can't believe you remember that."

"Of course I do. It's what I drew on when I had to teach myself to cook after Mom's arrest. Every week when you still . . ."

She trailed off, not wanting to scratch at a healing scab.

But it didn't matter.

"When I still lived at home." He studied her face. "I remember, too, but it's foggy. A lot of my memories of that time are, because it was so long ago. And . . . traumatic."

"Yeah, of course."

She didn't dare look at him. Didn't want him to be affected by her emotions.

"None of that was your fault. Not me leaving. Not Mother getting arrested." Delilah looked at him now. She couldn't not. "I've watched you since you've come here. I've seen your guilt in everything you do."

"No."

"Yes." His tone brooked no argument. "I should have said something. But . . ." He crossed his arms, looked out the window at the dark night around them. "I don't like to talk about them."

He didn't have to tell her he was referring to their parents.

"They . . . hurt me. Damaged a lot of who I was." He frowned. "I was a kid. I needed guidance. I needed love."

"You got neither."

"No. Nor did you."

She shook her head. "I still should have said something. I should have tried to get you money. Or—"

"You were a kid, Delilah."

"And then I was a teenager, Matt," she replied. "And then an adult. What happened with Mom . . . it was only a year and a half ago. I could have done plenty."

"Okay," he said slowly. "Why didn't you?"

"Mom . . ." She hesitated. But it was time to get it out. "Mom told me you were having a really hard time here. I believed her. I felt . . . guilty."

"For what?"

"I don't know. For still having the life you left behind?"

"A life that sucked. You know it's true," he said at her sharp inhale. "If anyone should feel guilty, it's me. I left you in that hell and started a new life away from all of it. Away from you."

She swallowed. "It's okay."

"It's not. It never was." He leaned forward. "I failed as your big brother. I'm sorry."

She bit down on her lip, relishing the pain. Focusing on it so there was no space for her bruised heart to spill through her eyes in tears.

He must have known it, because he gave her time. When the worst of it was over, when she released her lip, he pushed the plate forward and didn't continue until she was eating again.

"I know the power Mother had. She had it over me, too. The temptation of being loved by your mother, and by her, specifically, was a powerful thing. But it changed when I had Irene. I was terrified that she'd have the same power over my daughter. I got out. Far away. And I . . ." Pain shone in his eyes. "I left you behind."

"Your decision had nothing to do with me."

"No," he agreed. "But I wanted more for you. I still do."

She almost cried then, but he handed her the smoothie, so she drank instead. For the first time, she tasted the faintly bitter taste of spinach. Good. She'd focus on that little horror and not her brother's simple, breathtaking words.

"I wanted to come for you," he said softly. "So many times. But . . . I was afraid. Of her. Of them. And," he added, "of you. You used to look at me with the kind of adoration only young kids have. It would have killed me if you stopped."

"I wouldn't have. I loved you too much. I love you."

His eyes shone, but he cleared his throat. "Right. Enough of that." She hid her smile.

"Wait." He cleared his throat again. "I owe you a proper apology. I'm sorry I left you. I wish . . . I wish I'd come back for you."

"Me, too," she said with a hiccup. "I'm sorry you left me, too, but mostly, I'm sorry I didn't find you sooner."

He hung his head, took her hand, squeezed. They sat like that for a while before she said, "We should thank her. For bringing us together again."

He gave a derisive snort. "Yeah. Let's write her a letter. Be sure to address her by her proper title: Mother Felon."

Delilah gave a sharp laugh and slapped her hand over her mouth. But when she heard the rumble of Matt's laugh, too, she couldn't stop herself. The tension burst between them. Delilah could all but feel it seep out of her body, could all but see it as a puddle on the floor.

It reflected everything she'd felt about her estrangement with her brother: the guilt, the worry, the desire to make up for it. And now, her brother's acknowledgment, his apology, too.

"*She* was wrong, D," Matt said eventually. "*She* was the criminal. *She* hurt us. Sure, we hurt each other in the process, and Dad's somewhere in there, too, but Mom bears most of the responsibility for this. Especially for what she did to those people."

"I enjoyed the life she gave us," she said quietly. "With those people's money? I had a good life."

"Delilah," he said, voice grim. "I want you to hear me when I say this: You. Are. Not. Responsible. Punishing yourself for what she did, for the sake of the people she defrauded, isn't helping anyone."

"I'm not punishing myself."

He quirked a brow. And that brow was right.

She had been punishing herself. Still was. She'd rebranded it, called it "making up" for what she'd done, who she'd been, but that was only so she didn't have to face the truth of it.

Because facing the truth of it would be admitting that there was nothing she could do about her past. It was a terrifying, helpless feeling. Of course she hadn't wanted to feel it. Of course she wanted to believe that donating to the victims of her mother's crimes, helping everyone she could, could change the fact that, for a very long time, she'd been selfish.

Still was, if what she was doing, if how she was living, was so she could feel better about herself.

It would take some time before she could wrap her head around that.

"That's enough talking for tonight," she said decisively.

Matt let out a sigh. "No, it's not."

"What? No. I'm done. Help me clean up."

"I will." He gave her a steely look. "After you tell me what happened with Rowan. What did he do?"

"What makes you think it was him?"

"You're perfect," Matt said simply, without a hint of irony.

"I'm not—"

"Perfect," he said again and glowered.

They'd finally talked about their mother, about their past, about almost everything, and he still thought she was perfect.

She loved him. She loved him so much.

She exhaled. "You can't freak out about what I'm going to tell you."

"Have I ever?"

"You told me not to date Lucas. And Rowan. That's your way of freaking out."

The look on his face said, *Clearly I was right.*

His mouth said, "Fine."

And because she desperately wanted to talk about it with her brother, the man who stubbornly thought she was perfect, who loved her, who felt guilty about leaving her, who'd invited her to stay with him when her life had fallen apart, she told him what had happened.

Her heart warmed at his growls.

# CHAPTER

# TWENTY-FOUR

It was an ambush. He was being ambushed.

Mckenna had convinced Rowan to take Declan for his walk. He'd agreed. He was too tired to argue. He hadn't been sleeping well, and this time, he couldn't blame his son. It was his own mistakes playing in his head repeatedly, keeping him awake.

So he'd taken over the night shifts, and his fatigue was now physical, mental, and emotional.

Getting out of the house sounded like a good idea. Maybe some sun exposure would burn away all the embarrassment, the shame, he felt about everything that had happened with Delilah.

And if he was honest, about his grandmother's rebukes about how he was living his life.

Doubtful, but he had to try.

He'd made sure to walk in the opposite direction of Delilah's house and come back that same way so they wouldn't have to see one another. And when he got home, Corey, Lucas, and Matt were sitting in his living room.

Mckenna swooped in, took Declan from him, and went right back out the door.

He stared after her.

Someone—probably Corey—cleared his throat.

Rowan turned. Looked at the guys. His eyes settled on Matt. The man sat on his couch, arms folded, muscles tensed. His expression was unreadable, except for when his gaze met Rowan's and a quick *I want to kill you* flashed across his eyes.

Matt knew.

Shit.

"What are you doing here?" he asked, deciding to ignore this disturbing fact.

"You've made a mess," Corey said, opening his hands over his knees. "We're here to help you fix it."

"Really?" Rowan's eyes flickered over to Matt. "All of you?"

Corey and Lucas looked at each other.

Looked at Matt.

Matt stared at Rowan.

Rowan stared back out of pure pride.

"Yes," Matt said after a moment. He didn't offer anything else. It was probably for the best.

"What mess are you referring to, specifically?" Rowan asked, bravado fading.

"Well, we know you messed things up with Delilah," Corey offered. "How about Mckenna? How are things with her?"

"I don't know." He rubbed the back of his head. "Fine, I guess? I mean, there was an argument, but I think we came out on the other side of it relatively unscathed. She helped you with this, didn't she?"

"Yeah," Corey said. "Honestly I was curious about your relationship."

Lucas rolled his eyes. "Settle down."

"Hey, I'm in a relationship."

Everyone looked at Corey.

"You are?" Rowan asked. "How is this the first time I've heard of it?"

Corey blushed. *Blushed.* Rowan hadn't seen the man embarrassed once since they'd met, but a simple question had him blushing. Clearly, his partner was his weakness.

When Corey didn't answer, Lucas sighed. "It's fake. He and his ex-girlfriend pretend to be together on social media. He still loves her. It's a whole thing."

"*What?*"

"We're not here to talk about me," Corey said.

"Why not? Your situation is clearly more messed up than mine."

"Dude, your grandmother called Matt to tell on you. *Matt.*" Corey pulled a face. "She said you were moping about every decision you've ever made."

"An exaggeration," Rowan replied with a frown.

His brain was still getting over the fact that he'd spent so much time with Corey and he hadn't known his friend was in a fake relationship. Come to think of it, he knew nothing about Lucas's and Matt's personal lives either.

"Are you guys in a relationship, too?" he asked them.

"No, Matt and I broke up years ago," Lucas deadpanned. "Couldn't handle the moods."

"No," Matt answered, ignoring Lucas. "But we're not here about us. We're here for you."

Rowan was already shaking his head. "I don't need your help."

"Your grandmother called us," Corey reminded him.

"Your *grandmother*," Lucas emphasized.

The reminder did nothing for his ego. But at this stage, what was the point of having one? He already knew he'd been an idiot. Admitting that to his friends shouldn't be this hard. Especially if they wanted to help him.

He flopped down on the couch. "Yeah, I messed up."

They all nodded.

"I guess . . . I thought I didn't deserve it, you know? Any of it. You guys. Living here. Being happy. Her." He didn't have to clarify who he meant. "I got scared, and I made mistakes."

Corey let out a breath. "Man, I am so glad to hear you say that. I thought we'd be here all day trying to get you to admit it."

"We've already been here too long," Matt muttered.

"Hey, no one forced you to come," Corey told him.

"I had to," Matt grumbled. "I'm part of the club . . . or whatever."

"Ha!" Corey exclaimed.

Lucas laughed.

Matt ignored them.

"Delilah told you," Rowan said with a twist of his mouth.

"Yeah." Corey grinned. "The Single Dads Club. I liked it."

"He calls us that all the time now." Lucas rolled his eyes. "I guess coming over to help a friend with his kid can't only be friendship."

"Sure it can," Corey disagreed easily. "But when you add in the fact that we are all single fathers, that we help one another with our shit, and that we're raising our kids together, a club is better than friendship."

Matt swore. Lucas laughed again. Corey beamed.

Rowan would have enjoyed it more if the club hadn't come together because his life was a disaster.

"Okay, *club*," he said. "What do I do?"

"What do you want to do?" Corey asked.

Rowan shook his head. "No, no, no. If you're going to do some therapy shit on me, I'm out."

Lucas frowned. "Asking a question is therapy?"

Matt narrowed his eyes. "What's wrong with therapy?"

"Nothing's wrong with it," Rowan said. "But I already know what's wrong with me: I'm scared. I worked hard to get my parents' attention. I never did. Now, attention makes me uncomfortable, and I don't think I deserve it."

Love was a form of attention. Of validation. Of course he didn't think he deserved it after his childhood. But he did. He had to, if he wanted Declan to believe *he* did.

Rowan needed to accept love, attention, and happiness without sabotaging himself. If he didn't, he'd be teaching his son to repeat his mistakes. That was the last thing he wanted.

"You know," Corey said, "that makes me understand you a whole lot better."

"We're all messed up from our parents," Lucas added. "It's a part of life."

"None of you worry about passing that shit on to your kids, though," Rowan said. "You don't let it keep you from being happy. You've got your lives figured out."

There was a beat. And then they all started laughing.

Every. Single. One. Of. Them.

Even Matt.

They laughed so hard, so loud, that Rowan winced.

"Oh, ha ha," he said, standing. "Yeah, let's laugh at the new guy after he bared his soul."

"Sit down," Matt snapped. "We're laughing because you have no idea what you're talking about."

"Because none of you are keen on sharing," Rowan snapped right back. "You know Corey is still in love with his ex."

"Hey!"

"Am I lying?" Matt challenged.

"No," Corey said sullenly. "But you can't keep putting a man's business out there on the streets."

Matt rolled his eyes. "Lucas gets to see his kid for a weekend once every month, and it kills him."

Lucas tilted his head in acknowledgment.

"And my daughter has gone from a sweet angel to the bane of my existence." Matt rubbed a hand over his face. "Last night she told me she wants a belly ring. A piercing," he clarified, as if they didn't understand it, "in her stomach."

"In the skin above the navel," Corey said, ignoring the glare Matt gave him.

"Why would she want one?" Matt groused. "Why the hell would she want a piercing?"

"To make her feel sexy?" Lucas suggested.

"Confidence?" Corey added.

Matt looked at Rowan.

He wrinkled his nose. "Mckenna has a belly ring. I saw it when we were in school together, and I definitely remembered it before we slept together."

Matt exploded from the chair.

"Screw you!" he said, pointing at Lucas. "Screw you"—he pointed at Corey—"and *definitely* screw you." He pointed at Rowan, then began to pace. "None of that makes me feel any better."

"I take it you said no?" Corey asked.

He grunted a yes. "She isn't speaking to me."

They nodded. Of course she wasn't. She was a teenage girl who had been denied something she wanted. Matt kept pacing, but as suddenly as he'd stood, he lowered back to the couch. He threaded his fingers together and calmly addressed Rowan.

Which was creepy.

"None of us have it together," he said. "Our pasts affect how we are with our kids. So do our presents. But we don't let it affect *them*. It isn't their baggage to carry. So every day we show up and try to do better by them than our parents did by us."

He was right.

For the first time, Rowan realized how much pressure his desire to be different to his parents would put on his son. If Rowan focused solely on Declan, he *would* become obsessed. In a bad way. Declan would be the reason for his every emotion, for his every decision, and that couldn't be healthy. Not for him and not for Declan.

Now he could see why his grandmother was so worried. Now he could see why his friends were here. They wanted to protect Declan from him. They wanted to protect Rowan from *himself*.

"How do I fix it?" he asked roughly.

Lucas's tone was soft. "What exactly?"

"Everything. Fatherhood." He paused. "Delilah."

"You'll do what needs to be done with your kid," Matt said.

"And with Delilah?" Corey continued, as if he agreed with Matt. Their confidence in him . . . killed him. Meant the world to him. "Well, we can help."

"How?" Rowan asked again. "If it were easy, wouldn't you be back with your ex?"

Lucas tilted his head. "He's got you there."

Corey ignored them. "Do you love her?"

Rowan didn't hesitate. "Yes."

"So tell her. Admit that you treated her poorly. Promise to treat her better. Then do it."

"That's good," Lucas said. "You should say that to Becs."

Corey gave him the finger, but Matt spoke before he could retort. "Do you really love her?"

Rowan met his eyes. "Yes."

"Do you regret what you did?"

So he did know.

"Yes," Rowan said sincerely. "Everything about the way I handled that was . . . wrong."

"And you know that if we help you make this right and she forgives you but you hurt her again, I'll nail your balls to the wall?"

He stared.

"Say yes," Lucas stage-whispered.

Rowan resisted the desire to cover his penis with his hands. "Yes."

Matt looked pained. "Then we'll do it. Help you."

"This," Corey said, "is growth. I'm proud of you, man." He hit Matt on his back.

Matt sighed. "Don't be. I'm doing it for Delilah. She loves him, too, and his stupidity made her sad. We make her happy by making him less stupid."

They looked at Rowan.

"How?" Lucas asked the question they were all thinking.

"You grovel," Mckenna said from the doorway. She was watching them with an inscrutable expression. "You say sorry and you grovel."

Matt, Corey, and Lucas nodded. Matt said, "Thursday night. My house. Seven p.m." And then they were all gone, as if Mckenna were a repellent of men.

Rowan knew for a fact she wasn't and that at least Lucas didn't think so. His friend had looked back at Mckenna, his expression pensive, before he'd left. Rowan felt an odd sense of hope at that, then felt weird for thinking it.

"You're okay with this?" Rowan asked her.

She walked in with the stroller, waving a hand to tell Rowan to stay where he was. "He's sleeping. He'll be out for a while."

She looked at him thoughtfully.

"You know what people kept telling me every time I went out for a walk? And I do mean every time. Literally, every time I stepped out this house, someone told me what a good father you are. How lucky I am that my baby's father loves our son so much. How respectful and courteous you are and that someday, my son will see that and he'll be a better man for it."

Rowan waited, but his heart twisted. At the kindness of people who didn't even know him.

Although he supposed that wasn't entirely true. He was a part of the community now. At least, he tried to be. And he'd try even harder now.

"I know I'm lucky, Rowan. I've told you that. And honestly, I gave you enough trouble for wanting to be happy with Delilah when I first found out."

"You didn't. You made good points."

"Maybe I did. But I should have made this point: You're a great father, no matter your emotion. But it seems you're an exceptional father when you're happy. I want you to be exceptional. I want you to be happy. So you have my blessing. Not that you need it," she added quickly, "but you have it."

He didn't know what to tell her. Didn't know how to express how much her words meant to him.

But he didn't have to say it, because she hugged him, and he hugged her back, and then she cried, and he did, too, and he thought that sometimes actions were more important than words.

# CHAPTER
# TWENTY-FIVE

Delilah deserved a medal.

*How modest of you,* she thought with amusement, but she couldn't help it as she took in Sugarbush Park on the first night of the Founder's Day festival.

A large screen filled the space between two lampposts at the edge of the park. A string of light bulbs hung between the posts. They'd be turned off at exactly 8:00 p.m., when the movie started, but for now, they added brightness as the sun slid behind the ocean.

There were food trucks to the side of the park. Some for popcorn, snacks, and drinks; others for food. From where Delilah stood, she could see some of the townspeople getting ready for the beach bonfire that would start the celebration.

She deserved a medal because she'd managed all her duties with the help of friends. After her talk with Matt, she'd realized keeping busy had been an excuse not to deal with her emotions about Rowan.

What she hadn't known was how much it was affecting her body. Her mind. Running away from her emotions didn't mean they stopped chasing her. And when they caught up, as they had that day with Matt, they did more damage than if she'd faced them head on.

So she'd made an appointment with her therapist and had her first honest conversation about her feelings. With the rawness and strength she'd felt after, she'd called Wendy and suggested that maybe she'd been hogging all the good stuff with the festival.

Wendy had sighed in obvious relief and told Delilah she was glad Delilah had come to her senses. Between the two of them, they'd rearranged the responsibilities. Delilah had still overseen everything to do with the movie night, which had affirmed that she liked doing it.

She liked planning things, talking to people, being creative. She even liked managing the budget. It thrilled her to make things special. And every time she shared something she'd done with one of the planning committee members, especially if it hadn't been her responsibility, they'd thank her or tell her she'd made their life a little easier.

And she thought that, maybe, she could help people like this. She could help ease their burdens by doing something she enjoyed, something she was good at. It would have nothing to do with atonement.

The very thought of it helped her breathe easier.

That could also have been a result of the deliberate ways she'd begun to take care of herself. She scaled back on all the work she'd taken on. She ate all her meals, drank water, and checked in with Matt twice a day. He'd insisted and she'd complained, on principle, but secretly, she was glad to have someone hold her accountable.

She'd allowed herself to slip to the bottom of her priorities in ways she hadn't even realized. Part of stepping into a life that was both good and sustainable was realizing she couldn't do that anymore.

She had to take her emotions seriously. She had to look after herself. She had to deal with the trauma of a lonely childhood, of her adolescent mistakes, of absentee parents, of her mother's arrest.

And she would. Even if it meant more emotional breakdowns, more honest conversations with people she cared about, more therapy.

Delilah felt pretty good about it. But then, it had only been a week. She was very aware of how easy it would be to slip back into her previous coping mechanisms. Especially when the prospect of seeing Rowan this weekend had her itching to bury herself in work.

She didn't want to remember how she felt when he looked at her. She didn't want to remember his face every time he'd brought her lunch. Or how, when they'd had lunch together, he'd picked flowers for her. How he'd called her every night after work to make sure she got home safely.

She didn't want to remember his wonderful, happy baby. She didn't want to remember Rowan. Because every time she did, every time she thought of him, she remembered how much he'd done for her. How good he'd made her feel by doing those things, big and small.

How much she missed him.

Which was pretty annoying, to be honest.

But it was fine. She'd still enjoy the festival. Last year's had been her favorite memory of her first year in Sugarbush Bay. The comradery, the community, the feeling of coming together to celebrate their common love for the town . . .

She'd never been a part of anything like it before. She'd appreciated it the year before, but this year, she was even more aware of how special it was. How *lucky* she was. Nothing would keep her from enjoying this weekend. Not even the prospect of seeing the man who'd broken her heart.

"You did it," Matt said from beside her.

If she hadn't been used to her brother materializing when she hadn't expected him, she'd have been more disturbed by his sudden appearance.

Instead, she said, "I did not do it. In fact, you made me not do it."

"You know what I mean."

"I do." She patted his shoulder. "No need to growl."

"Are you petting me?"

"Yes. Because you're a good little doggy."

He narrowed his eyes, but she could see the smile at his lips.

"You're a good kid," he said suddenly.

The growl was still there, but now it was softer. She turned to see the sincerest look in his eyes.

A huge lump appeared in her throat.

"Why would you say that to me? You know I'm emotionally fragile."

"It's true." He kissed her forehead. "You're the best thing to come out of our family."

Now she put her hands on her hips, stared up at the sky, which was fading to dark blue, and blew out her breath.

"Damn it, Matt," she muttered.

"I'm not sorry."

She laughed. "I think you mean 'I *am* sorry.'"

"No."

She laughed again and bumped her shoulder against his.

He smiled. "Love you, kid."

"Love you, too."

He nodded, as if he already knew this. Neither of them said anything for a while.

The silence was comfortable. Familiar. She'd gotten used to it as they'd grown up. At first—and, if she was honest, often enough after—she'd filled the silence with her own chattering.

And he'd listened, even though he preferred the silence. But soon enough, she'd become quiet, too, and they'd enjoyed the silence together.

That hadn't changed. Neither had the bond she'd clung to during their years apart. If anything, it was stronger now.

Oddly enough, she felt like she owed her mother for that.

Before long, people started to arrive. Each time someone stopped to tell them what a great job she'd done, Delilah tried to explain she'd been one of many. No one believed her. Apparently Wendy had been singing her praises, something that Wendy insisted she deserved when Delilah confronted her about it.

"Do you think we got all those volunteers because they were feeling generous?"

"Yes," Delilah answered.

"Well, yes," Wendy allowed. "But they also did it because of you. You've done so much for everyone here. For the town. You've set an example many of us want to follow."

"Wendy," Delilah said with yet another lump in her throat. "Stop buttering me up."

Wendy laughed. "Oh, honey, I haven't even started."

After that, Delilah merely said thank you when someone complimented her, though she couldn't help the long-suffering sigh that accompanied the words. Matt grinned every time he heard it. He stayed with her throughout the night, as if he knew she'd appreciate the support.

Not even Irene's arrival changed that. He merely gave his daughter an appraising look—or perhaps a warning look—to which she rolled her eyes. But when she spotted Delilah, she waved excitedly.

"She used to be that way with me."

"Yeah," Delilah said. "But that was *before* she realized how uncool you are. I mean, what father says no to a belly ring?"

Matt groaned. "She told you about that?"

"Yes. And you're welcome, by the way. I told her about this girl in my high school whose belly ring got caught in her jersey and ripped out while she was making out with some guy. She was freaked out by that. I might have put her off piercings *and* boys. For a little while, at least," she said, considering.

"I owe you," Matt told her.

"You do."

His eyes flickered to something behind her—and lit with amusement. "But I've already paid you back. *You're* welcome."

He gave her the most self-satisfied smile before walking away. She tilted her head, watching him, before she turned to check out what he'd been looking at.

She gasped.

This was not happening.

It was not.

The bonfire had been dismantled.

It had been there a minute ago. Or had it? The last time she'd checked had been the start of the night. Someone could have done this right after, for all she knew. And that someone couldn't have been her brother, because he'd been with her the entire time.

Only he knew something about it. About these smaller collections of sticks that had replaced the larger stack of wood.

She would kill him.

Sure, she'd just thought about how far they'd come, and yes, they'd had a nice moment earlier. But she'd kill him for this. She'd mourn, of course, but she'd also dance on his grave. He deserved it for messing up all the hard work everyone had done.

Before she could commit her crime, she noticed that Corey and Lucas were there, too, standing behind the sticks, close to the ocean.

So. She'd have to become a mass murderer.

Honestly, they were making it easier for her. It wouldn't take that much effort to push them into the water. Holding their heads down might be a little more exhausting, but the pure rage pulsing through her blood would take care of that.

"Delilah."

She knew that voice. Heard it in her memories, her dreams. Hated that voice.

Loved it.

Just like that, rage turned into nerves.

She turned around.

"Rowan."

He looked good. He looked so *freaking* good. He wore shorts and a T-shirt . . . and that was pretty much all she could make out. There might have been something on the shirt, but she couldn't see him clearly with the moon shining directly behind him.

There was only his silhouette—the hard lines of his shoulders; the tuck of his waist; his strong jaw; his firm legs. Her mind filled in the rest, and the assessment told her *freaking good* was an understatement.

"Hey," he said, slipping his hands into his pockets.

Which was another thing she loved/hated: his endearing sweetness. His shyness. The effect of it after two weeks almost took out her knees.

"Hey," she said awkwardly. There was nothing else, only awkwardness. "Did you see what someone did to the bonfire? *Wow.* I better sort that out."

"I'm sorry," he blurted out, catching her arm. "I'm sorry for everything. I was an idiot."

"What?"

"I'm sorry." The words were more deliberate now. "For everything. I was an idiot."

Her eyes narrowed. "Were?"

"Am," he corrected obediently.

She had to purse her lips to keep from smiling. She would *not* smile at the man who'd had doubts about them—and voiced those doubts— while they were having sex.

"What exactly are you sorry for?" she asked.

"For not realizing what I had when we were together."

He spoke honestly—and *loudly*.

For the first time, she noticed that people were looking at them. Openly and unapologetically. Her gaze moved from Kirsten, who had a sleeping Robbie in her arms, to Wendy, who was standing with Jill, watching them as she ate popcorn, to Irene, who had her phone out and seemed to be recording this. Matt stood a short distance from Irene and nodded at Delilah.

What. Was. Happening.

"Rowan," she hissed. "Let's talk in private."

"No," he said in that same loud voice. "What I have to say, everyone can hear."

She stared.

"Delilah, I am an idiot," he called out, as if he were in a production of an outdoor play. "I fell for you after promising myself I wouldn't fall for anyone. I was scared, and I messed up."

Murmurs went through the crowd.

Delilah ignored it.

"I know all this, Rowan," she told him in a normal voice. Because she wouldn't be a part of whatever this was. Not when her heart pounded just hearing him say he'd fallen for her. "But I also know that I can't force you to be with me when your fears are clearly more important to you than I am."

"They're not," he said, softly now. "I . . ." He took a deep breath. "I've done a lot of thinking these last two weeks. And a lot of people did some talking. To me." He frowned. "At me."

She waited.

"I realized I was in love with you that night." He stepped closer. "It had been happening for some time, but I realized it then. I kissed you because . . . because I wanted to be in love with you. You're amazing." He shook his head, as if he couldn't believe it. "And you wanted me. And I wanted you. I wanted us."

"And then what happened?" she whispered.

"I saw you loved me, too." He took a step closer. "And I panicked. You're the right person, Delilah. You have been from the beginning. I didn't tell you how I felt about sex because I thought I was protecting you from how broken I was. But all I was doing was protecting myself."

He paused.

"When you looked at me after you came? It undid me. All of me. The love, but also . . . the insecurities. I let them take control. It was easier. It was familiar. It was stupid. I was pushing you away."

He loved her? He knew she loved him? She didn't know if that made what he'd done better or worse. All she knew was that this confession was chipping away at the anger she'd held on to. The anger that was easier to deal with than the hurt.

Hey. She was acknowledging her emotions, not turning into a perfectly adjusted human being.

"Rowan, I didn't ask you for anything. I never have. I wanted . . . I wanted us to be together. But I thought that's what you wanted, too.

I would have never . . ." She swallowed. "I wouldn't have let things go that far if I thought we weren't on the same page. And hearing it right after I realized I was in love with you . . ." Her eyes filled. "I don't feel like understanding why you did what you did. I want to move on from you doing it."

They were so close she felt the warm air as he exhaled. Could sense the faint tremble of his body.

"I can't hear what you're saying!" someone called from the crowd.

"You're not supposed to," she snapped back.

Rowan snorted. Delilah couldn't help the curve of her own lips.

"Sorry," she whispered. "I know you hate this."

"That's the point," he whispered back. "I love you more than I hate this."

Before Delilah could process that, a familiar voice said, "He's been miserable, darling. Please take him back."

"Gran!" Rowan shouted.

"It's true!" Linda said. "Mckenna, tell them it's true."

"It's true," another voice—Mckenna, Delilah assumed—called. Delilah squinted and saw the faint outline of a woman with a baby strapped to her chest. "And he would have taken his own sweet time dealing with it, too, if we hadn't given him a little push. You know how much he likes to punish himself."

"If it helps," Corey offered, "he admitted to being an idiot pretty much as soon as we ambushed him."

"He really does regret it," Lucas called.

"Okay, everyone," Rowan said loudly, "I think she gets it."

"We all get it," a voice in the crowd said. People laughed.

She quirked her brow at Rowan. "So this is what you've been dealing with, huh?"

"The punishment fits the crime," he said in a resigned voice. "But they're right. I have been miserable, because of my own actions. *I* pushed you away. I did it . . . before you could."

His voice broke, and Delilah's heart twisted. "I thought I knew all the ways my parents screwed me up. Turns out you only find out the really good stuff when you're worried the woman you love won't love you back."

"But I do," she whispered. "I did, then. You said you saw it."

"And I was terrified of losing it," he replied urgently, gripping her hands. "I had done nothing to deserve it. Nothing to deserve you. How long would it take for you to realize I'm not worth it, like my parents did?"

"Rowan," she breathed, but he didn't let her finish.

"And then I thought, well, even if that doesn't happen, didn't the way I feel about you mean I was just like them? It was the first time I'd ever loved anyone romantically. I suddenly understood what it was like to love someone so much you don't care about anything else."

"You worried you'd become like them," Delilah continued. "That you'd love me so much you wouldn't care about Declan anymore."

"Yeah."

She gave herself a moment to let the words slide into place before she spoke.

"Rowan, your pain is real and valid. And I'm sorry for it. But your fears . . . they are less valid." She paused. "Do you think there's a world where you don't care about Declan? Do you think there's a world where *I* would let that happen in the unlikely scenario it did?"

"I . . . no," he answered sheepishly.

"No," she repeated. "Two things can be true at once: you can be mine, and you can be Declan's. You can be Declan's first. I *want* you to be Declan's first. I've told you that. We're not your parents. We won't make their mistakes."

"Thank you."

So sincere, she thought. Only it was too late.

"I thought you knew that, Rowan," she said softly. "I thought you knew *me*."

"It wasn't about you."

"It should have been. You should have asked yourself if any of those fears you had about *me* were valid. But you didn't. Which makes this the second time you haven't trusted who I've shown you I am."

She should have given him a moment to think about that, but she had to get it all out before she lost her courage.

"I understood it the first time. We'd only known each other for a short while. I kept parts of my past a secret. It was fair of you to doubt me. But I thought we'd moved on from that. I thought you knew who I was. Who I worked—*work*—so hard to be. The same person I've been from the beginning, too."

Yes, she'd wondered about her own motives. Whether she was being generous and kind and helpful to make up for her past or because she wanted to be. But now she saw that those two could be true at the same time, too.

She liked who she was now. Liked that she was reliable and thoughtful. Liked that she cared about everyone she came across. Liked that she liked to help. She needed to learn how to be that person without sacrificing her own needs in the process, but she would.

Because she could see the first step was making sure the person she was in a relationship with saw the real her—and trusted it.

"We can't be together if we believe our fears about each other. Or ourselves," she added quietly. "We have to be able to communicate. We have to be able to tell one another when our issues trip us up. Which is my issue, by the way," she added with a wry smile. "I need you to believe in me. I need you to *see* me. If you don't . . . well, I think I might start to believe you instead of myself."

"I get it," he said, his voice thick. "I'm sorry, Delilah. I should have told you about the sex thing. I should have told you about everything. I was . . . I *was* scared. To trust myself. To trust us. But please, believe me when I say I would never have let it get that far if I didn't trust *you*."

He sounded so earnest. "By then it had become an excuse. To keep from being honest about my feelings, which would have meant dealing with my fears, too. I wish—" He paused to clear his throat. And then he coughed. Less than a second later, he shouted, "NO!"

Delilah stepped back as light burst around her. She started to turn, but Rowan gripped her arms. She could see his face now, courtesy of the light. His gaze was panicked. And beneath it, she could see evidence of his misery. The dark circles underneath his eyes. The lines etched into his skin. The tightness around his lips.

Her hands ached to touch him, comfort him. Tell him she didn't mean it and give him another chance.

But she couldn't. Not if she wanted to look herself in the mirror tomorrow.

"In my defense," Rowan said suddenly, "I was talked into this."

She frowned. "What?"

Then she heard the murmurs, the clapping. Someone was cheering. A voice shouted, "FORGIVE HIM, DELILAH. IT'S A GRAND GESTURE."

She tried to turn again, but his hands tightened.

"Rowan, what is going on?"

"Nothing."

"*Rowan.*"

"Fine."

He exhaled but didn't drop his hands. Pointedly, she looked at them. With a tortured expression, he let go. Immediately, she turned.

In the beach sand, blaring in bright, hot heat like the bonfire was meant to, were the words, *I'M SORRY, DELILAH.*

Well. At least now the sticks made sense.

# CHAPTER

# TWENTY-SIX

This was what he got. This was what he got for listening to his *idiotic* friends. None of whom were in a romantic relationship. Not a single one of them.

This was what he got for his desperation. A desperation that had grown throughout his conversation with Delilah.

"This isn't my fault," he said. "Corey said we needed to do something big to convince you I was sorry; Lucas said it needed to be something I wouldn't normally do. That's why we're doing this in public, right? And Matt suggested we go big and do it at the festival, and . . . it sounded like a good idea at the time," he finished weakly.

She wasn't looking at him but stared at the fire instead. The light flickered against the shadows of her face, and his breath caught. She was beautiful. Stunningly beautiful. Her face was a striking combination of angles and softness, her eyes bright and open, her hair fluttering in unruly curls around her face.

Had he thought she took his breath away? No, she *gave* him breath. Only around her did he feel the depths of his lungs. His fears robbed him of that. Took away the ease with which he inhaled; trapped the air so he could never fully exhale.

When he let himself simply feel—no logic, no thinking, only feeling—he knew Delilah was right for him. Knew they were right for one another.

Why else would he be this at ease with her? Why else would her words be ringing in his head, reminding him he'd failed at the one thing she'd always given him: The freedom to be himself? To be loved as himself?

He hadn't made her feel that way, and he hated it. Would spend the rest of his life making up for it.

If she let him.

Delilah angled toward him. "Whose idea was it to use the sticks?"

"Lucas."

"And the words?" She tilted her head. "Was that him, too?"

"No, that was me." This was mortifying. "With . . . um . . . approval."

She nodded and didn't say any more. The silence stretched longer than was comfortable, which explained why he was suddenly talking.

"Delilah, I have never loved anyone as much as I love you. I've never admired anyone as much as I admire you. You took a crappy situation and turned it into . . . this. You. And you're remarkable. I hate that you think I don't see that. I hate that . . . that you thought I doubted you. That I made you doubt yourself."

Slowly, her gaze traveled to him. It unlocked the restraint that had him pausing, and he was talking again.

"You're right, though. I should have trusted us over my fears. That was my mistake, one I promise I won't make again." He sucked in a breath. "If you give me another chance, I will spend the rest of my days proving that I want *you*, exactly as you are. We'll talk. I won't keep things from you. If I'm scared, we'll be scared together."

Even the thought of it made him nauseous, but it was worth it. She was worth it.

"If you're freaking out, we'll do that together, too. I'm an idiot, and I'll make mistakes, but I will always come back to you. Because I know what I'm fighting for. You make me happy," he choked out, offering her everything. *Everything*.

"Being happy turns me into the best man, the best father, I have been. Even if you don't forgive me, I want to say thank you for that. For showing me I can have it. That I deserve it. That it's possible."

He was breathing hard at the end of it. In, out, in, out, as if he'd run a marathon. And Delilah . . . blinked. She *blinked*. Once, twice, a flutter of lashes. Then she took a step back. Another. A third.

It hadn't worked. He'd put it all on the line, and it hadn't worked.

"That's some speech," she said, not looking at him.

"I meant it."

She nodded and silence fell. Even the crowd, which had turned into background noise as he'd focused on the conversation, had stilled. Everyone was waiting on Delilah. Waiting for her to stay or leave.

Rowan had no idea what she wanted to do. Not when she wouldn't look at him. Not when she didn't give him the chance to see what she was thinking.

So when she did, when she turned to him, his heart almost stopped.

Her face was open and soft. As open and soft as it had been, as she had been, before he'd messed up. He wanted to believe that meant she forgave him, that she'd give him another chance, but he wouldn't. Not until she said the words.

"I don't want to be collateral damage to your fears, Rowan," she said softly. "I want us to grow and heal together. But we need to choose it. Both of us need to choose it, because there are things I'm working through, too. We can't hold one another back. We need to move forward."

"Yes," he said quickly, eagerly. "Yes, please."

She laughed huskily. "What are you saying yes to?"

"To healing. Growing. To you. I choose you. I choose us. Declan. Our future."

The smile she gave him was a rescue boat to a man lost at sea.

"Great choice."

He had her in his arms before she could finish the words, his mouth on hers, finally, finally at home.

The crowd went wild.

People cheered. There were whoops from some of the guys, who he was willing to bet were his friends, and whistles. He thought he heard someone crying. He *distinctly* heard another complain that they hadn't heard enough of "the good stuff."

He didn't care.

"I love you," he said when they pulled apart.

"I love you, too." Her eyes were warm. "Don't break my heart."

"I promise." He kissed her nose. "You know you could have made me grovel for the rest of my life, don't you?"

"Oh, I plan to," she replied, hands gripping the front of his shirt. "I appreciate all this. The apology and the grand gesture. Which was very nice, if a bit misguided."

"You didn't like it?"

"No, I liked it. I also would have liked a nice honest conversation at my house. Or yours. Or the café. It didn't have to be public. It definitely didn't have to be at the festival."

"Matt," he growled.

She laughed. "You're lucky he didn't kill you."

"Good point." He paused. "I mean it, you know. I'm going to prove to you I'm the man you deserve. Bonus is that Matt will let me live."

She laughed again and turned to look for her brother. When she found him, he was watching them. He winked at his sister. Her smile widened.

"He loves me more than he hates you."

"I got that from the fact that I'm still alive."

"It took some convincing."

Rowan pulled her in tighter. "There you go, already saving my life."

"I can end it, too."

"Is that a reconciliation or a threat?"

"Can't it be both?"

He laughed. Even if she hadn't been joking, it wouldn't have mattered. He had no intention of screwing up again.

Not that he wouldn't make mistakes. He would. But he'd give himself grace when he made them. He wouldn't let his fears control him. He didn't have to. He had everything he wanted: a family. A community. A *life*.

His grandmother was beaming at him from the crowd. Mckenna gave him a thumbs-up, waving at him with her other hand, which had Declan's fingers wrapped around it. Corey and Lucas cheered by the fire, and Matt gave him a quick nod of approval.

He could never have imagined it. That made it so much better.

The rest of the night was full of people congratulating them, asking about a wedding that wouldn't happen anytime soon since they'd just started dating, and prying about what they'd said to one another. Delilah handled it beautifully, easily, and winked at him whenever she did, as if saving him the trouble of socializing was a pleasure.

The bonfire was put back together. Food was handed out. Drinks were consumed. The movie started only thirty minutes later than was scheduled. When it did, he and Delilah finally got the chance to sneak away, heading down to the river, where things were quieter.

"I'm still thinking about what you said. That whole thing about the punishment fitting the crime?"

"Yes?" he said slowly.

"If that were true, I think you should never orgasm again."

He opened his mouth. Closed it. Stilled.

"That was a joke," she said, stopping beside him.

"I know. But . . . we still haven't talked about it. Sex."

Her eyebrows rose. "Would you like to?"

"Yeah."

She turned to face him and took both of his hands. "I'm listening."

"I want you," he blurted out, buoyed by her support. "I don't want you to think any of what happened is because I don't want you."

She laughed lightly. "I got that from your enthusiastic responses." Her expression grew serious. "What I don't know is if you're okay with it."

He took a breath. "I am. Theoretically. I used sex as an excuse to avoid the real problem. I know that. But . . . I don't know if that knowledge will translate to when we're . . . together."

"That's okay," she said quietly.

"It's not. Not to me. When we were together at your house, it was all those things you said. Beautiful. Sexy. Fun. I've never experienced sex that way. And I want that for us. Without . . ."

"Without the interruption of last time?" she teased softly. "We'll have it."

"You sound so confident."

"Because I love you. I think you're hot. You touch me and I turn to flames. It's simple for me." She wrapped her arms around his neck. "But it isn't for you, and that's okay. We'll figure it out."

"I don't want my issues to overshadow our sex life."

She cupped his face. "Rowan, we'll figure out how to make love so that it's beautiful and sexy and fun and not complicated for you, too."

He closed his eyes. Leaned his forehead against hers. "You're incredible."

"An incredible kisser, too."

She'd barely finished the words before his lips were on hers. He sank his gratitude for her understanding, her kindness, into the contact. His love for her, his wonder at her.

He kissed her, hard and passionate, finally giving his lust free rein. It pulsed in his veins, through his body. Settled between his legs. He pulled her closer.

As he did, Rowan realized that it wouldn't be difficult to let go. Not at all.

There were no fears now. Only the woman he loved in his arms. Only their love and their need and desire.

It was freeing.

It was . . . wonderful.

"Oh," Delilah breathed when they finally pulled apart. "I think we're going to be fine."

He grinned. "Me, too."

With that, he swung her over his shoulder. Her shriek of laughter rang out into the night as he continued down the road.

"Put me down!"

"*You* told me to kiss you," he said and nipped at her side.

"And that's permission to kidnap me?"

"Kidnap you?" He stopped walking. "I thought we were going back to your place to explore how hot you find me."

"*That's* where you were going? What the hell are you waiting for?" she cried. "Go, go, go!"

He laughed, feeling light and free. What else would he feel knowing he'd be walking with her, flirting with her, laughing with her, kissing her, for the rest of the night?

For the rest of his life.

# ACKNOWLEDGMENTS

This book was a complete surprise to me. I had a vague idea for it a few years ago, but it was only when I sat down to write an entirely different book that I found myself writing this one instead. It's probably because at the time, I was in the throes of dealing with twin toddlers, and parenthood seemed (seems? Haha!) overwhelming and impossible and beautiful. I wanted to explore how you can fall in love in the midst of all that, and here we are. : )

Thank you to my agent, Courtney Miller-Callihan, for her unending patience and understanding. She didn't even bat an eye when I sent her the chapters of this book, even though they were very much not any of the ideas we'd recently spent a significant amount of time discussing. You are so appreciated.

To Lauren Plude at Montlake, for seeing this book's potential and making me believe it was as amazing as she said it was. I can't thank you enough. To both Lauren and Lindsey Faber, whose editing expertise propelled me to write the very best book I could. This is a story full of nuance and unconventionality, and I was sure I'd have to rein it in at some point. But I was fully supported, and I'm grateful to you both for allowing me to tell this story as authentically as it deserved.

To the team at Montlake, for helping me get this book into the hands of readers. I know how much work it takes, and I am so, so thankful.

To my friends and family, who offer me empathy and support despite not always understanding the ins and outs of publishing, I love you all. A special thank-you to Talia Hibbert, who helped me with the pitch for this book while being its biggest cheerleader, and Olivia Dade, whose unwavering love is a light I constantly look to.

To my husband, who is an incredible father and spouse and without whom I couldn't do any of this. Our kids and I are lucky to have you.

Last but not least, to my children: I adore you. May you grow up believing you deserve love in every possible way, because we've shown you that you do . . .

And because your mom writes about it. ;-)

# ABOUT THE AUTHOR

*Photo © 2022 ForeverYours Photography*

Therese Beharrie is a South African romance author of several acclaimed novels, including *And They Lived Happily Ever After* and her One Day to Forever series. She takes pride in writing diverse characters and settings, and her books are often recommended for their heart and banter. She lives in Cape Town with her husband—her inspiration for every hero—and two adorable baby boys. You can follow her on social media (@ThereseBeharrie) or visit her at www.ThereseBeharrie.com.

# SOCIAL MEDIA LINKS

Facebook: www.facebook.com/theresebeharrie

Twitter: www.twitter.com/theresebeharrie

Instagram: www.instagram.com/theresebeharrie

Goodreads: https://www.goodreads.com/author/show/15524274.
Therese_Beharrie